Skin Deep

Skin Deep

LAURA JARRATT

First published in paperback in Great Britain 2012
by Electric Monkey, an imprint of Egmont UK Limited
239 Kensington High Street, London W8 6SA

Text copyright © 2012 Laura Jarratt
The moral rights of the author have been asserted

ISBN 978 1 4052 5672 8

1 3 5 7 9 10 8 6 4 2

www.electricmonkeybooks.co.uk

A CIP catalogue record for this title is available from the British Library

Typeset by Avon DataSet Ltd, Bidford on Avon, Warwickshire
Printed and bound in Great Britain by the CPI Group

48089/1

MIX
Paper
FSC FSC® C018306

EGMONT

Our story began over a century ago, when seventeen-year-old
Egmont Harald Petersen found a coin in the street. He was on
his way to buy a flyswatter, a small hand-operated printing
machine that he then set up in his tiny apartment.

The coin brought him such good luck that today Egmont has
offices in over 30 countries around the world. And that lucky
coin is still kept at the company's head offices in Denmark.

For Mum, who taught me to read and so gave me the key
to a bottomless casket of treasure.

Rewind

The stereo thumps out a drumbeat. Lindsay yells and reaches into the front of the car to turn the volume up – it's her favourite song. The boys in the front laugh and Rob puts his feet up on the dash. I smile like I'm having a good time, squashed in the middle of the back seat with Lindsay dance-jigging around on my knee and Charlotte and Sarah on either side of me. I wish Steven would slow down because the pitch of the car round the country lanes makes my stomach lurch and I don't think he should be driving this fast.

Charlotte's giggling and rubbing Rob's head over the back of the seat. She likes him, I can tell. He rolls a joint and takes a drag, then passes it to her. She inhales the smoke right down. I shiver inside. Mum and Dad would go crazy if they knew I was in a car with people taking drugs, and if they saw me in Lindsay's halter-neck top and short skirt. Charlotte passes me the joint and I shake my head. She shrugs, her face scornful, and Lindsay grabs it and takes a few puffs before passing it on.

The car careers round another corner like we're on a track ride at the funfair.

I sort of wish I was at home, tucked up on the sofa with Mum and Dad and Charlie watching TV. But when the bottle of cider goes round the car, I drink as much as the others so they don't laugh at me for being the youngest. For being a stupid little girl. My eyes feel funny and heavy with the mascara Lindsay brushed on them earlier. I don't know who this girl is. It's not the me who stacks the dishwasher every night for Mum and helps Charlie paint his Warhammer figures at the kitchen table.

I drink more cider, but that doesn't give me any answers, just makes me feel a bit more like throwing up.

Lindsay leans forward and kisses Steven on the neck. Open-mouthed. Sucking hard. He'll have a bruise there tomorrow.

Rob laughs. 'Get a room!'

And Steven waves to him to take the wheel while he cranes round to catch her mouth.

The car swerves and my stomach clenches.

Sarah's quiet, probably miffed that Charlotte's after Rob and there's no one for her.

Lindz whoops as Steven takes the wheel again and floors the accelerator. The car surges forward and hurtles faster and faster down the road.

We hit a straight stretch and Steven spins the wheel from side to side, hands in the air, steering with his knees. Us girls scream and laugh all at once. I force my giggles out.

Something white swoops low in front of the car. Steven

shouts out and the car veers towards the hedge.

An owl!

He grabs the wheel and we shriek with relief. My heart steadies again though I feel sicker than ever.

'Fairy!' Rob jeers at him and Steven's face sets harder in the rear-view mirror. His eyes glitter and he slams down on the accelerator.

We're moving rally-car fast. The January frost coats the hedges in the headlights' beam as we flash past.

We wheel round another bend into the dip down to Harton Brook. Another twist in the road, and another.

The needle on the speedo reads 70 mph and the girls and I are really screaming. Steven's knuckles are white on the wheel and even Rob takes his feet down off the glove compartment.

We shoot over the bridge into the bend straight after it.

The stereo bass batters my ears.

And then . . . then the car feels different underneath me. The wheels . . . they glide and spin.

Bumps in the road . . . I can't feel them any more.

We're floating.

And I remember. Remember how Mum always nags Dad to slow down here. 'It's a frost pocket. There's black ice here,' she always says.

Suddenly Rob starts to yell and Sarah shrieks. And I know why the car feels funny. Why it's skating on the road.

Steven cries out, 'Shit! Shit!'

The car spins off the road, crashes down the steep bank into the field below.

We're not gliding any more and my bones shake like they're falling to pieces.

Thump . . . thump . . . thump from the stereo.

Screaming.

So loud.

I'm thrown upwards as the car turns over.

Then sent slamming down again.

The car rolls once more and my head hits the roof.

Blackness.

Dark.

So dark.

But it's not safe like it is when I'm snug in my bed. In my own little room.

This is choking dark.

Through it, the screaming reaches me again.

Deafening.

It won't let me stay, pulls me back to the sound.

I open my eyes.

I'm pressed up against the roof of the car. It's upside down. Charlotte's hanging over the back seat, her head half out of the rear window. Blood drips along the shards of the broken glass.

Her legs pin me to the roof and I can't move. My arms are trapped under her. I shove, but she doesn't move.

There's a sharp, bitter smell in my nose. I recognise it, but I can't remember what to call it.

Lindsay's not on my lap any more. She's in the front between the seats. Her eyes stare up, wide and glassy. Lifeless.

I wonder why it's so light, why I can see Lindz, and the panic rises in my throat.

I know.

Coils of light – orange flames – lick towards me.

An acrid stench of burning.

The screaming is coming from me now.

The flames touch me. I can't move away, can't get my arms free. They stroke my skin in a white-hot sear of agony.

The pain . . . oh God . . . the pain.

It goes on forever.

A voice yells, sobs, 'Hang on, I'll get you out.' A hand grabs my leg and pulls me hard and fast, away from the flames. Out from under Charlotte's body.

Rob yanks me out of the door. 'I'm sorry, I'm sorry, I couldn't get it open in time.' One arm hangs useless by his side. He puts the other arm round my waist and half drags, half carries me away.

I know I'm howling with the pain and I can't stop. Nothing's ever hurt like this before.

He collapses on to the grass with me. Steven's bent double beside us, rocking back and forth on his knees. Sarah's there too, whimpering and holding her head.

Rob looks at me. 'Oh my God, oh . . .' and he starts to cry too.

I let myself slide back into the dark again as the car explodes.

Eight months later . . .

1 – Jenna

Ugly people don't have feelings. They're not like everyone else. They don't notice if you stare at them in the street and turn your face away. And if they did notice, it wouldn't hurt them. They're not like real people.

Or that's what I used to think.

When I was younger.

Before I learned.

When I was small, my mother used to take me shopping with her. Thursday is market day in Whitmere and she bought her fruit and vegetables from the organic stall there. The stallholder had a purple-red birthmark running the length of his face and across his mouth. It made his bottom lip stick out, all swollen and wet like a lolling tongue. I wished Mum would buy our food from somewhere else because I had to try to forget his face whenever I looked at the vegetables on my plate or picked up an apple.

He couldn't speak very well either. I assumed he wasn't all

there in the head. Somehow not looking right made me think his brain was as wrong as his face. I could never stop staring, fascinated by how my stomach turned and how worms crawled along my spine when he sucked back on that flabby lip in a nervous tic. Mum told me off for it when she caught me.

She thought I was being helpful when I washed the fruit and veg for her at home. I never had the courage to tell her I was trying to wash him off them.

Once I asked her if we could buy our stuff from another stall. Why did we always have to go to that one? And she explained what organic meant, about pesticides and fertilisers and protecting wildlife. But she finished with, 'Besides, some people need our support more than others.' I never asked again, but I thought it was stupid because ugly people don't have feelings.

I know better now.

That's why on a warm day in early September, I wasn't there for the school photo. I was sitting on the canal bank instead. The Orange River we called it because of the iron deposits in the soil that leached out to stain the water a murky rust colour.

I'd skipped school for the first time ever. Mum would've written me a note if I'd asked her, but then I would've had to explain and see the understanding come into her eyes. See her blink to hold back tears.

I checked my watch. The girls would be in the toilets now doing their hair and make-up, squealing about how bad they looked. *As if*. Then they'd line up on the staging in the hall. Best faces for the camera.

Oh, they'd notice I wasn't there. But nobody would ask why. The teachers would be relieved because when they hung the photo in the school foyer, one face would be missing. I bet they'd even 'forget' to ask me for a note.

Ugly people don't have feelings. We're not like everyone else.

2 – Ryan

The water in this stretch of the canal was a funny colour – looked like Mum's carrot soup. I steered the boat along, hand resting on the tiller bar. From the time since we'd last passed a town, I reckoned we must be about ten miles from Whitmere. Time to start looking for a mooring. Didn't want to get too close. Towns meant trouble. Too many people.

I could hear Mum inside the boat, clattering around and singing some tree-hugger shit to herself as she made dinner. Not tofu again, please. I swear they made that stuff to convert vegans to meat. Cole had agreed with me about that. Tasted like candle wax, he'd said. But then if someone asked Cole what a vegan was, he'd say, 'It's someone who farts a lot.' Death by beans, he used to call Mum's cooking. It's not really true. We don't fart more than everyone else, but when he met us, Cole's stomach had some trouble readjusting after a life of eating dead cow.

I cruised on a bit further. Nowhere good to stop yet. Too far from any roads. I didn't fancy hauling my bike over four muddy fields in the middle of winter before I got to the nearest lane.

The smell of bean stew wafted out of the door and I listened to the familiar sound of water lapping on the boat hull as I scanned ahead. There were some houses coming up in about a mile – looked like a village. I squinted for a better view. Only a couple of the houses seemed to be near the canal. The rest were set back. There was bound to be a road nearby so this was a possibility.

I yelled into the boat. 'Might have found a spot.'

'I'll be there in a minute,' Mum called back.

She always got a buzz when we came to a new place. Me, not so much. Maybe I used to; now it was just same old, same old. This place could be different though. I had a plan for this one. I'd not told Mum yet, but even thinking about it made my stomach churn, in a good way.

It'd be better if Cole was still around to help me break it to her. He'd have backed me up, but he'd been gone a year now. He got tired of travelling, he said – found another woman to hook up with, one with a house and a couple of kids. Mum said I should forget him and move on. Travellers moved on – that's what we did. But moving on in your head's harder. I remembered stuff all the time. Things he used to say or do. Times we had a laugh together. Like when I told him about Chavez, the guy Mum was shacked up with before him.

Cole had frowned. 'Mexican?'

'Nah, from Bishop's Stortford. Real name's Jeremy, but he

changed it. Thought he was Che Guevara – if Che spent his life permanently stoned and bumming around on a narrowboat.'

'Sounds like a tosser to me.'

'They were all tossers before you.'

He'd winked at me, then raised his voice so Mum could hear. 'Yeah, well, you gotta kiss a lot of frogs before you meet the handsome prince, eh, Karen?'

Mum, predictably, freaked at him, yelling about women's emancipation and respect while we cracked up laughing. Then she threw cushions at us until Cole grabbed and tickled her, and made her laugh too.

I spotted a copse of willow trees on the bank ahead, and a bridge across the canal – a road. Were we too near the village? You couldn't see the houses from here and the footpath was so overgrown that I doubted anyone walked along it often. Cars going over the bridge noticing us? A risk – but the wall was high and if I pulled in just where that alder tree was, I reckoned we'd be tucked away out of sight. This might be it.

Mum came up the steps, shielding her eyes from the sun, and I pointed to the clump of trees.

'Perfect! My clever son!'

Her hands fluttered round my face, stroking it, touching my hair. She smiled and my stomach churned, in a bad way. That smile was too bright, too fixed. Not right.

'It'll be good here. I can sense it. There's good energy. The ley lines meet here and they're rising up to greet us.' She turned that smile on me. 'It'll be different here.'

I looked at her, wanting to say, 'Like you said the last place would be different, and the one before that,' but I kept my mouth shut. Couldn't risk unbalancing her mood. Besides, we needed to moor up somewhere and we needed money. Whitmere had a market where she could sell the jewellery she made. Maybe we'd make it through the winter before they moved us on.

I steered *Liberty* towards the bank. Mum sat on the roof, her bare feet dangling in the doorway. Silver rings on her toes, and in her nose and eyebrow. Hennaed hair glinting copper in the sun. The last of the New Age travellers, who never grew up.

'Feel that energy, Ryan, feel that energy.'

3 – Jenna

There's something about waking up early on Saturday morning before the rest of the family. The whole weekend stretched before me and, for a few hours, I had it all to myself. A quiet house. Peace.

My magazine had an article on how exfoliation made the skin glow and apparently people in French spas spent a fortune battering themselves with water jets, so I turned the shower up high enough for the water to sting my shoulders while I scrubbed all over with a loofah. But when it came to washing my face, I turned the spray down. Low pressure, cool water. I never forgot to do that. Couldn't.

I gave myself a scalp massage with the new hair conditioner, giving it time to soak in before rinsing it off. The bottle said it'd make my hair full and glossy. When I cleaned my teeth, I timed myself with a watch — two minutes like the dentist said. I had to do the flossing blind though; there was no mirror above the basin. I'd thrown the towel stand at it when I got back from hospital. Dad had taken the pieces away without a word. Nobody replaced it.

I sat down at my dressing table to put on the moisturiser and the sunscreen the dermatologist prescribed. It had to be done a certain way – tap the moisturiser in and then massage it thoroughly over the whole scarred area to keep the tissue soft and stop it contracting. The sunscreen was easier and only had to be smoothed over gently. My skin lived by this routine now.

I rough-dried my hair and gave it a quick smooth with the tongs, then threw on a pair of jeans and a T-shirt.

Raggs took one look at me coming down in my old 'walkies' trainers and ran around in circles chasing his tail. I grabbed his lead in case we needed it and stuffed it in my pocket with a couple of apples for the ponies and one for myself. He did his usual thing of hurtling down the garden and back to me again, over and over, as if he was on a bungee cord. I caught him up at the gate that led out into the paddock and down to the canal. The paddock was ours, two acres bounded by high hawthorn hedge to shelter the ponies. We bought the Shetland, Ollie, to keep Scrabble company when Lindsay's horse was sold. It felt like Lindz had died all over again when Clover went, but my dad said no father would be able to stand seeing his daughter's horse running in the field while she lay buried in the ground.

I whistled to the horses and Ollie headed over first, led by his greedy little tummy. Their velvet noses snorted at my hands as they chomped the apples. Raggs ran along the hedge line, nose to the ground as he followed rabbit trails.

I could see Lindsay's home clearly through the trees, a Georgian manor house that dwarfed our old farmhouse. There was a figure in the garden, wearing pyjamas and a brown robe. He stood and stared at the rose bushes, statue still. Mr Norman. I hadn't seen Lindz's dad for weeks. I watched him for a few minutes, wondering what he was doing, and then he turned and shuffled back into the house, slowly, bent over like an old man.

Best not to think of Lindz today. Not on such a peaceful morning. The pain was always there to catch me if I did, always too raw.

I patted the ponies' necks and followed Raggs down the field until we got to the thicket of trees that lined the footpath through to the canal. Not many people walked this stretch now it was so overgrown. Raggs disappeared into the undergrowth. He knew this walk as well as I did so I paid no attention and concentrated on picking a path through the nettles. The leaves on the willows above us were still pale green. They'd start to yellow soon, then fall. Raggs and I would kick them up as we walked. He hadn't seen leaf-fall before – this would be his first autumn. He'd love it.

I lifted a branch aside and came out on to the canal towpath. Raggs was already there peeing up a tree. I patted my leg and he fell in beside me as we strolled along the gravel path. But he stopped abruptly after a few metres, his whole body a line of quivering attention, and I looked up to see what he was watching, expecting to spot a heron or something.

Then I stopped too.

It wasn't a heron.

A narrowboat was moored up ahead of us and there was a boy on the bank washing the boat windows.

He was stripped to the waist and barefoot, wearing nothing but long shorts. His hair was the colour of the honey Mum bought from the farm shop, his skin tanned the same shade.

I ducked back into the trees, bending to grab Raggs's collar. We were going to go the other way *now*, but the stupid dog jerked away from me. I patted my leg frantically, but he ignored me. He took a few steps towards the boy.

'Come back,' I whispered. 'Come *back*.'

He fidgeted, dancing with his front paws on the spot, and then he made his mind up. He shot off towards the boat, yapping.

'No! Raggs! Heel! Heel!'

But he'd gone, leaving me cowering in the trees.

4 – Ryan

You have to scrub really hard to get splattered flies off windows. Especially when there's a week's build-up of suicide bomber insects mashed on the glass. Maybe if insects could talk it'd be different. Maybe they'd warn each other in hushed whispers about the danger of Light. Don't go there, one would say. My cousin went chasing Light. Always a fool, he was. Always after a new thrill and one day he never came back.

Then again, maybe not. The ability to talk didn't seem to make humans less stupid.

A girl's voice called out somewhere down the bank and I glanced up. Then a small ginger mutt came hurtling towards me out of the trees, barking like crazy. He slammed into my bucket, sending it into the canal, and then he cannoned into me.

'Ouch!'

His paws scrabbled at my legs as he bounced up and down, yipping for attention. I crouched down and he leapt on to my knee. 'Watch it, short stuff. Those are sharp claws.' His tongue slobbered over my face. 'All right, calm down. Where've you come from?'

'Raggs! Come back!' That voice again, sharper, panicking.

I rolled my eyes. What did she think I'd do with him? Wring his neck and throw him in the canal? Psycho narrowboat dog-murderer arrives in sleepy village – shock horror! We'd only been here two days. I'd expected longer before the locals found us and worked out we weren't on holiday. But that's villages for you. News travels fast and everybody knows each other's business. So much for Mum thinking here'd be different.

The dog wanted to stay in my lap and get his ears stroked, but even if he hadn't, I'd have hung on to his collar just to piss the girl off, stuck-up cow. Besides, he was a mad little pup and he might run into the canal. 'Can't have that, Shortie. We'd never find you in there. You're the same colour as the water.'

'Raggs! Raggs!'

'Dead obedient, aren't you?' I said to him as he paid no attention to the voice and tried to hook his stumpy front legs over my shoulders so he could wash my hair too.

The girl appeared from out of the willow trees and stormed towards us. There was something odd about the way she walked – head down, hair over her face, shoulders tense. From what I could see, she had potential though – medium height, slim, sort of graceful even though she stomped along with her shoulders round her ears. Shiny hair the colour of a wheat field.

'Hey, she's hot,' I whispered to the dog. 'Stay here.'

She stopped about halfway, shouting 'Raggs!' again, not that it did any good. Her voice hitched on the name like she was close to crying and guilt pricked at me. Maybe she was a stupid up-herself bitch, but she was a girl on a deserted canal bank with a stranger . . . I didn't like the idea I scared her.

'Nice dog,' I called out.

She didn't come any closer.

'He just wants to play,' I shouted, but she still stayed close to the treeline. I gave up and pushed the dog down. 'Go on, go back.' He paid as much attention to me as he did to her, jumping straight back on to my legs. I nearly picked him up and took him over to her, but I reckoned I was less threatening crouched down. She started towards us again.

'Raggs, come *here*!'

'Who trained him?' I said, grinning. 'Cos you should ask for your money back.'

'Raggs! Now.'

'I think you'll have to come and get him.'

'I'm sorry he bothered you,' she muttered when she got close enough for me to hear. I opened my mouth to say, 'It's all right, no worries,' but the words choked in my throat when I saw the face behind the curtain of hair.

Jesus, her face . . .

The right side was chewed up by a wide scar running across her cheek, down her jaw and neck and disappearing into the collar of her T-shirt. Fuck, that was a mess. Not an old scar

– still purple-red angry. But not brand new either as it was all healed up. The skin there wasn't smooth like it should be, but rippled and puckered, especially on her neck.

What in hell had happened to her?

I didn't see the rest of her face at first. The scar was all I could see, my eyes drawn to it like a driver rubbernecking at a crash scene.

She bent down and snatched the dog from me. That broke my trance and I caught a flash of her eyes springing tears before she turned away with the dog under her arm and hurried off.

I scrambled up. 'Hey, no harm done. He was only playing . . .'

She all but ran down the path away from me.

No wonder she didn't want to come over and get the dog. She must get that all the time – idiots staring at her with their gobs open, like Frankenstein's monster had just lumbered into view.

You utter, utter dick! Why did you have to stare like that?'

Should I run after her and apologise? But what would I say . . . 'Hey, I'm sorry I stared at your face' . . . Hardly.

She disappeared into the trees.

I felt like shit. She only looked about fourteen and I'd made her cry. I should be ashamed of myself.

And I was.

I fished the bucket out of the canal. She'd gone and there was no way of making it right even if I had a clue where to start.

'Ryan, I've got some tea for you here. Take a break,' Mum called.

I went inside and Mum handed me tea in an enamel mug. I examined it. 'What is it?'

'Nettle.' She beamed at me. 'Very cleansing.'

Urgh! Gross. Reminded me of green piss. Not that I'd ever tasted green piss, but I reckoned nettle tea was how it would taste.

'Did you finish the windows?'

'No, I knocked the bucket over. I'll go back out and do it.'

'Drink your tea first. And you can tell me what you think of some of my new designs.' Jewellery kit was spread across the table: stones, beads, silver wires and torcs and catches, leather cords.

I sat down on a floor cushion. No chance of chucking the tea in the canal then. Mum held up a silver torc with a jade stone carved into the shape of a dragon.

'It's great, Mum. You should make more of those. They'll sell for sure.'

'Good. It took me ages to get that right. Very delicate job, especially the tail. What's wrong with your face?'

'Nothing. Why?'

'You keep rubbing it.' She put her fingers on her right cheek. 'Here.'

I flushed hot. 'I do?'

She poked her tongue between her teeth in concentration as she threaded red beads on to a leather thong. 'Mmm.' Her hair was piled up in a scrunchie on top of her head. She looked like a pineapple.

'Mum, if you get injured, like an accident, they can do plastic surgery to take the scars away, can't they?'

'Yes, but I don't think they can make them disappear. Sometimes perhaps, but not always.'

'What would give you really bad scars?'

'I've no idea. I once saw a child with a terrible scar from pulling a hot pan off the cooker. Why?'

'Just wondered. I'll go and finish the windows.'

I filled the bucket again at the sink and managed to chuck the nettle tea away at the same time.

As I scrubbed the rest of the insect debris off the windows, I couldn't get the puckered skin on the girl's face out of my head, or the look in her eyes when she'd turned away. She'd have been pretty before that. Nothing incredible, just normal average pretty like a lot of girls are. Kind of cute in a quiet way. If I ran into her again, I wouldn't stare. After all, I used to hate it when kids stared at me and Mum.

5 – Jenna

I towed Raggs down the lane away from the canal and we looped through the village so I didn't have to go near that boat again. The stupid dog kept pausing to look anxiously at me and I tried to stop the tears rolling down my cheeks.

Even before the accident, that boy would be out of my league. I guessed he was a few years older than me and he was tall, around six foot, but he didn't have that stretched-out look boys have when they've grown too fast. His shoulders were too broad for that and he had a whippy muscled thing going on that made me wonder if he worked out. The honey-coloured hair was streaked blonder on top and his nose had a touch of sunburn as if he spent a lot of time outside. He wasn't boy-band pretty, but nobody would've thought him anything other than good-looking. Especially without a shirt.

If my feelings had gone away when I became ugly, life would be easier, but the wobble in my tummy when I saw a boy like that was still there. Even though he looked at me like I was a monster.

The tears fell faster, blurring the road ahead. 'It's all your fault, you useless dog! I told you to come back. I hate you!'

Raggs pulled out of the clump of brambles he was nosing in and ran towards me, his tail wagging.

'Come on, you. We're going home.' Forget the weekend stretching ahead of me. I wanted to go home and crawl under my duvet and hide. Forever.

We passed Charlie in the garden where he was kicking a football around on the lawn. 'Want to be in goal?' he yelled as he dribbled the ball along on spindly ten-year-old legs.

'No!'

He stopped and stared at me in surprise as I hurried into the house, leaving Raggs behind with him. 'Jen, what's up?'

I slammed the back door and ran upstairs.

In the bottom of my wardrobe, right at the back and wrapped in a towel, I'd hidden a make-up mirror, the only mirror I still had. I knelt down and unwrapped it with shaking hands. A wave of nausea rose up when I looked in it. It was as bad as ever. Like a horror film. The ugliest thing I'd seen outside the movies. No wonder that boy had looked disgusted. I bet he'd wanted to throw up at the sight of me. I did.

Better to have been Lindsay. Better to be dead than look like this.

The thing that lived inside me since the accident woke again. The thing that chewed me with grinding teeth. I wanted to hurl the mirror across the room. Scream. Break everything in sight. Rip the curtains down. Smash the window. Let the animal thing out.

But good girls don't do that, don't make a fuss, don't upset parents. And I was a good girl so I curled up on the floor and sobbed silently instead.

When they took the bandages off in hospital for the first time, my dad had looked at me and cried. In fourteen years I'd never seen my dad cry, but he sat there and wept as if something inside him had broken. Mum tried to make him to stop, but he couldn't so a nurse came and led him away gently. They weren't sure they should give me the mirror after that. Mum and Dad were supposed to support me, but that wasn't going quite to plan. I had to look in the end though. It couldn't be put off forever. I told them that.

'Now remember, you've still got a lot of healing left to do. This graft needs to take and it'll be a while before the colour fades. The mask will reduce the scarring as long as you wear it properly. In a year's time, it'll look very different,' the nurse said.

Mum's hands trembled as the nurse raised the mirror to my face.

I looked in it and any shred of hope I had was butchered.

They gave me a jab to calm me down and the counsellor

came later. Her face swam woozily in front of me. 'Jenna, I need to check first that you understand what the doctors have told you about your burns.'

Yes, I'm not stupid. Third degree. Full thickness burns. They've been through all this with me when they harvested my skin for the grafts, and then again afterwards.

It means the burns are skin deep.

And beauty's skin deep.

Mum knocked on the door. 'Jenna, I'm going to the library. Do you want to come?'

No, I never wanted to leave the house again.

But that wouldn't do. I'd promised I'd go out when the mask came off after those six long months. They'd been patient and hadn't hassled me before that, but now they took every opportunity to get me out of the house. Refusing would lead to one of those conversations I didn't have the strength for.

We got into Mum's red Corsa and she drove carefully into town, making a fifteen-minute journey last twenty. She always expected me to be nervous in cars now, but I wasn't. How much worse could it get?

Once we were in the library, she left me alone in the Fantasy section while she headed for the Crime and Thriller shelves. I found something I liked the look of and settled into a comfy chair to check it out. I hated taking a book home only to find it was unreadable so I always flicked through the first chapter before deciding.

I heard a voice at the desk counter next to me. 'Is the craft shop closed?'

I looked up sharply. The boy from the canal . . . He was still in the shorts, but he had a white T-shirt on now.

'Yes, the lady who runs it has gone for lunch,' the librarian replied. 'Can I help?'

'My mum makes jewellery. I was going to ask if you'd be interested in a sample,' he said, pulling a pouch out of his pocket. I wondered if I could slip away out of sight or if moving would make him notice me.

'You'll have to talk to Clare about that. She'll be back in twenty minutes if you want to wait. Feel free to browse.'

Urgh! Now I had to move. I got up as stealthily as I could and ducked into an aisle. I sat down close to the shelf and let my hair fall over my face as I pretended to read.

Footsteps sounded on the cord carpet, the soft pad of trainers coming closer. And then . . .

'Oh!' He walked into me as he came round the corner and knocked the book from my hands. It skidded under the shelf.

'Oh, sorry!' He crouched down to fish the book out. 'Didn't see you there. Are you . . .' He tailed off and I waited for the shudder.

He grinned at me.

What?

'Hi again!' He pulled my book out and handed it back to me. 'I'm glad I've bumped into you . . . well, fallen over you! I wanted to say this morning, only you ran off . . . that . . . your dog . . . it's fine. Dead friendly, isn't he? I like dogs. Sorry if I came over as rude.'

I was too shocked to move away or speak. And . . . and he was looking me full in the face . . .

He had nice eyes – a sort of brown colour, warm and smiley. He'd looked at Raggs that way too.

He went on. 'You surprised me, that's all. The scar' – he touched his face – 'took me by surprise. I didn't mean to be rude, honest.'

I gaped at him. Nobody ever, *ever* mentioned the scars. Their eyes slid away or they turned aside or they pretended they couldn't see them at all. But nobody ever acknowledged them directly. Even my own family avoided talking about them in front of me, apart from those humiliating and painful times when Mum felt it was necessary for a serious chat about my progress. But in the way that he'd just done? So blunt? So matter-of-fact? No, nobody did that.

He scratched at his neck. His grin was sort of lopsided this time. 'What I mean is, sorry if I screwed up.'

Screwed up? Oh yeah, you did that. For a few minutes in eight horrible months, I'd forgotten my face and enjoyed something as basic as taking the dog out. And then he'd made me feel like an ugly freak. Which I was, but I didn't want to be reminded of it . . .

I blinked hard and opened my book, hoping he'd go away.

'Good book? You read any of his before?'

I shrugged, unable to get words out, not knowing what to say if I could. Charlie aside, this was the first boy to talk to me since the accident. I avoided them at school and I'd have been shy of this one even before the accident. Close up, he was even cuter – the kind of boy girls would be drawn to like a magnet. My skin felt scratchy with nerves at having him so close, and having his eyes on my face.

'I've read a couple. Not bad. He goes on a bit though.' The boy chuckled. 'So, do you come here often?'

Oh, I got it. That's why he was talking to me. I was a joke. One big bloody joke. Talk to the freak and laugh behind her back about it later.

I scrambled up. 'Fuck off!'

'Hey, what's wrong? I was –'

'*Fuck off!*'

People turned to look at us and the shameful tears came again as they stared. As he stared.

I ran to find Mum.

She hurried towards me as I burst into the aisle. 'Jenna, was that you shouting? What on earth is wrong?'

'I want to go home! I want to go home *now*!'

'Calm down. What's happened?'

'Now!'

From the corner of my eye, I could see the boy watching us, but he melted away when Mum stuffed her books on to a shelf and shepherded me to the door.

When we reached the car, she hesitated. 'Are you sure you want to go home?' she asked. 'Only . . . well, Dad's having one of his meetings.'

'Oh, so that's why you wanted me out of the house. I should've guessed.'

'Darling, I know it upsets you and –'

'I want to go home!'

She winced and put the car in reverse. I stared out of the window as we drove home in silence.

Dad's meetings. His campaign group. The sorest of sore points. He hadn't even had the courtesy to tell me about it. I'd found out when I came across a discarded newspaper. I came down one morning to find he'd rushed out and left the local rag open on the table by accident. I was folding it up when I saw the headline on the front page:

STRENTON MAN TAKES ACTION AGAINST THE MENACE OF DANGEROUS DRIVERS

I frowned and sat down to look at the article, my skin flushing and crawling the more I read:

Local businessman Clive Reed has taken his campaign to Parliament after enlisting the support of Whitmere M.P. Trevor Davies.

Following the car crash that led to the death of two teenagers and left his fourteen-year-old daughter horrifically disfigured, Clive Reed has been campaigning for action to be taken by county police to combat dangerous driving on our roads. The outcry caused when the eighteen-year-old driver of the car, Steven Carlisle, also of Strenton, was given a suspended sentence has made him even more determined to bring the issue to national attention. Carlisle was driving under the influence of alcohol and drugs, but walked free from court in June after the judge heard a range of character witnesses speak in his defence, including representatives from Whitmere Rugby Club. Carlisle received a lengthy driving ban, but with local opinion running high, Mr Reed's pressure group has swelled in number.

David Morris, whose daughter was one of the two girls who died in the accident, has given the campaign his full support. 'Clive has been amazing,' he said. 'After Charlotte was killed my wife and I were too distraught to organise something on this scale. Clive's made people around here sit up and realise that we need to do something to keep our children safe.'

Mr Reed spoke to our reporter yesterday. 'This verdict is a travesty of our justice system. The only fair result would have been a custodial sentence. We are now seeking a review of the handling of this case and we're calling for tougher sentencing and a greater police presence on our roads.' Mr Reed's distress was clear as he added, 'I would hate for any other parent to have to go through what we have all suffered.'

I was shaking when I stopped reading, and I was shaking again when Dad got home that evening and I confronted him. 'When were you going to tell me?' I asked as I threw the paper down on the table.

He sat down wearily. 'When we thought you were ready.'

'Horrifically disfigured – you let them print *that* in the newspaper. And down here' – I prodded the paper – 'it says a photo of me will be used in your leaflets. You're going to put my photo in there. Without telling me. Without *asking* me.' My voice rose to a scream. 'What the hell gives you the right to do that?'

'That was taken out of context,' he protested. 'It was only a suggestion from Charlotte's dad. He thought it might help. Your mum said it wasn't the right time to talk to you about it. We wouldn't have done it without —'

'Oh yes, like you told me about this whole campaign?'

'Jenna, for God's sake, we have to do *something*. That boy has ruined your life!'

The words were out there, though he looked like he could have bitten his tongue off for saying them. I got up and ran blindly to the door. He followed me up the stairs, putting his foot in my bedroom door as I tried to slam it.

'Jenna, I didn't mean that your life is over. Of course not, it's all ahead of you. But look what he's put you through, the pain, the operations. You could have died too!'

'You didn't even wait until the mask is off.' I tore at the plastic mould on my face, but he grabbed my hands to stop me. 'It's me who has to wear this. Me!'

He hung on to my wrists. 'Don't. You'll hurt yourself. It'll be off soon. You'll get back to normal then, see your friends.'

'Oh yes, except my best friend is dead! It won't be back to normal for her, will it? It won't ever be normal.' I hated Dad then. I'd heard him talk to Mum about how Lindz changed after her mum left and seen the frown crease his forehead when we went out together. He thought she was a bad influence. He couldn't see her the way I did. How she glowed brighter than other people and that I wanted to sparkle like her.

'But you're alive, Jenna. Thank God, you're alive.'

'Yes, and I wish I wasn't!'

Dad let me go and backed away. Mum came running upstairs and pushed him aside and he left me for her to deal with.

What he said stayed with me. There was no way out of this. I couldn't go running to my parents and have them make it better like when I cut my knee playing with Charlie when we were little, or when I got stuck on my maths homework. This was never, ever going to go away. Like the man on the market stall, I'd be stared at. I'd be *wrong* all my life. No going back. No making me right.

Too soon we pulled into the drive. Mum had to park on the lawn because there were so many other cars there.

'Why is he having it here?' I muttered, wanting to know, but not wanting to speak to her either.

She hesitated before she answered. 'Last time they met at the village hall, but the cars were vandalised. Paintwork keyed and the tyres let down.'

And I knew who'd have done that. We all knew.

'They'll be in the kitchen,' Mum said. 'Go in through the front door and straight upstairs if you don't want to see them. I'll bring you a hot chocolate.'

Charlie was doing trumpet practice in his room so I lay on my bed with my iPod turned up high to drown him out. Sometimes now I scared myself. Sometimes I couldn't hold it in and go back to being Mum and Dad's normal Jenna, even in the safety of my home. I wasn't sure if any of that girl was still left. Perhaps the thing inside me had eaten her all away. Maybe I only acted at being her now.

Before the accident, I used to daydream about meeting a boy who didn't want Lindsay or a Lindsay wannabe. He only wanted me. That was crazy thinking because Lindz was catnip for boys. She could get anyone she wanted. I'd watch her go into action, torn between admiration and jealousy, knowing I could never be like that. When she wanted the rich and unattainable Steven Carlisle, she'd even hooked him. But this dream boy would only be interested in me. We'd do regular things like go to the cinema, bowling with friends, hold hands, kiss eventually. Things I was ready for. Things Mum and Dad would be happy with. Things Lindz would laugh at as babyish.

And sometimes, after the accident, I used to dream it could still be possible. That someone would see past the scars and not care about them. Hopeless dreams. Stupid little girl dreams.

Dad sat on my bed and I jumped. With my headphones on I hadn't heard him come in.

'We're having coffee and cakes. Come down and say hello.'

I turned the iPod off. 'Why? So you can exhibit your freak to the crowd?'

His eyes registered his hurt and disappointment. 'Where did

36

that come from? Have some manners. Those people down there care about you. You've known most of them since you were a little girl. They're doing this for you.'

'If they care then they should leave me alone, like I want.' I reached to turn my iPod on again, but he snatched it away.

'Don't be so selfish and rude. I want you down there in five minutes.'

So five minutes later, I went down to play the part of Daddy's good, tragic little daughter. I smiled at the people while they smiled at my left ear. Mrs Crombie from the village shop cut me an enormous piece of chocolate cake and pressed me to eat it. Charlotte's dad asked me heartily how school was going, which was brave of him, I guess, considering. Mrs Atkins from Belle Vue Cottage told me about her new kittens.

'Does it make you sick to look at me?' I wanted to ask. But Mum and Dad would never have forgiven me if I did, so I put the old Jenna on for them until I could escape back to my room.

Later, when they'd all left and the coast was clear, I crept down to the kitchen for a glass of milk. Mum and Dad were in the sitting room whispering to each other. I paused at the half-closed door to listen.

'I'm worried, Tanya. She hardly comes out of her room. She won't talk to people unless we make her. She never sees her friends. You said it would be different once she took the mask off.'

'It's only been a few weeks. She needs time to readjust. She's gone back to school. That's a start.'

'But it seems as though she's getting worse, not better. And what was all that about in the library today?'

'I don't know. She wouldn't tell me.'

'I know you're worried too. I can see it in your face. She's shutting herself off from everyone. I don't want her getting like that poor bastard next door. He's practically a hermit since Lindsay died.'

And I couldn't stand to hear any more after that. I slunk back upstairs, the milk forgotten. Back to the safety of my room where I could lock the door on them all.

6 – Ryan

I snuck out of the library after the girl and her mother left.

Outstanding success there. Major league. I'd made her cry again. Only this time I didn't have a clue why.

She was crazy. I hadn't done anything.

If I saw her again, I was going nowhere near her.

I stood in the town square and pulled the sketch map out of my pocket. How did I get to the canal from here? When I looked up to get my bearings, three lads hanging around a black car were staring at me, narrow-eyed. I stared back at them just long enough to let them see I'd noticed, then I leaned against the lamp post next to me and examined the map. Just another set of small town lads who thought they were hard men. I found the street I needed and set off. I could feel their eyes following me and they straightened and stiffened as I passed them, but when I carried on ignoring them, they turned back to the car. It's all in the body language, Cole said, in the way you stand, the way you walk. Get it right and they won't touch you.

I never got it right before Cole came, but he sorted me out

39

all right. He'd ridden into our lives four years ago on a Harley. We'd moored up by a skanky little place off the Llangollen canal – Mum's Welsh phase – and Mum and I had gone to the Co-op to get some supplies in. The shop assistant followed us round from the moment we entered the shop. My face heated up as Mum strolled around filling her basket with lentils, carrots and peppers and the woman behind us watched, scowling.

'Mum, hurry up, please.'

'Quiet, Ryan. Don't rush me.'

'Can I wait outside?'

'Oh, go on then. But don't wander off.'

I went outside and sat on a bench. Some boys my own age, around twelve, kicked a football round the empty car park. It looked like a laugh, but I didn't go over to join them. No point.

Quarter of an hour later and Mum still hadn't come out of the shop. The boys noticed me and looked over, moving together into a pack, muttering. It set the hairs on the back of my neck on end. I knew this script, but Mum had said don't wander off.

They came over, swaggering more the closer they got.

'You a gyppo?' one called. He was shorter than me, but stockier.

I shook my head.

'You look like one. Don't he look like one, Rhys?' He turned to the boy nearest.

40

I balled sweaty hands into fists. I didn't look like them, for sure, in the tie-dyed crap Mum made me wear back then.

'Can't you speak?' the third asked, stepping closer.

'Yes.'

'Ha! He's English. An English gyppo.'

'I'm not a gyppo.'

The five surrounded me. The one called Rhys slapped me on the head. I scrambled up, meaning to make a dive over the back of the bench and run into the shop, but the stocky one grabbed me and kicked me in the knees.

Crunk!

I hit the pavement hard and brought my arms up to protect my face. The first kick wasn't as hard as I expected – a taster. Maybe they hadn't done this before. But it landed in my stomach and winded me all the same.

'Go on, Huw! Boot him!'

The second kick slammed into my arms as the boy aimed at my face.

I heard them laughing.

'Gyppo!'

'English bastard!'

'Kick his head in!'

Feet hit into me from every angle, in my back, my legs, my arms still curled around my head, my chest, stomach. I never got a chance to hit back.

Please don't let Mum come out and see this. Please.

But please make it stop . . .

The feet kept kicking. Above the sound of their laughter, I heard another roar. An engine. Coming closer.

The kicks to my front stopped suddenly.

'Brave little shits, aren't you? Five on one.'

The kicks behind me stopped as well.

'Get out of here. Unless you want to take me on too.'

Feet slammed on tarmac, running away. Big hands hauled me up.

'You all right, kiddo? Let me see.'

He pulled my arms away from my face. A big man in leather trousers and a vest, tattoos down both arms – bands of Celtic knots, brown hair pulled back in a ponytail, and a beard. His chest hair poked over the top of his black vest. The Harley engine thrummed next to us.

'Getting a bit of hassle?' He grinned at me and wiped blood away from my nose with his hand. It was hot from the sun and as hairy as the rest of him.

I nodded.

'No harm done?'

'No, I'll be OK.' I sat up properly. 'Thanks.'

'No worries.' He held out his hand for me to shake. 'Cole.'

'Ryan!' Mum shrieked as she dropped her bags and ran towards us. 'What happened?'

Cole stood up. 'He had some trouble with the local kids, but he's fine.'

Mum stopped in her tracks.

He looked at her. She looked at him. And that was that.

A week later he moved in.

I walked through the town, keeping an eye open for craft shops for Mum. There were a few potentials. I scribbled the names down. Better give her something to sweeten her up because when she found out what I was planning, she'd go mental.

The town looked like most of the country towns we stopped in, except for the lake on the edge of it – the mere that gave it its name. There were a few streets of shops and a mixture of houses, from the big, posh places to pokey cottages. You could probably walk from one end of it to the other in under half an hour. I passed the edge of a council estate and then I turned into a lane with a sign pointing to Whitmere Marina.

The boatyard was bigger than I expected, but there didn't seem to be much going on there considering how many boats they had in. A ginger cat eyed me from its sunbathing spot on top of a van. There was an old guy in the dock area working on a flue on the roof of a narrowboat, his bald head burnt red. He looked up as I went over, squinting his eyes before he shielded his face from the sun.

I decided to get in first. 'Excuse me, is the boss about, please?'

He looked me up and down. 'Aye, lad, over there, back of that shed sorting a delivery.'

'Thanks.'

The shed turned out to be the size of a small barn. There was no sign of life at first so I stepped inside and spotted a man at the back bending over a crate and counting out rope fenders.

'Hello?' I called.

He straightened up. 'Yeah?'

'Sorry to disturb you. Um, have you got a minute?'

He laughed and put the fender down. 'That depends on how much you're spending.' He strolled over, dusting his hands off on his jeans. 'What can I do you for?'

My stomach steadied when I saw the tattoos up his arms and the ring through his eyebrow. He was around Cole's age, with a big build like him.

'I'm looking for work. I wondered if you needed any help.'

He looked around. 'I don't see any sign up advertising a vacancy, do you?'

'No.' I shrugged and tried a smile. 'Thought I'd ask though, just in case.'

He snorted. 'How old are you?'

'Sixteen.'

'Ever worked in a boatyard before?'

'No, but –'

'Ever *worked* before?'

I hung my head. 'No.'

In the pause that followed I got ready to apologise and get out of there. There were other yards I could try, but this was the closest. He broke the silence in the end with another laugh.

'Guess you won't have picked up any bad habits then.' I looked up quickly and he winked. 'Come on, convince me.'

I took a deep breath. 'Um . . . er . . . I'm looking for work with boats because they're what I know about. This is the first place I've tried and it's a big site so I thought there was a chance you might have some jobs that needed doing. I'm good with narrowboats. We've had one all my life and I've been brought up around them and I do all the work on ours and I'm not scared of hard work or getting my hands dirty and –'

'Woah! Slow down!' He held up a hand to silence me, but he smiled. 'Are you a local kid?'

'Ah . . . no . . .' This would be the difficult bit.

He frowned. 'Moved here recently?'

'Yeah.'

'So where did you come from?'

I heaved a sigh. Might as well leave now. 'Nowhere. We move around. We're here for the winter.'

He rubbed his chin. 'You're a traveller?'

I nodded.

'You got a police record?'

'No.'

'Cautions?'

'No, nothing like that.'

'So you said you had a boat. You mean you live on it?'

'Yes, me and my mum. She makes jewellery. Good stuff, not rubbish.'

His lips pursed together in thought. 'You were honest about it. You could've lied,' he said finally.

'I don't lie.'

'I wasn't looking for any help, but now it's sitting here offering itself up, I could do with another pair of hands around the place. Tourist season's nearly done and I'll have boats coming in for full maintenance soon. I can take more if I've got someone who knows what they're doing.' He nodded slowly. 'You don't look like you'd faint at pumping waste out or fall over with a bit of heavy lifting.'

I shook my head, and then wondered if I'd got that the wrong way round. Maybe I was supposed to nod.

He got the message though. 'Can't give you a contract. You'll be casual labour, but I'll send you on your way with a good reference when you leave, if you've proved yourself.'

'That's fine with me.'

'You're polite enough too. I could use you in the shop on Saturdays. We get a good bit of passing trade in at the weekend. Can I trust you with the till?'

I set my teeth together. 'Yes, you can.'

He laughed. 'I see you can keep your temper too. That's important with customers, especially some of the stuck-up sods you get round here. Peace, lad, I'm not stupid. I can spot trouble when I see it and I don't see it in you. I'll give you a go if you want. It's good to see someone your age getting off his arse and looking for work.' He held his hand out. 'I'm Pete, and that's Bill over there.'

A grin broke over my face as I shook hands with him. 'Ryan. And thank you!'

My first job! Yes!

7 – Jenna

On Monday morning, Charlie and I waited for the school bus at the crossroads on the edge of the village. He nudged me with his elbow as the bus came into view.

'What?'

'Will you look after my case for me on the bus?'

His trumpet case – he had a lesson today. Mum and Dad wanted him to learn an instrument so, of course, he'd picked the noisiest one he could. 'What do I get in return?'

He grinned at me, the blond curls he hated plastered down with gel because Mum wouldn't let him cut his hair short enough to get rid of them. 'I'll wait until you go to feed the ponies to practise tonight.'

'You're on.' Charlie was not a natural musician. When he practised, we all suffered.

The bus drew up and Charlie abandoned me to sit with his friends. I made for a window seat at the front, putting my bag and Charlie's case beside me so no one could sit there, and I took out a book. Now I didn't have Lindz to talk to, I always read on the bus. The journey from Strenton to school took forty-five minutes, the bus winding down narrow country lanes to pick up in Whitmere and all the villages. I looked out of the window occasionally to see where we were, but otherwise I kept my head down.

Charlie paid me no more attention as he got off the bus than he had when we were on it, except to grab his trumpet as he went past. Big sisters were fine to play with at home, but were to be ignored at school in front of mates. The Prep department was in a different building to the Upper School and he and his crew ran off to play football in their yard before the bell went. I headed round the side of the building to the girls' locker rooms. The noise hit me as soon as I went in, all the post-weekend chatter about who'd done what, with who and when. I hung my coat up and collected some textbooks I needed for the morning. This area was only for Year 10 so everyone here knew me; it was safe.

Walking out into the corridor was different. A bunch of younger girls stopped at the sight of me, their mouths screwing up before they turned away. And then the whispers . . .

When would it stop? We'd only been back a couple of weeks and I was still a novelty – Shrek Goes to High School. But would they ever get used to me?

A couple of Year 8 boys pushed into me, not looking where they were going, and I shoved them out of the way before they knocked me over. 'Eww, that's disgusting,' the geeky spotty one muttered to his friend. 'She should put a bag over her head or something.' Even a minger like him found me repulsive.

The second boy sniggered and I couldn't stand the idea of them following me down the corridor so I veered into the girls' toilets and locked myself in a cubicle.

I leaned on the door for support as I waited for my pulse to slow and the usual choke of anger and humiliation to die away. Walking down that corridor was the hardest part of the day and every time I did it, I had to fight back the memory of the first day back at school after the accident.

The locker room had been bad enough as girls from my year rushed over to say, 'Hi! We missed you . . .' before their voices tailed off. Their eyes widened in shock, even though they all knew what had happened to me. But knowing it isn't the same as seeing it. I saw the thoughts flash through their heads: if that happened to me . . . oh God, I'd die . . . it's . . . it's . . . They tried to pretend they weren't horrified, but they couldn't hide it. I didn't know what to say to them. I wanted to run out of the building and phone Mum, then sit in the field and cry until she came to get me.

But she'd talked me through this so many times and I didn't think she'd come for me anyway. She'd call the school and they'd send a teacher to find me. They'd already offered to get my form tutor to meet me from the bus, but I didn't want that. To be escorted down the corridors would only make people stare even more – Exhibit One, Fugly Scarface with Mrs Barker as bodyguard. Instead Beth had met me at the lockers and linked her arm through mine to march me to the form room.

When a new girl gasped at the sight of me, Beth's face set as stiff as the plastic mask I'd discarded only the week before. My heart raced so fast I felt faint and I needed her arm to stop me falling. The corridor went quiet – a Mexican wave of silence spread along it as people saw us coming.

Stop looking at me! Leave me alone! I screamed it so loudly in my head that I was scared for a second I'd yelled it for real.

Everyone around me took on that blurry quality as if I was sleepwalking through a nightmare. Fuzzy blobs of faces, staring bulbous eyes. Beth half-dragged me down that corridor; I couldn't have done it by myself.

I took a deep breath and opened the toilet door, remembering just in time to look away from the mirrors. Another deep breath, and I stepped out into the corridor again.

Beth was sitting on the desk in the form room changing the cartridge in her fountain pen. She looked up as I walked in and I sensed she had news. Big news.

'Jen, hi!'

'Hi, good weekend?' I sat down on the desk next to her.

'Yeah, the battle re-enactment was brilliant! The best I've ever been to.' Beth's parents were members of a historical society who dressed up and did role plays of famous events in the area. This meant Beth wasn't exactly the coolest girl in school. Tramline braces, glasses and hair that wouldn't be tamed out of a frizz by even the hottest straighteners didn't help her case either – Lindsay used to be really catty about that – but we'd been friends since our first day at school and I liked Beth no matter what anyone said. 'I had this amazing costume – an amber underdress and a blue one over the top with this neat belt made of rope. Mum did my hair in plaits with ribbons wound in them. It looked totally authentic.'

She was not this excited just about a costume. There was more. 'And?'

She giggled. 'I met this boy . . .'

'Yeah?'

'Mmm, and he's a really nice guy.'

Well, good for her. I'd met the biggest jerk on the planet myself.

'His name's Max and he's in Year 11. And he's asked me to go to the society's harvest dance at the end of the month. I told you about it, remember? The one with the medieval theme.'

She still had more to spill, I could tell. 'Yes, I remember. And?'

Beth went red. 'Oh . . . he kissed me.'

'No way! You jammy cow. Is he fit?'

'I think he is,' she said guardedly. That meant no, I decided.

That meant Natasha Green and her friends – the bitch queens of our year – wouldn't think he was. They'd raise perfectly plucked eyebrows at him and laugh when Beth was out of sight.

'What's he look like?' After all, she could lie if she wanted. I'd probably never see him.

'About that height.' She pointed to an averagely tall boy chatting to a girl outside the classroom door. 'Brown hair. He's got a lovely personality.'

Which meant he must be hideous. Not that Beth and I were in any position to be critical because neither of us were likely to trouble the modelling world any time soon.

'Is he local?'

'He lives near Whitmere, but more your side than mine. He goes to Badeley College – boards in the week and comes home at weekends.'

'Badeley?'

'Um, yes. I asked him if he knew Steven Carlisle and he remembers him from before he got excluded. His older brother's on the rugby team with Steven, but Max says he doesn't like him much.'

I sniffed. 'Max's brother has good taste.'

'Have you seen him around lately?'

'No, but I think it was him vandalising cars at Dad's campaign group meeting.'

'What's he doing now?'

'Still working for his dad. Anyway, I don't want to talk about that loser. So, you haven't met Max before?'

'Not exactly. I've seen him at other events, but I've never had a chance to talk to him. Parents around – just too embarrassing. But it was so mad on Saturday with the battle going on that we ended up spending loads of time together because my lot and his lot were on the other side of the field. We got on really well and when our side was celebrating at the end of the battle, he kissed me.'

'Properly?'

'Not at first. He snuck it in like it was part of the re-enactment. But I didn't object, so . . .'

'And how was it?'

She grinned. 'Awesome!'

I prodded her. 'Bitch! I told you you'd get there before me.'

'Jen, maybe you should come to the next one. I know it's not your thing, but . . .' She hesitated. 'It's something to do. Get out, go somewhere new, you know.'

'Yes, I'd go down a storm.' I pointed to my cheek. 'Authentically blown up with a musket ball.'

Beth flinched. 'Don't say that. I didn't mean that and you know it.'

'Sorry,' I mouthed at her as our form teacher came in and we scrambled off the desks hastily before she went mental at us for sitting on the furniture.

8 – Ryan

On Monday morning, I lifted the bike off the boat with my ears still ringing from the sound of Mum crashing about in the kitchen. She hadn't said a word to me since I got up, not even when she slammed a bowl of soya milk porridge under my nose and shoved a tub of salad in my rucksack. I cycled the eight miles to Whitmere and freewheeled down the long hill towards town, rattling over the last stretch of cobbles. As if my nerves needed any more jangling.

Eight fifty. I was early.

Pete stuck his head out of the office. 'Mornin'. And a filthy one it is. Come in for a brew before we get started.'

I parked the bike up by the side of the Portakabin. Pete handed me a mug of tea when I went inside. Bill nodded to me, puffing up a cloud of blue smoke from his pipe.

'See that semi-trad outside?' Pete pointed out of the window.

I looked out at a yellow and black narrowboat hauled up into dry dock. 'Yes.'

'Needs an overhaul – do the works on her. You any good on the painting side?'

'Yeah, not bad.'

'The arty stuff?'

I nodded.

'Good, because I'm not. Bill normally takes that side of things, but he's got a lot on so I'll let you have a go with this one. You give me a shout to check your work regular, mind. I can't afford for you to be making a mess.'

I hovered by the sink, gulping hot tea and agreeing.

He threw an amused glance up to the ceiling. 'Sit down and drink it, lad. You're making Bill nervous.'

I shuffled over to the spare chair. I'd never seen anyone look less nervous than Bill did, sucking away on his pipe.

Pete's mouth twitched. 'Got first-day jitters, eh? I still remember my first day at work. Apprentice in a car plant in the Midlands. I was bleedin' terrified.'

Bill laughed, a phlegmy rattle. 'Aye,' he said, stretching his legs out. 'I were an electrician. Big firm up north of here. They used to torment us new lads something chronic.' He stared at me, eyes narrowing in weather-beaten skin as he took another draw on the pipe. 'Let's hope this 'un's better than the last, Pete. Terrible trouble, he were.' He took his pipe from his mouth and leaned closer to me. 'Drove us to beyond what a man can endure. Drove us there over and over again until we couldn't stand no more. We 'ad to do something! We buried him under the storage shed,' he said in a croaky whisper. 'His bones is still there.'

56

My mouth fell open, until I caught his eyes crinkling up with laughter and I snapped my jaw shut again. Bill winked.

Pete slapped the desk and his laugh boomed out. 'Your face . . . priceless!'

Bill creaked to his feet and patted a heavy hand on my shoulder as he took his mug to the sink. 'You'll do all right, lad. Never worry.'

All the same, it was stressful that morning. I was desperate to get everything right and just as desperate not to be a nuisance. I kept thinking of Cole too. I guess that was from being around Pete and Bill. They reminded me a bit of him and his mates. And they loved those boats. Cole had been like that with the bike.

After he moved on to the boat with us, he decided he needed to take a trip over to Shrewsbury and he took me along riding pillion. Mum was so loved-up that she let him talk her into letting me go as long as he rode slowly. It might have been slow to Cole, but to me it was like we were an arrow flying through the air. He'd bulked me up in his spare leathers so I didn't look so much like a kid to any passing road cops who might pull us over to check he had permission for me to be on the bike. We travelled down country lanes for miles, my arms round his waist for balance, and I learned which way to tilt as we cornered and how far to lean out.

We stopped at a council cottage in a large plot just outside Shrewsbury. 'This is Jeff's place,' Cole said, holding the bike while I scrambled off. 'Jeff!' he hollered to a small man fiddling with a bike engine outside the house.

The guy came over. 'Cole, mate, how's it going?'

They clapped each other on the back and chatted for a few minutes about people I didn't know, until Jeff asked, 'So, who's this then?'

Cole slung his arm over my shoulder. 'This is Ryan. He's part of why I'm here. Me and his mum have a thing going and we're together now. But she lives on a boat. Moves about.'

'Ah!' Jeff said, and I couldn't understand why he sounded so sympathetic. 'How much do you want?'

'Nothing, man, nothing. Just look after her for me. Take her out. Keep her ticking over.' He looked like someone taking his dog to the vet for the last time.

'Cole, what are you doing?' I interrupted.

'Must be a special woman,' Jeff said.

Cole's arm tightened round me. 'Yeah she is, eh, Ryan?'

'Er, yeah, of course. But what're you doing?'

'Can't take a Harley on a boat, son.'

'You're leaving it here . . . no, you can't . . .'

'Jeff's an old mate. I wouldn't want to see her with anyone else.'

Jeff wheeled the Harley towards the garage. 'Any time you're around, you drop in and take her for a spin. She's still yours. And when you want her back —'

Cole held up a hand in warning.

'Oh, yeah,' Jeff said, glancing at me. 'No, you won't, course.'

'Are you sure?' I asked.

He smiled briefly. 'It's only a bike, kiddo.'

But I think he left a piece of his heart in that garage. I hope he went back for it when he walked out on us.

Pete sent me into town to the bakery at lunchtime. He told me to get something for myself too and there was no way I was getting that tub of quinoa and lentil salad out of my rucksack in front of them. *Sorry, Mum . . .*

She hadn't talked to me properly since I told her about the job. Said she hadn't raised me to be part of The System. But I didn't care. I was finally having a go at real life.

It felt like a rebellion too. Especially as I watched the woman slapping greasy bacon on to white baps. I'd eaten meat before, but not since Cole went. He used to fall off the vegan wagon sometimes and take me with him for a burger. On my birthdays, he'd take me down the pub for a meal. We'd eat a packet of Polos between us on the way home so Mum wouldn't find out.

When I got back with the food, Pete took the change from me without checking it and shoved it in his back pocket. I wondered if he'd count it later when I was out of sight. 'Your tea's on the side, lad.'

This time I sat down without being told.

'You're travelling people then,' Bill said, licking his fingers as he finished the roll.

'Er, yeah.'

He filled his pipe with tobacco from a cracked leather pouch. 'All boat people was travelling folk once,' he remarked. 'The barge men. Used to carry goods all over this country on the canals. Lived on the barges with their families. The kids used to work too. Back in them days, the barges was pulled by horses. No engines then. So when they got to a tunnel, the horse couldn't tow them through, see. One of the little 'uns would unhook it and lead it round and the other kids would lie on their backs on the wings of the boat with their dad and push against the tunnel wall with their feet. Legging, it were called, and they shoved the barge through that way. Damned hard work. My granddad grew up on one of those barges. Told me some fine tales about it.' He smiled. 'Aye, all the boatmen was travellers once.'

Mum had a face like she was chewing on a rancid nut when I ducked my head in through the door and came down *Liberty*'s wooden steps. She didn't say a word.

'Hey, you've been busy!'

She had rows and rows of finished necklaces, earrings and bracelets laid out on the folding table, and a pile of the dragon torcs. She must've been at it all day without a break. A twitch ran up my spine. Not a good sign . . .

'I had to do something to keep busy instead of sitting here worrying about you,' she snapped.

I thought of the food she'd made me, cast on the roadside halfway between here and Whitmere for the birds to peck at. She'd been on her own all day. I couldn't remember the last time she'd been alone for so long – not since before Cole left. I thought of how never being away from her suffocated me and how I'd felt free today. And then how different it must have been for her, sitting here polishing stones until I came home . . .

I sat down beside her, guilt knifing me. 'Today went fine. It'll bring in some extra money anyway. Mum, these are great. Really great. Want a hand with anything?'

She took a breath in and combed her fingers through her mess of hair to loop it back. 'I'll start dinner. Tidy up for me and bag the finished ones.'

'Want me to put the price labels on?'

'Yes . . . yes . . . OK.' She hesitated and forced a smile. 'It was strange here without you today.'

I fished in my pocket and pulled out the bus timetable I'd picked up in Whitmere on the way home. 'Got this for you. There's a bus that runs through the village. Maybe you could go into town tomorrow and give those shops I told you about a try. And you could find out about the market. Do some shopping too?'

She nodded and put the timetable on the pinboard.

'It's an OK town,' I said as she got a pan from the cupboard and took ingredients from the fridge. I thought I saw tofu and shuddered. 'Plenty to look at and you'll like some of the shops. Bet there's even somewhere you can get some new supplies . . .'

I wittered on while she got dinner ready. The more I talked, the more she relaxed, so in the end I babbled on about nothing just to drive the day's silence away for her.

9 – Jenna

***Thursday was Charlie's football night so I came
home from school alone.*** I picked the letters up from the
doormat and went to put them on the hall table, but a folded
sheet of paper caught my attention. It was an A4 sheet folded in
half, with the shadow of dark lettering showing through. I
opened it.

Letters cut from a newspaper were glued on in a message:

UR A DEAD MAN

Steven – I knew it was from him. I headed for the hall chair
before my legs gave way under me. *Don't overreact – this is typical
of him. Always shouting his mouth off.* It didn't mean anything, I
told myself, trying to calm down. He was trying to scare us,
that's all. For all Steven Carlisle thought he was a big man and
not a stupid boy, when the car had crashed, he'd lain crying on
the grass. It was left to Rob White to pull me and Sarah out while
Steven whimpered and did nothing. He'd never have the guts to
do anything to Dad, no matter how much he might hate us.

I tried to put it out of my mind and focus on my homework.
If only Dad would drop this stupid campaign. It'd alienated most

of the village against the Carlisles and while I didn't care how that affected Steven one little bit, I did care if it kept people talking about the crash. All I wanted now was for it to be forgotten – as much as it could ever be possible for the village to forget Lindz and Charlotte's deaths.

I never did understand what Lindz saw in Steven, apart from the looks of course. He thought the world rotated on its axis for him alone and treated everyone as if they should agree with him.

The scrape of a key in the front door lock meant Dad was home. I ran downstairs. Mum was with him. I handed him the note. He read it and passed it to Mum. His face didn't flicker. He picked up the phone from the hall table.

Mum's hand flew to her mouth as she read the note. 'Clive, what are you doing?'

'Calling the police. I'm not having that little thug try to threaten us.'

'Are you sure that's a good idea? Maybe it would be better to ignore him.'

'Dad, let it lie, please.'

He dialled the number for the police station and walked off into his study with the phone.

'Come on, let's go and pick some apples,' Mum said. I knew she was only trying to distract me, but I didn't mind being distracted right then.

We walked down the garden to the two apple trees by our

vegetable patch. Mum held the basket while I reached up and picked the ripe ones from the lower branches.

'Get that one. No, up a –' Mum stopped suddenly.

I followed the direction of her eyeline over the hedge and into next door's garden. Lindz's dad was standing there, staring into space. We watched him for a while, but he seemed frozen to the spot. Mum put her arm round my shoulders. 'Come inside,' she whispered.

'Do you think we should say hello?' I whispered back.

She shook her head uncertainly. 'I think we'd better not, Jen. Last time Dad and I tried to speak to him, he got very upset. I don't think he's well at all just now. We might make him feel worse and we don't want to do that.'

Maybe I was like Lindz's pony – too much for him to see. I sort of understood that. I think perhaps I understood it better than anyone.

Charlie's friend's mum brought him home after football practice, and he came stomping into my bedroom, mud-spattered.

'I got dropped from the team for the next game,' he said, flopping on to my bed. Normally I'd have yelled at him for messing my duvet up, but he looked too upset.

'Why?'

'Doh – someone else was better than me.'

I put my homework down. This was going to take a while.

'You've trained loads. Maybe you had an off day.'

He prodded my teddy bear in the eye with a stiff finger. 'I was beyond bad, and anyway, it's not the same now.'

'Don't do that to Barney. It's not his fault. Why isn't it the same?'

'Because you used to be in goal for me before and I could practise shooting better.'

'You said I was rubbish in goal!'

'Yeah, you are, but it's still easier when you have a goalie to aim around, even if they are useless.' He prodded Barney again viciously. 'You never do anything with me now.'

That was true. I'd hardly spent any time with him since the accident. 'I was worried about getting my face hit by the ball.'

He pouted. 'It's better now though and you still don't do stuff with me, even other stuff, not like we used to.'

I hadn't realised he'd missed that. Maybe I had been too wrapped up in me. Most little brothers would have sulked like anything over how much attention I'd had over the past months, but Charlie hadn't. 'OK, so tomorrow night when you get home, we'll practise your shooting. How about that? And we'll keep doing it until you're so awesome, they can't wait to get you back on the team.'

His face lit up. 'Thanks, Jen! Maybe you're not the suckiest sister ever.'

'Thanks, Charlie. Your compliments slay me.' I laughed and

shoved him off the duvet. 'Now go shower – you're minging.'

He stuck his tongue out and tried to rub his sweaty, muddy shirt on me, then trotted off to get cleaned up.

I finished my homework when he'd gone and went for a long soak in the bath before I went to bed. I fell asleep almost immediately.

A couple of hours later, something woke me with a start. I saw the landing light go on under my door. Dad shouted, 'Stay in bed. I'll sort it out.' He thundered down the stairs. I heard him swear briefly and threw the front door open. Mum yelled, 'Clive, don't go out there,' but I heard the crunch of his feet on our gravel drive, then Mum's feet running downstairs too. When I crept to the top of the stairs and looked down, I saw the hall carpet was covered in broken glass. A brick lay on the floor by Mum's feet and the window beside the door was smashed.

Dad came back in. 'No sign of them now. And no sign of a car. That proves it was someone local.' He snatched the phone up. 'I'm calling the police again. Friendly chat, they said. Warn him off. That didn't do much good. He needs locking up.'

'I'll go and check on the kids,' Mum said. 'Ask the police to keep the noise down if they come out. It's school tomorrow.'

I scooted back to the bedroom. Charlie had slept through it all. If the roof blew off, he'd not wake. I pulled the covers over my head and pretended I was asleep because I was too angry to talk to Mum about it now. Angry with Steven Carlisle for being

67

walking, breathing scum, and angry with Dad for getting us into all of this. The police wouldn't find any evidence that Steven was involved – he'd have an alibi for sure.

Mum hovered in the doorway for a few minutes. I could sense she was unconvinced by my act, but she closed the door quietly and left me.

I burrowed my head into the pillow.

The helicopter engine buzzed loudly in my ears. Lindz laughed. 'Come on, do it! Do it!'

I'd had this dream before. Always the same. She always laughed. Always ran forward to the open side of the helicopter with a big grin. Flung herself out into the sky, shouting 'Come on!' as she fell away from me.

And I always followed. Sick, knees weak, but I followed.

We fell through the sky together, pulling the cords of the parachutes at the same time. Hers never opened, but she still smiled, that same wild grin as she plummeted down to the deserted forest beneath, the canopy of the trees a rippling ocean of green.

It looked peaceful. I always thought that.

Until Lindz hit the first tree. She died a different way each time. Sometimes she hit her head. Sometimes she fell feet first. This time her neck snapped back like a broken doll as she plunged into the trees and disappeared.

I floated after her until my parachute got caught in the branches and I hung from the harness. The canopy snapped back into place above me — nobody would see me from the air.

Below, far below, Lindsay's body lay on the ground. But me, I dangled there. Suspended in the trees where nobody would ever find me.

10 – Ryan

Does any pay packet feel as good as your first?
Especially when you get a ten quid-bonus for keeping the shop customers happy. Pete was impressed with how patient I was with the old ones and how that made money land in his till. I tried to tell him it wasn't difficult, talking to them about all the bargeware stuff because Mum was into all that, but he waved me off with a laugh and told me to enjoy the rest of the day.

I cycled into the town square and went into a craft shop with a jingly door curtain made of metal bells. Some of Mum's jewellery was on sale in a locked counter on the desk and two women were bending over, examining it. 'Ooh, Sandra, these are lovely. New in?'

'Yes, I'm rather impressed with that range too. Very high quality and all handmade locally,' the woman behind the counter answered. She looked up sharply as she noticed me. 'Can I help you?'

'I'm looking for a present,' I said. 'Joss stick holders?'

She smiled, the kind of smile a security guard gives you when they're watching you, and she pointed me to a rack at the back.

'You'll also find a wide selection of fragranced sticks,' she added, sounding like an advert.

I ignored the usual brass holders – boring – and rooted around until I found a painted one Mum would like. Her old one had got broken a few months ago and she'd been sticking incense sticks in a blob of Blu-tack ever since. I picked up two packets of joss sticks to go with the holder.

'Do you gift-wrap?' I asked the woman at the counter when I went to pay.

'Yes, an extra pound if you want curling ribbon and handmade paper.'

'Yes, please.' It'd cost me more to buy the stuff myself and I'd probably mess it up.

'Are they selling well?' I pointed to the jewellery display as she made curls of silver ribbon with the scissors. How did women know how to do that stuff? I'd cut my finger off or something if I tried that.

She gave me a strange look. 'Yes.'

'My mum makes them.'

Her face changed – a smile spread over it. 'Ah, you're Karen's son! She told me about you. Working at the marina, aren't you?'

'Yes, just finished for the day.'

'Are these for your mum?'

'Yeah, I thought I'd get her something with my first week's wages.'

She got that cooey expression like the old ladies in the boatyard did when I helped them. 'No charge for the wrapping then.' She dropped her voice to a whisper and nodded over at the two women who were now looking at sequined cushions in the corner of the shop. 'Those two have just spent fifty pounds each on your mum's work. That's a nice profit for both of us. Tell her to bring more in on Monday if she has any.'

I couldn't wait to see Mum's face when I got back with a present and good news, and I belted back to Strenton. I stopped at the bottom of the hill up to the village to strip my T-shirt off. Summer seemed to be lasting forever this year and the afternoon sun beat down on my shoulders as I powered up the hill, standing up on the pedals for better leverage.

Strenton came into view and I pedalled harder. I whizzed over the crown of the hill and then zoomed down the narrow lane that wound along to the canal cut-off at the bridge.

I saw something move by the hedge in a field to my left.

What the . . .?

Shit!

A flash of orange scudded in front of my wheels.

I swerved the bike across the road away from it, fast as I could. Jammed on the brakes. The tyres hissed on the road and I sailed over the handlebars.

The bike went sideways and I carried on forwards. I hit the road on my side and yelled in pain as bare skin ground against tarmac.

11 – Jenna

Saturday afternoon I trotted Scrabble through the village. Raggs ambled ahead of us, sniffing interesting dog smells, cocking his leg every few metres and generally mooching around. Strenton was quiet and empty except for Mr Ardwell trimming the privet hedge in the front garden of his black and white cottage. He waved as I passed. There were less than two hundred houses scattered in and around the area and everyone knew everyone else. Probably down to what they had for breakfast. Last year, when Charlie had been rushed into hospital to have his appendix out and I'd been dispatched to the village to buy him some comics, eight people had stopped me to ask how he was before I reached the shop.

We turned into Tenter Lane and I slowed Scrabble to a walk. The Grange, where the Carlisles lived, lay to the right and from Scrabble's back I could see over the high holly hedge into the grounds. Outside the garage block, a boy was washing two cars. Even from this distance, the way he held the hose and soaped the bonnet, his whole body language, said he was bellyaching about doing it.

Steven Carlisle. Official bad boy of Strenton even before he'd trashed his new car that night last January. Outrageously good-looking, and he knew it.

Lindz used to say a boy can be good-looking and he can be hot, but that one doesn't necessarily lead to the other. Steven was both, she said.

Up until last autumn, we'd never seen much of him except at a distance. He was three years older than Lindz, four years older than me, and he'd boarded at Badeley College. His dad owned a nationwide chain of home-furnishing stores and both his parents were away a lot on business. At Christmas, the family went skiing in Switzerland. In the summer, they stayed in their villa in the south of France. Easter was the only time we saw him around, until last November when Badeley threw him out in his final year of sixth form. We heard it was drugs. Rumour had it that it wasn't the first time, but whatever the reason it was never made public.

So there he was, back in Strenton with nothing to do. His dad made him go to work in the Whitmere office of the family business, fuming after all the money he'd spent on Steven's education. That was how Steven had met Rob White, working in the delivery depot shifting boxes. Rob supplemented his wages by pedalling gear small time and Steven had just found his next supplier.

We met him one Saturday morning when Lindz and I drifted

along to the village shop. Steven was outside on the bench, rolling a cigarette, with a face that said he was about to die of boredom.

Lindz's eyes opened wide at the sight of him, a huge present just waiting for her to unwrap. He did look impressive though. Six foot two and shoulders that looked like he played rugby, which we later found out he did. Blond hair and blue eyes and the remains of his French tan lingering. He had cheekbones to die for and a full mouth that might've looked a bit too girly if it wasn't set in a permanent sneer.

Good-looking – tick.

Hot – tick.

Badass attitude – double tick.

'Wait for me,' Lindz muttered and she strolled over to him, leaving me pretending to read the notices in the shop window. 'Hi, I heard you were back,' she said.

He gave her a 'Do I know you?' expression that would've withered me. Lindz just reflected it back at him until he laughed and leaned back in the seat to stare up at her with more interest. 'How do you not go crazy in this place?' he asked. 'It completely sucks and I've only been back a week.'

'Don't you know that in villages you have to make your own entertainment?'

I spun round, hardly believing my ears. She couldn't really have said that, or meant it how it sounded. But I saw from her face that she did.

And Steven knew it too.

They were hardly apart after that.

But he never even went to her funeral.

We took the bridleway back towards the house and once past the woods, Raggs scented home and scampered ahead. I opened my mouth to shout him back . . .

Too late.

Something hurtled past the open gateway. I heard a simultaneous crash of metal and Raggs setting up a volley of frantic barks.

I jumped down from Scrabble's back and hauled him to the open gate, looping his reins quickly over the gatepost before I ran into the lane.

'Oh, I'm so sorry! Are you . . .' The words died on my lips. A bike was sprawled on the road in front of me, wheels spinning, and to my left a boy groaned on the ground with Raggs running round him like a mad thing.

The boat boy . . . oh God, no . . .

I stared at him, my stomach sinking into my riding boots, and tried to wish myself invisible. Raggs stopped running in circles and leaped on him, licking his face madly.

'No! Gerroff!' He shoved Raggs away, but not roughly.

I ran over and clipped the dog's lead on. 'Um, are you all right?' Then I noticed what he was lying in. *No . . . oh no . . . let me die now* . . . A pile of horse droppings. A pile I was pretty sure Scrabble had made earlier. My dog had knocked him off his bike and now he was lying in my horse's muck.

He sat up with a wince – didn't he ever wear a shirt? – and wriggled his legs. 'Yeah, I'm fine.'

I clapped my hand to my mouth when I saw his back. 'Oh my God! You're really bleeding!'

He peered over his shoulder. 'Eww!' When he looked at the ground behind him in disgust, I braced myself for a hail of abuse. 'Aww, no, I didn't . . .'

Sorry, sorry, sorry . . .

He turned back, looked up at me and burst out laughing. 'Guess at least I got a soft landing, huh? Good aim!' He scrambled up, gritting his teeth. 'Are you all right? You're white as a ghost.'

'You're bleeding,' I said again stupidly.

He scrunched his face up and twisted round in an effort to see his back. 'I'll heal – no big deal.' I gave up waiting for him to explode. It didn't seem as if he was going to. Instead he grinned ruefully at me. 'Look a right mess, don't I?' Then his eyes widened. 'Oh shit!' He hobbled over to his bike and yanked a gift-wrapped parcel out of the rucksack on the back. He felt it over carefully and relaxed. 'It's not broken.'

'Is it a present?'

'Yeah, for my mum.' He tucked the package back into the rucksack and picked his bike up.

77

I swallowed hard at the sight of the blood trickling down his back, mixing with blobs of horse muck. It must hurt a lot more than he was letting on. 'Is your bike damaged?'

'Nah, it's a heap of old junk anyway. Looks all right.' He wheeled it a few steps. 'Yeah, it's fine.' He smiled at me again. 'No harm done.'

'Thank you . . . for not running my dog over.'

He frowned and shook his head. 'As if I'd have run into him if I could avoid it. What do you think I am?'

Was he cross? He didn't look cross. I hadn't meant to insult him. 'Sorry, it's just . . . it's my fault and I feel bad. And your back . . . is there someone in on your boat who can help you clean it up because it's really dangerous to get dirt in cuts and you should get it seen to as quickly as possible. It could get infected. My house is just here if you want to come in and wash it off . . .' As soon as I said it, I wanted to snatch the words back. Stupid, stupid, stupid. He'd think I was coming on to him . . .

'Oh no, that's . . . er . . . nice of you, but I, er . . .'

My face burned. 'I only asked because you're bleeding really badly, and do you even have a shower on a boat? And . . . and you won't report us to the police for having an out of control dog, will you?'

'God, no!' He looked like I'd suggested he ate babies. 'Of course not.' He chewed on his lip and watched me from under his lashes, which fascinated me because really that was a girl's thing to do, but it didn't seem girly at all when he did it. 'Sure, we've got a shower. It's got everything you get in a house.'

He said it significantly, like I was supposed to understand something from that. I didn't.

'We live on the boat,' he said after a pause. 'All the time. We're not really supposed to be moored down there.'

I got it, finally. 'Oh . . . oh right. Look, my mum and dad are out if you're worried about awkward questions. They've taken my little brother ice skating and won't be back for ages.'

He had an odd look on his face. It was only later that I realised properly what it reminded me of. A few years ago we'd visited a nature reserve with Dartmoor ponies. If we approached very quietly and held our hands out, and waited, and waited, then sometimes they would come to us. With that same wary look in their eyes that the boat boy had as he said, 'You won't say anything about our boat, will you? I don't want you to lie, but –'

'No. Are you kidding? My parents would go ballistic if they knew I'd let Raggs run off and cause an accident.'

A lump of horse turd fell off his back. He stared at it solemnly and that appeared to decide him. 'Er, can I come in after all? I stink, and Mum's wound up enough about . . . stuff . . . without me coming home like this.'

I pointed him through the garden gate leading off the paddock. 'That's the back door. I'll be one minute,' and I jogged Scrabble down the field to the loosebox. He wasn't too sweaty and it was so warm I decided that he could dry off in the field without a rub-down. By the time I got to the house, the boat boy had found the outside tap. He was crouched underneath the stream of cold water, trying to sluice the muck off his back without getting his jeans wet. His screwed-up face said how much it hurt.

'You could have done that inside.'

'Don't want to drop crap all over your house.' He shifted his shoulder to angle the water stream on to a dirtier part.

'Um, you've got some in your hair.'

He groaned and stuck his head under the tap. 'Has it gone?'

'Nearly. Not quite. No, left a bit.' I gathered up my courage as the water missed the spot again and grabbed his head, manoeuvring it into place. I gave his hair a quick rub to get the muck out, but it wasn't coming off his back at all.

'You'll get it on your hands,' was his only response. No 'eww, don't touch me, Shrek – you make me vom'.

'It's no worse than mucking out. Besides, it's my fault.' I took the opportunity to have a closer look at his back. 'Look, this is no good. Hang on.'

I left him under the tap and went inside the house. Hopefully Raggs wouldn't bounce around and annoy him too much. The stupid dog had done enough damage already. I grabbed Mum's antiseptic handwash and two clean tea towels from the kitchen and ran back out.

The boy was still wriggling about under the tap. He twisted

his arm into a contortion over his back to try to get the muck off.

'Um, would you like me to do that?' I asked, my skin running hot and cold with embarrassment.

He looked up. 'Yeah, thanks.' He said it as if it wasn't an issue, being touched by a strange girl with a crisped face.

I soaped a blob of handwash into his hair and rinsed that out first. His hair kicked up at the edges when it was wet, hints of curl.

Breathe in . . . breathe out . . . breathe in . . . try not to act like a complete loser . . . keep your cool . . .

Then, hands shaking, I started on his back. 'This is going to sting, but –'

'Be fine,' he said, his head upside down beneath the tap.

I'd never touched a boy like this before – a real one that is, not a kid like Charlie. I knew they were supposed to feel different to girls, but I'd not really grasped what that meant until I was soaping his back. He felt . . . amazing. Soft skin stretched over taut muscle that made his body feel hard in a way mine didn't. I shouldn't notice that, but it was impossible not to and my fingers didn't want to leave his skin.

He scrunched his face up as I cleaned his shoulder.

'Sorry.'

'It's all right,' he said through clenched teeth.

I soaked one of the towels under the tap and used it to swill him off until his back was clean and free of blood, but he was a mess – raw patches down one side and his shoulder and elbow mashed up. 'This does look awful, you know. Maybe you should go to hospital.'

He stood up, his head dripping, and took another look. 'It's only a few grazes. Looks worse than it is.'

'If you wore a T-shirt, it wouldn't have been half so bad.' I passed him the dry towel for his hair.

'I like not wearing a T-shirt,' he protested.

I checked out an eyeful of tanned chest and flat stomach. Who wouldn't like him not wearing a T-shirt? 'I suppose I could dab some antiseptic on and try covering it with gauze if you want.'

He grinned encouragingly. 'That'll do.'

He followed me into the kitchen and his eyes grew very big. 'Wow, this is massive.'

As I opened a cupboard to get a bowl, I caught sight of my reflection in the leaded glass – I'd forgotten not to look, and I jerked back.

'Are you OK?'

He was right behind me. I could see his reflection too. I shut the door quickly and rummaged in a drawer for the Dettol and first-aid kit. When I turned round, he was sitting on a chair watching me.

He touched the right side of his face. 'What happened?'

Direct again. Like nobody else would. And he was looking straight at me.

'Don't answer if you don't want to.'

Somebody braver than me said the words with my voice. 'A car accident.'

'It wasn't long ago, was it?'

'Earlier this year.'

I turned away and filled the bowl with water and Dettol. The water clouded up and the smell of disinfectant wafted around the kitchen.

'My name's Ryan. What's yours?'

'Jenna,' I said, unrolling gauze.

I borrowed somebody else's legs to walk over and put the bowl on the kitchen table.

'I was dead lucky with the name, you know. Mum nearly called me Anarchy.'

I choked. 'She nearly called you what?'

'No, you heard right.' He sounded gloomy, but I could see he was hiding a smile. 'Anarchy. If I'd been a girl, I would've been Liberty. But I wasn't so she used that on the boat instead.'

'What changed her mind? About Anarchy.' I dipped a length of gauze in the water and dabbed the top of his shoulder, intending to work my way down the cuts. He tensed. 'Did that hurt?'

'No, it's not you. I was thinking what a lucky escape I had.'

Liar!

'She said the runes told her not to.'

'Er, pardon?'

He sighed. 'The runes. They're an ancient Viking alphabet.

She does stuff with them, throws them around. She says they tell her things.'

I grabbed a fresh piece of gauze and moved to the next patch of scraped skin. 'Do they?'

'No, it's a load of hippy crap.' He paused and I wondered if I'd hurt him again. 'But then they did tell her not to call me Anarchy so they can't be totally useless.' He tilted his head back and looked up at me, faking relief, and I saw his eyes were a warm hazel. 'Don't you like ice skating? You said the others had gone skating.'

'Oh, er, it's OK, but . . . I had homework.'

'So you'd have gone with them if you hadn't?' He hissed a breath in as I cleaned over the bruised shoulder blade.

I had the oddest feeling he knew I wouldn't so I didn't answer and concentrated on getting some stubborn grit out of the wound.

'Don't you go to college or school?' I asked after a while.

'Never did.'

'What, never?'

'No. Mum did home tuition with me. She thinks schools brainwash you.'

I changed the water in the bowl at the sink. 'That's weird. Oh, not your mum! But never having gone to school. I can't imagine it. How do you make friends?'

He shrugged, forgetting his cuts, and then looked as if he wished he hadn't. 'You make friends with other traveller kids when you stop up for a while. Like when we had to put the boat in dry dock for repairs and we'd go and stay with friends of Mum's for a bit.'

'Why only traveller kids? Here, put your elbow in the bowl and let it soak.'

'Because other kids don't want to know you.' His forehead creased into a frown and his voice took on a trace of hostility. Bitter, even. He cocked his head on one side and looked at me. 'You know when I saw you down by the canal, I thought you were being snotty with me because of that. At first.'

I shook my head vehemently. 'I didn't realise you lived on the boat. I thought you were on holiday.' I knew what he meant. I'd heard people talk about travellers: thieves, live like pigs, violent, not to be trusted. But I couldn't match any of that up with the boy in front of me. 'No, it wasn't that.'

'Yeah, I know.' He smiled and I dug my nails into my palms because I knew he knew the real reason I'd snapped at him that day.

'Have your family always been travellers?' I asked, to take the attention away from me.

He shook his head. 'We're not Gypsies or traditional travellers. Mum got into it after uni. She went on the road at first, then she lived in a teepee for a bit, then she got the narrowboat. She's into New Age stuff. There were a lot of them travelling back then, and they all hung out together. But most have packed it in now. There's less of us every year.'

I vaguely knew what New Age travellers were, but not much more. 'So don't you mix with the other kinds . . . um, Gypsies and . . . ?'

'Nah, different culture. They stick with their own and we stick with ours, what's left of us.' He didn't seem to like talking about this much and I got a feeling, when he started looking round the kitchen, that he was trying to find a way to change the subject. 'This is big. You must get lost in here. Ours is tiny.'

He smiled at me again. Lindz would have said he looked hotter with the brooding face he had a minute ago, but I liked the smile better. He sat placidly as I dabbed cream on his cuts and stole sneaky looks at his profile. He didn't have a model face like Steven Carlisle. His jaw was too narrow for that and his nose tilted up too much – not a ski jump, but a definite lift. He wasn't as bulky as Steven either, but whatever – he was gorgeous.

'You're really good at this,' he said.

I wished he'd stop smiling at me because every time he did I felt like a wobbly jelly being smacked with a spoon. It was infectious – made me want to smile back at him, but I was too shy to do that. 'Charlie, that's my little brother, is the most accident-prone thing on the planet. He's always falling out of a tree or something. If Mum's not home, I have to patch him up. Dad's useless with blood.' I taped the last piece of gauze on. 'All done.'

'Brilliant. Thanks.' He pulled a T-shirt out of his rucksack and eased it on.

I rolled my eyes. 'Better late than never. You could still get attacked by another crazy dog before you get home.'

He shivered, playing along. 'Yeah, and yours is out there waiting to pounce. I'd better go. Mum'll be freaking about where I am.'

I opened the back door and scooped Raggs up as he burst in. 'Thanks for not being mad at me.'

He shook his head. 'It was an accident. Forget it. Bye, Shortie.' He patted Raggs on the head, picked up his bike and wheeled it off, waving as he disappeared round the side of the house.

I closed the door and sat down in a daze with Raggs on my knee. 'OK, he is so not what I expected.' Raggs licked my chin. 'He's . . . he's just nice. Even after what you did, he still made a fuss of you. And he didn't stare, you know. He looked at me like there wasn't anything different about me.' Only Mum and Dad and Charlie and Beth managed that and it had taken them a while. And yes, he'd talked to me like I would to Charlie, and no more than that, but he'd actually *talked*. Properly.

Stupid, the curl of warmth bubbling inside me. I tried to stop it, but it wouldn't quite be frozen out.

12 – Ryan

***Bill and I unloaded a delivery of engine oil outside
the shed.*** He puffed as he bent to pull bottles from the box.

'I'll do that,' I offered. 'You price them up and I'll carry
them over to the shop.'

'Thanks, lad.' He checked his watch. 'Not long to clocking
off now.' He stretched to relieve his cramped back and then
groaned. 'Oh lord, here's trouble.'

A girl in school uniform strolled towards us, her white shirt
undone at the neck and her tie loosened. Her skirt ended halfway
down her thighs. Nice legs! Bit tacky though. She was orange
with fake tan and the big gold hoops in her ears nearly brushed
her shoulders.

'Who's she?' I hissed.

'Sadie, Pete's daughter. Sixteen going on thirty,' Bill said out
of the side of his mouth.

She came over, swaying her hips more now she'd spotted us.

'Dad around?' She spoke to Bill, but her eyes were on me.

'In the shop,' he grunted.

'Who's this?'

'New lad.'

'Mmm, I can see that. Doesn't he have a name?'

'Ryan,' I replied.

She looked me over like I was a choc ice she wanted to lick. 'I expect I'll see you around, Ryan. I come down here a lot.' She sauntered off towards the shop, casting a look back to make sure I was watching.

'Aye, comes here a lot when she wants something,' Bill growled. 'Put a bloody T-shirt on, will you? That one'll eat you for breakfast. And her dad don't like no one messing around with his little girl so watch yerself.'

What was it with people nagging me about my shirt? I looked down at myself as I pulled the T-shirt on. Nothing wrong there. I looked all right. Not bad, not bad at all.

When I got home that evening, I headed for my usual after-work shower while Mum made dinner in the kitchen. I could see a bit of me in the steamy mirror as I dried off and that looked OK, but it was only the top part of my chest. I headed to the kitchen for a second opinion.

'Mum, am I too skinny or too fat or all right?'

'Beautiful,' she said, chopping peppers and not even looking.

'Will you look, please?' *I do actually look different to when I was ten, you know.*

She turned. 'Perfect. Who is she?'

'Nobody. Just asking generally.'

She raised an eyebrow. 'Generally perfect then. Gorgeous. Pass me an onion.'

'Mum!'

She rinsed her hands under the tap. 'Come here.' They were cold and wet when she grabbed my face and turned it from side to side. 'Yes, perfect covers it.'

'You're my mum. You have to say that. Try to be objective. Can I have some weights for my birthday?'

'What for?'

'Duh! To build my muscles up.'

'We'll see.' She turned back to chopping the peppers.

They must teach mothers to say that when they're giving birth. Like it's the last thing they learn before they push you out into the world. 'When your kid asks for something you're not going to let them have, just say "We'll see" and that'll shut them up.'

'What about just a few dumb-bells then?'

'Ryan, go away and do something constructive. Read a book.'

'Exercise is constructive.'

'Pass me the onion. There's some exercise for you.'

'Fine! I'll buy them out of my wages.' I stomped over to a chair and flopped down. Yes, it was childish, but she never let me do normal stuff. Cole'd had weights. It was OK for him. He didn't have to be friggin' *sensitive*.

This was kind of a big deal with me. After Cole walked out, Mum got hammered. She didn't do that often. 'All men are bastards, Ryan,' she'd said, sitting on the end of my bed swigging a bottle of wine. 'But you're not going to be. That's why I've brought you up to be different. To be in touch with your feminine side. To appreciate women and their power. To be sensitive.'

I was a *boy* though, and I liked it. I'd had my first shave last month. Did she even know that?

She went on and on. 'Women are the strong ones. That's why men feel threatened by us. They're weak so they want to be in control all the time. To take us over. They wage wars. Murder. Abuse. Because deep down they're jealous of our power to create. All men can do is destroy.'

Thanks for that, Mum.

'But you'll be different.'

So why did she always go for men like that? She never picked a man like the kind she said she wanted me to be. If they were such bastards, why did she keep choosing them?

I bet the orange girl wasn't bothered if I was sensitive. Bet she was just interested in what's in my pants.

That was the thing with girls. They loved the whole traveller thing. Everyone else hated us, but when I told girls I lived on a boat, they couldn't get enough of me. I found that out at the first biker festival Cole took us to. He always covered for me with

Mum. If she'd known what I was up to, she'd have gone mental and lectured me for eternity about respect and the sacredness of women, babbled about moon goddesses and all that. But Cole just grinned and asked me if I had enough johnnies.

I got up and stood over Mum's shoulder, frowning. 'What're we having for dinner?'

'Couscous and tofu and red pepper salsa.'

I tutted. Loudly.

'Ryan, if you're not going to do anything useful, you can arrange my beads for me. I want to do some more work tonight. I was meditating earlier with the quartz and I felt inspiration flow into me. I want to channel it before it dissipates. And the moon is full tonight. It's a powerful time.'

For fuck's sake! Why couldn't I have a normal mother and a normal life?

The orange girl, Sadie, came to the boatyard again the next day. I knew she would. She arrived just as we'd closed and I was cycling up the lane. She stopped when she saw me coming and stood waiting, hand on hip. She must've rolled her skirt up because it barely covered her bum today. Great legs – not too thin, not too fat. Pity about the orangeness, but you couldn't have everything.

'Your dad's still in the yard.'

She leaned on my handlebars. 'I didn't come to see my dad.'

Result! I was in there.

'You want to buy me a milkshake?'

She didn't hang about.

I waited, as if I was thinking about it. 'Yeah, all right.' I got off the bike and wheeled it up the lane. She walked ahead, letting me get a good view of her legs and I didn't waste the opportunity. Her tits weren't that big. It looked like she had one of those push-up bras on, the kind that leave you disappointed when they come off. Probably padded too. We went on up to the shops, her silent and showing off, me silent and appreciative.

'What flavour?' I asked as she slid into a table by the window at the burger bar.

'Strawberry.'

'Want anything else?'

'No.'

When I came back with the drinks, she watched me as she tore the top off the wrapper around the straw. Then she slid the paper slowly and deliberately down the length of the straw. She stuck the straw into the shake and sucked hard on the end. I wanted to laugh at how obvious she was being, but that would've wrecked my chances.

'You doing anything tonight?' she asked.

I shrugged. 'Not much.'

'Nothing to do round here anyway.' She stirred the shake with the straw. 'It's a dump.'

I nodded. I'd been through some dumps and Whitmere wasn't one of them. Quiet, yes, but she had no idea what a dump was. Wasn't going to argue though.

'It's got even worse lately. We can't even get in a car now without the police pulling us over and hassling us.'

I said nothing, just let her keep talking.

'All year it's been this way. Since some dumb posh kid from one of the villages put his car into a field. He was off his face.' She checked I was listening and I nodded so she went on, satisfied. 'So were the others in the car. Two girls got killed and another got her face fried when the car caught fire . . .'

Jenna?

She'd said it was a car accident. And she'd said it was this year. It had to be the same accident. But off their faces? Jenna didn't look the type. Too much of a little girl.

'Which village?'

'Strenton. Why?'

So it was Jenna. But she was so quiet. It didn't fit. Unless she'd been different before the accident. But even so . . . 'No reason.'

'I've got to go soon. You want to meet me later? Hang out?'

'I don't think your dad would like that.'

She peeked up at me, sucking on her straw for a moment, before she said, 'My dad doesn't have to know.'

'I can't lose that job.'

I didn't want any trouble with Pete. I liked him and I liked the job. But Sadie wanted to get together with someone so it might as well be me. And she liked having to do a bit of work to get me now. She liked the challenge. But she'd turn the tables later and want me to be the one doing the running.

My one talent – reading girls for stuff like that. If you watched people enough, you picked up things like that. Body language, little looks, the way things were said – people gave themselves away. And I'd seen Mum play those games over and over again.

Sadie reached across and put her hand over mine. 'Hey,' she said, her hard edge hidden away, 'we can go somewhere quiet if you like. Where we won't get seen by anyone. Just you and me. Dad'll never know.'

I bit back a smile. 'OK.'

Home and a shower and dinner. Then I broke the news to Mum. 'Going out now.'

'Where?'

'Into Whitmere.'

'Ryan, I've been on my own all day!'

'Am I not allowed to have a life?'

And I left, not waiting for an answer.

Sadie was already at the bus stop on the edge of town when I got there. I was ten minutes late. Deliberately. She waved a bottle of vodka and a torch at me. 'This way,' she said, and led me down an overgrown path to a field at the back of the town

Rugby Club. A large hut stood at the rear of the ground in overgrown grass. She reached up to the window in the wooden wall, standing on tiptoe, and prised it open. 'It's been broken ages,' she said with a giggle. 'I don't think they know. They don't use it any more. Give me a leg-up.'

I stirruped my hands and she stepped up, opening the window wider and wriggling through with her mini-skirted bum in my face. She held the window while I vaulted up and squeezed in.

The hut was dry and smelled of leather and dried mud. There was a pile of old kit bags in the corner and she sat on it and opened the vodka. She took a swig and passed it to me. I drank and she rubbed her arms, watching me.

'Are you cold?' I screwed the cap back on the bottle.

'Mmm.'

I sat down beside her and handed her the bottle before I pulled her into my lap and wrapped my arms round her. 'That better?' I rubbed her arm, and then let my hand slide round . . .

'Yeah,' she said, breathing a bit faster.

I nearly put myself off then wondering if her tits were orange too. Did she put the fake tan all over them? Or, when I got her bra off, would they stand out white against the orange like poached eggs in reverse?

She felt good though, warm and enthusiastic. I leaned back against the hut wall and took another drink. She gulped down more after me. I didn't kiss her, just looked at her, not smiling, not saying anything, not doing anything until she got nervous and leaned forward to kiss me. I moved my head away. She stopped in confusion and I waited for a moment until she frowned and pulled back. I laughed and grabbed her and kissed her.

Ten minutes later, I found the fake tan did go all the way. And the bra was padded.

We got dressed quickly afterwards. It was cold. She snuggled up against me to finish the vodka. I cuddled her for a bit. She didn't expect me to talk, just grunt while she went on and on about her friends and stuff and . . . I'm not sure what because I stopped listening. I kissed her again in the end to shut her up.

We both played it cool when we left the hut and walked back up to the bus stop slowly.

'Do you live far?' I asked. It was past eleven and I wasn't going to let her trail down some dark street on her own.

She pointed to a road about fifty metres away. 'Just down there.'

There were plenty of streetlamps. 'Go on, I'll wait until you get round the corner.'

She hesitated. 'See you around?'

'Yeah,' I said, leaning against the bus shelter.

She opened her mouth, then closed it without saying anything and hurried off.

I bet myself a fiver she'd be outside the marina again tomorrow.

Mum was waiting up when I got back. 'So who is she?' she asked, twisting a jewellery clasp fiercely.

'No one special. I just went for a drink.'

She didn't look right. Something about her eyes. 'I don't want you out drinking. You're only sixteen, Ryan.'

'Since when did you care about the law?'

'It's not the law I care about.'

Her hands shook on the pliers as if they had cramp. Piles of bagged up work by her feet. I definitely didn't like the look of this.

'Mum, I don't want to fight. I'm tired. I'm going to bed. OK? I've got to get up for work tomorrow.'

'You stay home tomorrow night.' Her hands fumbled on the pliers and she dropped them.

I bent and picked them up and packed them away in her toolbox. Then I gathered up her equipment. 'Yeah, course. I'll come straight home after work and help with dinner. We can go for a walk after.' She'd been stuck on this boat too long. It drove me nuts. What did it do to her? 'Why don't you go to bed too? I'll make you some camomile tea.'

I lay awake in bed for a long time. If Sadie turned up tomorrow, I'd blow her out. Mum needed me. Sure, I could explain, but Sadie wouldn't be interested, not in my real life. It was her fantasy she wanted. Being blown out wouldn't wreck that. Me babbling about Mum would. That was the thing about the girls who chased me. They lived in their own little worlds in their heads. They made their own realities and I was just there to make them feel good. It didn't bother me. I never got attached. It was just sex.

Sadie did turn up the next day and waited for me at the top of the street. And I did blow her out. Said I had other stuff on and maybe another time. She acted like she wasn't bothered, but I saw the shock on her face, and then the hurt before she hid it. I didn't feel proud of myself.

But Mum looked better when I got home. Calmer. We made dinner together. We went for a long walk and looked out over the village from a distance.

'You were right. It's pretty,' she said, and she hugged me. 'My special boy!'

I felt guilty for feeling suffocated again, but I hugged her back because I loved her. And I didn't understand how those two feelings could sit in a person side by side.

13 – Jenna

I'd discarded a pile of clothes on the bed before I finally decided what to wear. When I sat down to straighten my hair, I did it by touch alone. I was good at that now. But eventually I couldn't put the moment off any longer and I got the hand mirror out from the wardrobe.

This was the first time I'd used the make-up since the dermatology appointment at the hospital after the mask came off. I went through it all in my head, trying to remember exactly how to use each product.

'First,' the nurse had said, 'you put on a fresh layer of moisturiser and let it sink in for a couple of minutes. This one's much lighter than your massage cream.' She smoothed some over my face and it felt light and cool.

She arranged some pots in front of me on the table. 'The next part we do in three stages. We start with some concealer. You can do this in small sections so by the time you have to look at the whole of your face to put the foundation on, it's already looking better.' I swallowed and kept my eyes on the pots. She patted my hand. 'It helps some patients, until the colour settles down. I'll start off and then you have a try.'

'All right,' I mumbled. What I really wanted to do was get up and run out. The thought of touching my skin in that way, paying it so much attention, turned my stomach. It was bad enough when I had to do the massage twice a day, but at least then there was no mirror and a thick slick of cream under my fingers so I couldn't feel my face properly.

She dipped her finger into the tub and dotted some yellowish gloop on to my face. I watched as she rocked her finger over my scars. 'This is called stippling and it works the concealer into all areas equally.' I had a try, less successfully, and she dampened a sponge. 'Foundation now. This is much lighter so we're going to pat it all over your face, like this. Be careful not to drag at the skin or it pulls the concealer off.' She picked up another pot and passed it to me. 'Last stage. This one is a different shade and heavier. You only put this where you need it, but I like the mix – it gives a better result.' She nodded her approval as I stippled the concealer in and pointed out where she thought I'd missed a bit. 'Close your eyes now. I'm going to whisk some powder over your face to take the shine off . . . OK, now have a look.'

I opened my eyes. It did look a little better, but the right half of my face still reminded me of fingertips after a soak in the bath. No amount of make-up could take that away.

*

Two months on, and I looked at my made-up face again. I hadn't done such a bad job on it. I slipped some silver hoops in my ears and ran the straighteners over my hair one last time. Perfume was out because it irritated my neck, but it didn't matter because I'd put on plenty of body lotion after my shower.

A car hissed on the gravel as it pulled up and I ran downstairs, putting my shoes on at the bottom step. Mum hovered with my coat.

'I don't need it. I'll be in the car.'

'You look lovely. Have a great time,' she said, fussing with the wispy scarf covering the scar on my neck.

Dad came into the hall. 'Now if there's alcohol, remember you're not to –'

'Clive, she knows. It's the first time she's been out in months. Don't nag her. The bar's soft drinks only tonight, I told you.'

'And if there are drugs,' he went on, ignoring her, 'then you call me on your mobile and I'll come and pick you up. You have got your mobile? Is it charged?'

'Yes,' I snapped, my stomach a whirlpool of nerves, and I ran out of the front door before I was tempted to escape upstairs and lock myself in my room.

'I'll have her back by half eleven,' Beth's dad called to mine as I got in the car.

Whitmere Rugby Club often had social events on, but this was the first time they'd had one for under-eighteens. Tonight was part of their twentieth anniversary celebrations and Max had got us the tickets. He and Beth had gone to the harvest dance the week before and were now officially an item. Beth saw it as her best opportunity to drag me out of the house. 'You'll get to meet Max,' she said when I protested and tried to duck out of it. Normally if I put her off she gave up, but this time she nagged until I agreed.

Beth checked her phone as we drew up at the clubhouse. 'Text from Max. He's here and he's waiting for us at the bar.' She leaned forward to peck her dad on the cheek. 'Bye, see you later.' She looked good tonight – she had her new contacts in and she'd done her hair differently, scrunching it so it curled.

The veranda at the front of the building was full already. Boys passing bottles around that they hid in the plant pots when they'd taken a drink and girls comparing outfits. I recognised a few of them from school.

We passed a couple on a bench by the door. The girl caught my attention because she wore the shortest, tightest white dress I'd ever seen and white platform heels with laces that criss-crossed up her legs to mid-calf. She was with a boy who had his arm round her and was muttering something in her ear while she rested her hand on his leg in a possessive way. She was pretty, but she would've been nicer with less jewellery and bottled tan. It made her look cheap.

I stumbled as I saw the boy's face.

Ryan?

It was a couple of weeks since I'd last seen him. He looked different somehow. Perhaps it was the smart clothes – black trousers and a narrow-fitting black shirt shot through with faint pinstripes of white. But his face looked different too as he spoke to the girl. A harder expression that made him look older and . . . and a little bit scary.

He glanced up when he heard my heel scuff the ground. His eyes widened and he smiled. 'Hi,' he mouthed. The girl scowled at me until she got a good look at my face and relaxed.

No, I'm not a threat to you, am I?

'Do you know him?' Beth whispered as we went up the steps to the door.

'I've run into him a few times. Why?'

'Is he nice?'

'Yes, why?' She could not seriously be on a match-making mission.

'Because that girl he's with is a Class A1 bitch. *And* she's slept with half the town. Her name's Sadie. My cousin told me about her. She's best friends with Sadie's little sister. You should warn him about her.'

'I don't know him *that* well.'

Yes, good one, Beth. I could just picture it. 'Ryan, I thought I'd better tell you that your girlfriend is a slut. No ulterior motive of course.' He'd really believe that.

'Oh, look, there's Max!' Beth pointed to a boy at the bar.

I got a good look at him before he saw us. He was a nice surprise. I'd built up a dread in my head that he looked like a cross between a Munchkin and Lee West in the year above us (who had so many spots that his face could be used as a join-the-dots puzzle). But Max was mostly spot free and wasn't exceptionally ugly or exceptionally gorgeous. He looked like any other average boy. I let my breath out – I wouldn't have to lie to Beth. 'In the blue shirt? He's much fitter than you made out.'

Beth glowed. 'Come and meet him.'

Max's face lit up when he saw her. He slipped his arm round her and kissed her cheek. Jealousy spiked through me. What I wouldn't give for a boy to look at me like that. Beth did the introductions: Max, his older brother, two other boys they knew. All had been pre-warned, that was obvious from the way their gazes slipped over my face and moved to rest on safer ground, carefully not staring.

Max bought me a Coke. His brother and the other two lads talked about rugby while Beth and Max chatted about the battle re-enactments, trying to include me with an occasional comment like, 'You should have seen his face, Jenna, it was so funny!' But they were just being kind. Anyone could see they were only interested in each other, and I didn't understand or care about what they were talking about. I stood smiling vacantly and twisting my glass of Coke in my fingers, wishing I'd never come.

I retreated to a dream world where I lived on a desert island and there were no people, only dogs and Arab horses to keep me company. No school to face, no parents feeling guilty when they saw me, no disgusted looks, no sniggering behind my back. Sun, sea, miles of white beach, palm trees for shade, all for me . . .

Then I noticed Beth start backwards, her mouth opening in surprise. Her eyes flashed to mine and I spun round before she could put out a hand to stop me.

Steven Carlisle.

Standing in the doorway with a girl on his arm. A slim blonde in a beautiful green dress. The kind of girl every other girl in the room wanted to be.

Beth grabbed my arm. 'Jenna – God, I'm sorry. I should have thought. But he's over eighteen. He shouldn't be here.'

'He's on the team. His dad gives money to the club,' I replied dully. 'He can probably do as he likes.'

Steven sauntered through the bar with his newest girlfriend clinging adoringly. He walked through groups of people, pausing to speak to a chosen few, until he got to the bar.

Where he saw me.

He stared.

His lip curled as if he'd seen something white and pulpy under a stone.

And then very deliberately, he turned his back on me.

He bent his head to catch something the girl said and laughed loudly.

Beth yanked me by the arm. 'Jenna, come away.' I let her pull me into the next room where it was quieter.

'He should be dead,' I hissed. 'He should. Not Lindz. And not Charlotte.'

'Jen, let it go. He's not worth it.'

'But Lindz is.'

Max hurried in after us. 'Are you OK? He's cleared off on to the veranda where the team are. He'll hang out there most of the night, I reckon. We'll just avoid him.'

The DJ turned the volume up and a group of people drifted on to the dance floor. 'Come and dance,' Beth said, more to distract me than because she really wanted to. I let her talk me into staying on the floor for a few tracks and we danced while Max shuffled around apathetically as boys do when they're not sure what to do with their arms and legs. But it was hot under the lights as the floor got more crowded and I began to worry that my thick layers of make-up would melt and run. I made an excuse in Beth's ear about needing to cool off and retreated to a table by an open window where she could still see me.

An R&B track came on and the girl in the white dress ran in through the French doors dragging Ryan behind her. I shrank back in the chair and bent my head over my drink. When I sneaked a look up, they were dancing together. He rested his hands on her hips and she was wiggling between his legs, slammed right up to him. She was a good dancer. When the track ended, he grabbed her hand and pulled her back outside.

I sat back and watched the glitter ball spin above the floor. Laughter drifted across from people at the other tables and through the open window from outside. Beth waved at me and I waved back, but I wished she'd leave me alone. I watched the clock on the wall. The minutes ticked by painfully slowly and I willed the hand to move faster so this could be over.

'Hi.' A boy slid into the seat next to me. 'Not dancing?'

'Taking a break.'

'Me too.' He leaned towards me so I could hear him over the music and I smelled cider on his breath. 'What's your name?'

'Jenna.'

'Hi, I'm Ed. Are you here with your boyfriend?'

How much had he been drinking? Couldn't he see straight? 'No, with friends.' I waved vaguely at the dance floor.

'So your boyfriend's not here?'

'I don't have one.'

'No way, I can't believe that. Obviously you haven't met the right guy yet.' He grinned as if he'd said something really witty. His face had that odd look that boys' faces go through. One year they look like Charlie, all cute and babyish; then they come back after the summer holidays and they've changed, but they haven't got where they're going yet. They look funny, kind of like a werewolf transforming in a film. Their noses don't fit and their jaws are a different shape. Weird. Still, I was in no position to be fussy and I really should know better.

'Obviously not,' I said, forcing myself to smile back.

It turned out he was in the under-fifteens rugby team. He told me all about it, match by match for every game this season. I did interested noddies, but I hadn't a clue what he was talking about. All the magazines said boys like to talk about themselves and girls should encourage them so I did try. He never asked anything about me, just bragged about his rugby tries. It crossed my mind that he might be trying to impress me, but that was just silly.

'You want to get some air?' he asked. 'It's stuffy in here.'

At that moment, Steven Carlisle appeared in the bar, looking towards the dance floor, so I nodded automatically and followed Ed outside. Beth gave me a delighted thumbs-up.

'Round here,' he said. 'It's quieter.' He walked round to the back of the clubhouse. After the heat inside, the cool air nipped my face. My ears rang from the music. The change in temperature and the darkness made me dizzy, and I leaned on the wall and closed my eyes to stop my head spinning.

'Hey,' Ed said, too close. When I opened my eyes in alarm, he was only centimetres away.

'What –' I started to say, but his mouth pressed down on mine.

In the films when a guy kisses a girl, he touches her face. Ed didn't touch mine. The cider on his breath was stale and sour and it made me want to heave. He stuck his tongue in my mouth, jamming it in, wet and slippery and . . . horrible.

It isn't supposed to be like this. I'm supposed to like it. What's wrong with me?

He grunted and leaned against me. I didn't know what to do so I stood there with my mouth open and my hands hanging by my sides. His hands fumbled with the hem of my top and then slid under. He grabbed my breasts and squeezed as he pushed his tongue deeper in my mouth. The thump of the music inside beat into the back of my head through the wall while he made strange, panting noises. But when he started to rub against me, I couldn't stand it any longer.

I shoved him away hard. He didn't expect it and I caught him off balance, enough to make a gap between us so I could break free and run. I couldn't stop to explain. What could I possibly say? Frigid, that's what they called girls like me. Maybe Steven had damaged more than my face when he crashed the car. Maybe something had gone wrong inside my head too. A scarred freak. A scarred, frigid freak.

Beth wasn't on the dance floor any more. I pushed through the crowd to look for her so I didn't have to be alone when Ed came back in. People jostled around me, muttering angrily as I squeezed past without waiting for them to move.

I heard Beth before I saw her, standing by the bar, talking to Max. 'She's so different now. Won't go out. Won't do anything. She thinks everyone is looking at her.'

'Yeah, but they are,' Max replied.

'But they'd get used to it. She doesn't give them a chance. She doesn't talk to most of the people at school any more. It's like she's forgotten how. You can't have a conversation with her. Even with me she's not the same.'

Not the same? Of course I'm not the same! You try walking around like this and see how normal you are, you stupid, thick cow!

Tears stung my eyes. Beth was supposed to be my friend and there she was telling a guy who didn't even know me all that stuff that should be private.

I heard Steven Carlisle's hateful laugh across the room and there he was again, his arm round that girl like it would've been round Lindz once.

Got to get out of here.

I began pushing through people again until I got to the veranda, but Ed was out there with a bunch of lads. I stopped, uncertain where to go next.

'Come on, you owe me twenty quid,' Ed said, laughing, to one of the others.

'What, you actually did it? You kissed her.'

My breath stopped.

'Yup, so hand it over. And give me a drink. I need it after that.'

The other one pulled some notes out of his wallet. 'Go on then, what was it like?'

'Gross. She was totally up for it though. Thought she was gonna eat my face off!'

His mate laughed. 'Fair play, man, you win! How did you manage to do it?'

'With my eyes shut, you dick, how do you think?'

I reeled away from the door. Tears spilled over and ran down my cheeks as I blundered towards the main entrance. I didn't know where to go or what to do, but I had to get out. My heels slipped on the steps as I ran out and I nearly fell, but I caught the handrail to save myself.

The laughter and music echoed after me as I stumbled down the path.

'Hey!' a voice called behind me as I ran faster, blinded by tears and the darkness after the lights inside.

Useless, stupid freak. Nobody would kiss you unless they were paid to.

'Hey!' the voice called again. A male voice. And then, 'Jenna, wait!'

I kept running.

'Jenna, stop.' The voice was close and a second later, he'd skirted round in front of me. I tried to veer to the side, but he grabbed my arms. 'Jenna, woah, what happened?'

Ryan.

'What's the matter?'

'W-w-w . . .' I couldn't get any words out.

He pulled me towards him and put his arms round me. My nose squashed against his shoulder. 'Sshhh, sshhh.'

He was big and warm and solid and I didn't have enough energy to fight so I leaned on him and sobbed.

He stroked my hair. 'Jenna, tell me what happened? Has someone done something?'

'Who-who'd w-want to do anything t-to me?' I hiccuped against his chest.

He hugged me tighter. 'That's bullshit. Tell me what happened.' He ducked his head down and tugged mine up. 'Was it that guy from the accident? He's here, isn't he? Someone pointed him out to me.'

I shook my head. 'Nothing to do with him. Please let go. I want to go home.'

'Not until you tell me what happened.' He patted at my face with the cuff of his sleeve, mopping some tears up. 'Come on, someone's upset you and I want to know.'

'I can't . . .'

'Yes, you can,' he said firmly, 'and you're going to.'

I started to cry again. How could I tell him *that*?

He cupped my face in his hands . . . he cupped my face . . . 'You tell me right now! Don't look like that. Just tell me – go on, spit it out.'

You're touching my face.

'Jenna!'

'A boy in there . . .'

'Yes?'

'He was talking to me, then he took me outside and . . .'

'And?'

'He kissed me.'

'That's not all he did. What did he do?'

My face crumpled. 'Put his hands up my . . . my . . .'

He put his arms round me again. 'All right, don't cry. I get it. What then?'

'I pushed him off and I went back in. Then I heard him talking to his friends, telling them about it. I-I can't tell you the rest.'

'Course you can. Was he saying it was more than it was?'

'Yes.'

'Dickhead.' He rubbed my back for a moment, then pulled away. 'What're you not telling me?'

He wouldn't stop asking questions and I ran out of words except the truth. 'He did it for a bet. For twenty pounds. Because I'm . . . I'm . . .'

Ryan held me at arm's length. 'What? He did *what*? What's his name?'

'Ed. Why?'

'What colour shirt is he wearing?'

'Blue and white check. Ryan, what –'

'Wait here. Have you got a coat inside?'

'No . . .'

'Wait – I'll be back in a minute.'

He jogged off to the clubhouse. As he got near, a girl's shrill voice shouted, 'Ryan, what're you doing? Come back here. Don't you ignore me!'

I took my shoes off and ran down the grass. When I sneaked round the side of the building, I could see the girl in the white dress grab at his arm, but he shook her off. He vaulted over the rail on the veranda. A few girls squealed and got out of his way.

I crept closer.

He walked up to a group of boys with a figure wearing a blue and white checked shirt in the centre. 'Are you Ed?'

The boys moved and I saw Ed nod. 'Yeah, why?'

Ryan's fist smashed into his face and Ed hit the floor with a crash.

14 – Ryan

Fucking pondlife. Sometimes there aren't words enough to say how you feel and only a smack in the mouth will do.

He'd gone down like a pro boxer had hit him.

Quite proud of that.

The other lads stared at me, too shocked to react.

'Whichever of you dicks gave him the twenty quid, you were robbed. He never got near her. She blew him out and laughed in his face.'

I bent over the kid on the ground and he cringed away. 'Tosser!'

'What's going on here?' The guy Sadie pointed out earlier, the one who crashed the car, came out. 'Who's he?'

'He just floored Ed,' one of the lads said.

'What? And you lot stood there and let him?'

They shuffled and glanced at each other. One stepped closer to Carlisle and muttered something at him that I couldn't catch. Carlisle looked back at me and curled his lip like he was the big man. He gave Ed a hand to pull him to his feet.

Yeah, you're something, you are. Real special. I looked him up and down like he did me. 'Fuck you,' I said, giving him the finger, and turned to vault back over the rail.

I heard a scuffle behind me.

'Steve, leave it. He's going. Probation, remember?'

'No, who the fuck does he think he is?'

I cleared the rail and walked away. Sadie grabbed at my arm again as I went to pick my coat up from the bench. 'Don't you dare walk out on me,' she shrieked before I had a chance to explain anything. I caught a glimpse of Jenna's face peeking round the corner at us.

'I'm taking her home. You've got mates here. Hang out with them.'

'Are you mental? I mean, look at her, for Christ's sake. You are not leaving me to take *that* home!'

I spun round and she shrank back. 'You selfish bitch!'

'Fine, screw you then!' she yelled, backing away. 'But you go and that's it. You're dumped. You are so dumped!'

'So? Am I crying?'

Carlisle came up now, followed by a few of his mates. 'You're not going anywhere. I want a word with you. I've just been hearing all about you, pikey.'

Sadie had a big mouth, I realised. Of course she'd bragged – she was that type.

He swaggered up to me, his back-up waiting a few metres away. Sadie retreated behind them to watch. 'I get the impression, pikey, that you think you can stroll into our club and insult one of us and we'll let you. But I'm here to tell you, you piece of shit, that you're wrong.'

'Oh yeah? But you're not bothered about what one of you did to deserve it?' I folded my arms. He was bigger than me and he had his mates, but my temper was still spiked from what Jenna had told me.

'No. He's drunk. Being one of the lads. He didn't know she'd find out and what's it got to do with you anyway?'

'She's a friend.' Well, not exactly, but she did help me clean up that time and I reckoned she was all right.

He laughed. 'And does her dad know that? Have you met him? He'd be really interested in you. Having a piece of traveller trash on his doorstep and hanging around with his precious little pet.' *Thanks, Sadie.* 'I bet the police will be interested to know about you squatting there too. No one will sleep safe in their beds once they know there's a gyppo nearby.'

Here we go again. Always the same. Do you know how many times I've met you in different places? I put my best bored face on. 'Are you going to blag on all night or is there a point to this?'

That threw him. Obviously I wasn't supposed to answer back. I was supposed to be intimidated. 'You stay out of our way because if you mess with any of us again, I'll make so much trouble for you . . . .'

'If your mates don't upset mine then I won't need to mess with you, will I?'

He took a few steps closer and shoved me hard on the shoulder. 'That little bitch deserves all she gets, stirring her dad up to get the village against me. So what if Ed did it for a bet? She's lucky somebody normal will go near her. I wouldn't do it no matter how much you paid me.'

The surge of anger swept through me so fast it left me shaking. Jenna was hearing all this. 'You're some piece of work, you are. You think you can make trouble for me – ever stopped to think how much I could make for you? I know people who'd take you apart if I asked them to.'

He took a step back. He hadn't thought of that and I must be bluffing well enough to fool him. 'I don't know what you see in that bitch,' he snarled. 'Or have you got some sick thing for shagging ugly –'

He didn't get to finish because I dived on top of him and took him down.

I only got a couple of punches in before he fought back and flipped me off him. He was stronger than me and the first time his fist collided with my jaw was like being hit by a train. The pain seared up the side of my face and blinded me so I didn't see the next punch coming. His knuckles smacked into my cheek, smashing my head to the side.

Gotta get up or he's gonna destroy me.

I could hear his mates egging him on, eager to help if he needed them.

'Not so mouthy now, are you?' he said with a laugh as he brought his fist down towards my face again.

But I saw the blow coming this time and twisted. His knuckles missed and crashed into the gravel instead. Punching the ground hurt, and I saw the pain flash across his face so I added to it and whacked him in the mouth with my own fist.

I hit him hard enough to knock him clean off me and his mates roared with anger as they piled towards me.

'Lads! Pack this in! No more!' a voice bellowed behind them.

Carlisle scrambled up, clutching his face and spitting blood from a split lip.

A man pushed through Carlisle's mates and put himself between us. He grabbed Carlisle and pinned his arms. 'Let it go. You can't afford more trouble.'

He was a big guy – looked like a rugby player too – and Carlisle knew him because he stopped struggling to get to me.

The man turned to look at me. 'You, get out of here. Now. Before I call the police and have you removed.' The rest of the lads were standing back and letting him deal with it so I guessed the club must have put him in charge tonight. Time to exit. As I got up, Carlisle snarled at me over his shoulder, 'If I see you again, you're dead.'

I thought about flipping him the finger again, but I remembered Jenna, left waiting on her own, so I gave it up and walked off just slowly enough to piss them all off.

15 – Jenna

'Let's go,' Ryan said. I winced as gravel cut into my bare feet and he waited for me to put my shoes back on. He ruffled my hair. 'You saw all that, didn't you?'

'Yes,' I said quietly. I wasn't sure what I felt after seeing him act in that way. Was I a bit afraid of him now? Maybe.

He sighed. 'I told you to stay put.'

'Sorry.' My voice came out even quieter, almost a whisper.

'I'm not mad at you,' he said, bending his head to see my face. 'Did I scare you? I'm sorry if I did.'

'Where are we going?'

He laughed. 'No idea. We'll decide when we get to the road. How are you supposed to be getting home?' He sounded almost like the boy who'd fallen off his bike again. Almost, but not quite.

'My friend's dad's picking me up at eleven. I can't go home earlier or Mum and Dad'll know something's up and I can't face explaining.'

He squeezed my shoulders. 'Let's go and get a coffee then and wait it out. Oh, and we missed the buffet!' He rummaged in his pocket. 'Yup, got enough to buy you a burger.'

'I've ruined your night.'

'No, you haven't. It wasn't that good there.'

'But your girlfriend?'

'She's not my girlfriend.'

I lapsed into silence, not sure how to respond to that.

'There's a burger place down the street. There?'

'OK.'

He ruffled my hair again and I realised was still shaking.

16 – Ryan

Jenna was on the phone when I got back with the food. 'No, I'm fine. I'm with a friend . . . Having coffee. We're only ten minutes away. I'll talk to you later . . . Yes, I'll call you. Oh, I don't know. Half an hour – we'll sort it out then.' She snapped the phone shut. 'My friend Beth. She noticed I'd gone.'

'Here – burger, fries, coffee, donut.' I sat down opposite her. 'Is she the one you're going home with?'

Jenna nibbled a chip unenthusiastically. 'Um, to be honest I don't really want to talk to her at the moment. I heard her saying stuff about me to her boyfriend.'

'Yeah?'

'She said things I wish she hadn't. About how I've changed and how I don't talk to people any more and . . .' She put the chip down half-eaten.

'Is it true?'

Her lips trembled and she pressed them together. 'I guess.'

I peeled the foil lid back from the ketchup tub and picked up her discarded chip. I blobbed some ketchup on the end and I wafted the chip towards her mouth. 'Open!'

She looked at me like I was crazy. 'No.'

'Open or I'll do aeroplanes.'

She almost smiled. 'You'll do what?'

'Aeroplanes. Didn't your mum ever do that when you wouldn't eat?'

'No.'

'You never had to eat tofu, that's why.' I zoomed the chip around in the air. 'Rrrrrrmmm, rrrmmm, corner to the left, loop the loop . . . and . . . coming into land.' I popped it into her mouth. 'Now have I got to do that with every one or are you going to eat them?'

She swallowed the chip and picked up another. 'I'm not three, you know.'

'Whatever.' I bit into my burger. 'Oh, that is *so* good!'

'Huh – and I get told I don't get out much.'

'Yeah, well, I'm vegan.'

'Er, right.' Her eyebrows shot up. 'Lapsed, right?'

'Very. Oh God, this is better than sex!'

She giggled. 'I wouldn't let that girl hear you saying that.' Her smile faded. 'She looked really pissed off. She will forgive you, won't she?'

I scoffed the rest of the burger down. 'I doubt it. And even if she does, who says I'm interested?'

'But she likes you. She wouldn't have been so annoyed if she didn't.'

'She'll get over it.'

'That's not very nice,' Jenna said in a small voice.

'Yeah, well, she wasn't very nice to you.'

'I knew I'd ruined your night.'

'You haven't. Shut up and eat your burger.'

'If you speak to her like that, I'm not surprised she dumped you.'

'There, see, she's had a lucky escape. Feel better now?'

She hid a laugh behind her hand and ate her burger while I devoured my fries.

'Do you ever talk about the accident?' I asked as she sipped coffee.

'No.'

'Tell me about it.'

'No! I hardly know you.' Her hand started to shake on the cup.

'I'm a good listener. Maybe you should.'

'Why?' Jenna slammed the cup down and a little pool of coffee slopped up out of the plastic drinking hole. She gestured to her face. 'So you can satisfy your curiosity about what made *this*.'

'They're just scars. They're not you.' I mopped the coffee up with a paper napkin. She stared at me, big blue eyes filling up again, and I felt like a shit.

'If they're just scars, why do people stare? You stared. Why do people act differently around me? Have you got any idea what it's like to walk down the street and have little kids point and ask their mums why you look horrible? And have nobody be able to look at you properly because you turn their stomach?'

'You don't turn mine. I stared because I didn't expect it. And then I thought whatever did it must have hurt really bad, and how I'd been wrong about why you wouldn't come to get your dog. And that I was a dick. But I didn't feel sick.'

She buried her face in her hands.

'No, don't!' I scooted round on to the bench seat next to her. 'Look, don't cry. I keep making you cry and it makes me feel like a right bastard.'

'Why did he do it?' she mumbled through her fingers.

I rested my elbow on her shoulder and stroked her hair. It felt like the silk Mum made her jewellery pouches from. 'Because he's a complete and utter wanker. Did you like him a lot?'

She shook her head. 'No, he was boring and . . .'

'Uh-huh, and?'

'I hated kissing him. See? I'm a freak.'

I did try not to snigger, but I couldn't keep it in. 'Was that your first kiss?'

'Shut up!'

'OK, that means it was. Oi, look at me. I'm not laughing at you. Him, yes, but not you.' I shrugged. 'Don't blame you for hating it. I'd hate it if he kissed *me*.'

She made a surprised noise that I decided would've been a

laugh if she wasn't so upset. Good – she thought I was funny.

'So what didn't you like about it?' I whispered in her ear. 'Go on, tell me. Give me details.'

That stopped her crying – she jerked her head out of her hands. 'No!'

I grabbed her. 'Tell me or I'll tickle.'

She struggled to free her arms. 'Stop it. Let go.'

'Did he put his tongue in your mouth?'

'Yes. Yes, he did. And it was gross. All right? Happy now? Let me go!' I released her and she slid to the end of the bench. 'You're horrible!'

I leaned on the table and grinned at her. 'You didn't like it because he was useless at it. It's not you, it's him. Doesn't know how to do it properly. Bet you a fiver I'm right.'

Her forehead crinkled up. 'You think?'

'No. I know.'

'How?'

'Nobody who knew what they were doing would stick their hands up your top that fast. Trust me. He's the freak, not you. Ugly bastard too. You can do way better than him.'

Her mouth twitched and I nodded solemnly at her. She bit her lip. Then she couldn't hold it any longer and she burst out laughing.

I winked. 'Better. Now you gonna tell me or don't you trust me?'

She eyed me exactly as if she didn't trust me. 'It's not that. I told you, I don't talk about it. Not to anyone.'

I patted the seat. 'Yeah, but I'm different. And I'm just gonna go on and on at you until you do tell me. So come here and get it over with.'

She sighed hard, but she shuffled back towards me and I angled round so I blocked her from anyone else's view. 'Right, look at me. Nobody else in here can see you. Just me. I want you to tell me the whole story. As long as it takes. I'm not going anywhere. We've got loads of time.' I flicked her under the chin with my finger. 'Tell me. Please? You'll feel better afterwards, I promise. And if you don't you can thump me.'

Jenna frowned. 'I don't want to thump you.'

'Yeah, but I'll let you. I'll sit here and you can pound on my head and I won't say a word. Won't make a sound. I might cry a bit, but I'll do it silently. How often do you get an offer like that?' She was wavering, trying not to smile . . . I got a buzz from seeing that – strange. There was no way I was giving up now. I looked down at our legs nearly touching. She hadn't moved away so she didn't feel that uncomfortable with me. I could feel her watching my face so I glanced up at her from under my lashes – that worked on girls sometimes. 'Please? I'll feel a failure if you don't.'

Her resistance crumbled and she looked away in a hurry.

OK, so you like me doing that, do you? I'll remember that. Why I should want to remember I wasn't sure, but never mind — I was concentrating on her, not me.

She sighed. 'All right, if it shuts you up. I don't want to, but —'

Yes! Got her! 'Just get it out, the whole thing. Don't stop and think. Go for it.'

She fixed her eyes on a spot behind me. 'OK, I guess it starts with Lindsay.'

17 – Jenna

I didn't want to talk about this at all, but he was so persistent and I didn't want to be as rude as I'd have to be to get him to back off. Not after he got punched for standing up for me.

'Lindz was my best friend ever since we moved to Strenton when I was seven. We used to do everything together. She was a year older than me and she was the most alive person I've ever met. She never walked anywhere, she always ran. But when she was twelve, her mum walked out. It was the talk of the village because everyone thought they were the perfect family. Lindz's dad ran all the village events and her mum organised the fêtes and knew everyone. But one day, Mrs Norman just left out of the blue with a man she'd been seeing for over a year. No one had suspected a thing. She wanted to take Lindz with her, but Lindz didn't want to go and live in a flat in Stoke and lose her pony and all her friends.'

Ryan swallowed some coffee and nodded at me. Either he was good at faking or he really was interested.

'She went a bit mad after that. Lindz, I mean. Sort of off the rails. Hanging around with lots of boys, and drinking. And she was a year older than me so . . .'

'You got left out?'

'A bit. Then last year she got together with Steven Carlisle after he was kicked out of school. She was majorly into him and I saw less and less of her. I missed her, you know, because we used to tell each other everything.' I paused, remembering back to when I was twelve. 'We even shared blood once. We cut our hands with a vegetable knife and mixed it like American Indians do. A bond. Something no one could take away. Look, you can still see the scar.' I held my palm up for him to see the tiny faint line there.

'So just after Christmas, when Steven got this flash car for his eighteenth birthday, she asked me to come out for a ride with them, and I went.' I took a breath in and my chest felt tighter. 'Because I wanted us to be close again. There were two other girls with us. Charlotte was from Strenton too, but I didn't really know Sarah.'

He nodded.

'Steven had a friend, Rob, with him. They were in the front with us girls in the back. They were passing vodka and a joint around and we were all a bit out of it.'

'Carlisle too?'

'Uh-huh, and he was driving fast. Way too fast, showing off.'

I found it hard to speak now and Ryan ducked his head down

to catch my eyes. 'You OK?' He handed me the coffee cup and I took a few sips.

'Thanks.'

I fiddled with the lid on the cup, snapping and unsnapping the tab. Somehow that helped. 'There isn't much more. Basically Steven lost control, ploughed the car off the road. Sarah had a seat belt on and she got out OK. So did the boys. Charlotte and Lindz were killed. They told me the car rolled a few times, you see. Then it caught fire. Rob pulled me out, but not before this.' I waved at my right cheek. 'The car blew up. I . . . I . . . still have nightmares that I didn't get out in time and I'm in there when it blows.' I scratched at my hands, not able to stop myself. 'I don't know why I'm telling you this.'

He reached over and twizzled a strand of my hair round his finger.

'And I don't know why you're listening.'

'What happened next? Why is Carlisle on your case?' he asked as if he hadn't heard me.

'He was charged with dangerous driving. There was a court case. His dad hired a very good lawyer and Steven got a suspended sentence. People in the village were really angry. Some of them set up an action group. My dad heads it up. It sort of gained momentum and spread. People from Whitmere and other villages got involved.'

'And what happened with you?'

'Me? Huh! Hospital, skin grafts, operations, counselling. I had to wear a compression mask over my face for six months after the last graft to help the healing.' I tucked my feet up on the seat and wrapped my arms round them. 'I'm supposed to keep going for counselling, but all the talking in the world can't make *this* right. They just say, "Oh, Jenna, you have to come to terms with it," but I can't. I can't! And I'm so angry. I'm so, so angry and I have to pretend I'm not because they all want me to get better. But it's not their face, is it?'

He shook his head. 'No, it's not.' And his eyes stayed on my face, like he understood.

18 – Ryan

She was breathing fast like she'd run a long way.
She looked out of words and out of energy – smaller and paler than ten minutes ago, curled into a little ball on the seat. I wanted to hug her, but I didn't know if she'd let me.

Oh bollocks! I can't just sit here.

I put both arms round her, pulled her almost on to my knee. She was as taut as fence wire.

'What're you doing?' she squeaked.

'I'm giving you a friggin' hug because you need one. What do you think I'm doing?'

She slapped me on the chest and half laughed. 'I don't know. I'm sure you could be doing something better than sitting here with me.'

'Hang on, I'm thinking . . . er . . . er . . . nope. Not coming up with anything.'

'I don't believe you.'

'Hey, it's not every day I meet someone who catapults me into horseshit.'

That did make her laugh, reluctantly at first, but then

properly. 'I so don't get you,' she said.

'You're in good company. I don't get me either.' Christ, I meant that too. How had she got me to say that? Then I realised something. 'Hey, you know your friend said you never talked.' She stopped smiling. 'You talked to me OK. Didn't you?'

She screwed up her face. 'Mmm.'

'Your nose scrunches up when you do that. Like a rabbit.' I grinned. 'Or a pig.'

She stopped doing it immediately. 'You're the pig . . . Oh no! Beth! I was supposed to phone her again to sort out what's happening later.' She rooted in her bag for her mobile.

'Are you going home with her or are you calling your parents to get picked up?'

'I don't know.' She tapped the phone in her fingers. 'I don't want to see Beth because she'll be all . . . pitying.' She spat the word out. 'But Dad . . . Oh, I don't know, what should I do?'

I turned my pockets out on to the table. 'I haven't got enough for a taxi.'

'There aren't any around here anyway.'

'I'd walk you home, but it's too far. You wouldn't get a quarter of a mile in those heels.'

'You'd walk me home?'

'Course I would.' Mad girl, as if I wouldn't. 'Hey, can you ride a bike?'

'Yes, why?'

'Got an idea. I'll take you home on mine. Call your friend and sort it.'

I could see why she didn't want to tell her dad. Like how I never wanted to let on to Mum when I'd got beaten up by some townie.

She rang the number. 'Beth, it's me again. Listen, make an excuse to your dad. I'm getting a lift back with someone from Strenton. OK, yes, I'll call you when I get back so you know I'm all right . . . No, I'm not with anyone dodgy.' I sniggered and she thumped me, trying not to laugh. 'Talk later. Bye.' She put the phone down. 'So what's your idea?'

'I've got – Ow!' She'd grabbed my hand.

'Oh my God, Ryan, why didn't you say something?' She glared at my mashed knuckles.

'It's nothing. I'm not bothered.'

She pushed past me and marched to the counter. I heard her order two coffees and ask for a cup of ice. She came back with a pile of paper napkins. She unfolded a couple on the table and tipped some ice on to them, then rolled them up to make an ice pack. 'Hold that on your hand. I feel awful for not noticing earlier. Do you need some for your face too?'

'Nah, it's no big deal. He missed me mostly.'

'Do you always do this?' she demanded.

'What?'

'Get people to offload on you, but everything to do with you is "no big deal".'

'I don't know.' Did I?

She tossed me a sachet of sugar to go with the coffee. 'If I had to do it, I think you should.'

'Eh?'

'Your turn. You made me tell you stuff. Now it's your turn.'

'Nothing to tell. I'm boring.' There was no way I was telling her personal things.

She sighed in exasperation. 'You're annoying. Even more than Charlie and I thought that was impossible. That's not fair.'

'I don't *talk* to girls.'

She did the rabbit thing again with her nose. 'What do you do with them then?'

She walked right into that one. I leaned back in the seat and raised my eyebrows and waited until she got it. She coloured up and fiddled with the lid on her coffee cup. 'What about your girlfriends? You must talk to them.'

'I don't have girlfriends. Just girls I, er, hang out with sometimes.'

'Urgh! That is such a Neanderthal attitude.'

'Yeah? Better than being bloody *sensitive*.'

She blinked. 'What?'

'Nothing,' I said, tipping sugar into my coffee and stirring it viciously. 'Anyway, I thought you were supposed to be quiet and shy and –'

She huffed. 'You wanted me to talk. Your fault.'

'Huh! I've created a monster.'

Jenna jumped like I'd slapped her. I didn't understand why for a moment, until she put her hand to her cheek to cover it. Then I got it. 'Oh, fuck, no, I didn't mean it like that. Don't be stupid.'

But she was already up and grabbing her bag and pushing past me without a word to rush out of the door.

I threw my coat over my arm, picked up the coffees and hurried after her. She was standing in the street dithering over which direction to go.

'Don't you dare run off! I'll catch you anyway,' I barked. 'You totally overreacted. You know I didn't mean it like that.'

She hung her head. 'I'm sorry,' she mumbled. I thought I heard her sniff too and I felt like a shit for shouting at her.

'Hold the coffee.' Christ, she was hard work. I shoved the cups at her and put my coat round her shoulders. 'Now give it back to me and put this on. It's cold.'

'But then you'll be –'

'Just do it, Jenna.' I snatched the cups back. 'Come on, we're going home.'

She trailed after me down the street, slipping her arms into the coat sleeves. I paused to hand her coffee cup back when she was ready. 'Thanks,' she said, head still down, and we walked on in silence.

I had the craziest idea. I knew how to convince her for sure that the guy at the Rugby Club was a human turd and that she wasn't disgusting. Because she wasn't. Yes, the scars were bad, but you got used to them after a while and the rest of her face was cute. She had this funny smile, shy and cheeky all at once. It got to you. And those big blue 'cuddle me better' eyes. Plus she fitted under my arm just right.

All I had to do was kiss her and I could make it all go away. I'd kissed loads of girls. I was good at it.

But it was a dumb idea. Jenna wasn't like the others. You couldn't kiss her and walk away. She wouldn't understand that.

She tugged my sleeve. 'Ryan, I'm sorry. It wasn't your fault. It was mine.'

I sat down on a garden wall. 'What was all that about?'

She sniffed and rubbed her nose. 'Shrek.'

'Eh?'

'It's not worth explaining. But in films, have you ever noticed that scarred people are always the baddies? They're always evil like Joker in *Batman*, or Scar in *The Lion King*. I never noticed it before the accident, but it's true.'

'Can't say I have, but then we haven't got a TV.'

She stared. 'You don't? Oh! That is weird.'

I sighed – yeah, wasn't everything about me weird? 'It's all right, I understand, but you can't expect everyone to tiptoe round you. If they don't mean it that way then don't take it like that.'

She sat down next to me. 'Sorry. Again. I'll try. I know you're right.'

I rested my arm on her shoulders. 'We friends?'

'Do you want to be?' She stared at her feet while I bit back a smile.

'Yup, do you?'

She nodded.

'OK, we are then.' I hugged her briefly. 'Go on then – three questions and I'll answer them. And that's it.'

She sipped her coffee. I checked for signs that she thought she'd got one over on me, but I didn't see any. She really wasn't at all clued-up yet.

'OK, first one. What were you doing there tonight? I'm guessing you don't play rugby. Did you go with the girl who isn't your girlfriend so I don't know what to call her?'

'Yeah. I've hung out with her a few times and she had a spare ticket. She nagged me so I went. Her dad owns the boatyard where I work so I hope she doesn't screw that up for me.'

Jenna groaned. 'See, I told you I'd messed things up.'

I butted my shoulder on hers. 'No, you haven't. Pete would go mental over me seeing her so you've more got me out of trouble than into it.'

'Did you like her though, Ryan? Really?'

I thought about it. 'Nope. It was just sex.' She looked down quickly. 'Hey, she didn't really like me either. She got what she wanted and she saw what she wanted to see. If she knew the rest, she'd already have dumped me.'

'What do you mean, the rest?'

I scratched my neck a bit. 'Oh, stuff.'

'Hey, come on – you said three questions.'

'You've had three.'

'And you've got to answer them. Spill!'

I gulped some coffee down and burned my tongue. She waited. 'My mum. Sometimes she's not very well.'

'Oh. Do you have to look after her?'

'Yeah.'

'What's wrong with her?'

'I really don't want to get into this.'

To my surprise, she put her hand over mine where it rested on the wall, taking care not to touch my cut knuckles. Thin little fingers with no strength in them. She didn't say anything, but sat there watching the cars go by. Waiting.

'Do you know what bipolar disorder is?' She shook her head. 'Manic depression?'

'I've heard of it, but not really.'

'It's a mental illness. People with it go through phases where they get really low and then others where they're high. Not normal ups and downs. Totally extreme and when they're

141

like that they're not in control. They do strange stuff.'

'And that's what your mum's got?'

'Yeah.'

'Is it . . . Is she . . .'

'Is she dangerous?' A bubble of anger rose inside, blocking my throat. 'No, she's not!'

'I was going to ask if she's going to get better,' she said softly.

It was my turn to stare at my feet in the stupid shoes left over from when we'd gone to Cole's friend's wedding last year. They were a bit tight; I'd grown again.

'No,' I said finally. 'Not better. She controls it. Most of the time. But when she gets bad, you have to watch her. Gets carried away, does things she wouldn't when she's well, but she's not dangerous.'

Jenna took hold of my hand properly. 'Don't tell me if you don't want. It's OK.'

'I don't mind,' I said, which was true, but I didn't know why because I usually would. 'Don't really know what to say though.'

'How long has she had it?'

'Always. Since before she had me.'

'What about your dad? Doesn't he help?'

I shrugged. 'Never met him. He was just some guy she got together with for a while. She does that in her manic phases. Goes out, gets a guy, shacks up with him. Then he gets fed up and clears off. That time she decided she wanted a baby so she

142

made sure she got pregnant before he walked out.' I looked up and Jenna tried to hide the appalled look on her face, but she wasn't quick enough. 'Look, I love my mum! She's been a good mum. She can't help being ill, and she's not nuts. She's got a degree in philosophy from Oxford. She taught me at home. She taught me loads up until I went and got this job. She's not a scrounger. She earns money and looks after me and —'

'Ryan —'

'And people look down their noses at her, but she's not doing anyone any harm. She's living what she believes in. That's nobody's business. And the stuff I do wrong isn't her fault. She'd kill me if she knew some of it —'

'Ryan, shut up!'

She didn't look appalled any more. I didn't know what it was on her face, but I realised she had my hand in her lap now, nestled between both hers. I took a shaky breath. 'Sorry, I don't know where that came from.'

'I think it's called being bottled up,' she said. 'When was the last time you talked to anyone about it?'

'Not sure. Sometime last year. Before Cole left.'

'Who's Cole?'

'A guy Mum lived with. He stuck around for a few years.'

'And you liked him.'

'How did you know that?'

She smiled. 'Your face. Do you miss him?'

'Suppose. He wasn't like all the others. We used to do stuff together. He'd take me places, like we were a proper family. I wish he was still around. There's things I want to ask him sometimes.'

'It sounds like you two were close.'

'Yeah, maybe. He helped me a lot.'

'How?'

She was so far over her three questions now, I'd lost count, but the answers slipped out anyway like I didn't realise in time to stop them. 'With lots of things. Like when I was younger and kids used to pick on me, he said to me it's all about attitude. If someone's going to give you trouble, get in first. Hit 'em hard, hit 'em fast. Don't let them see you're scared and they'll back off. And he taught me to defend myself.'

Jenna smiled. 'It's a good thing he did if you go around hitting guys twice as wide as you.' I laughed. She still had hold of my hand. I guess I liked it. Felt good.

'Come on, better get you home now. Don't want you getting in trouble for being late.'

She waited while I got the bike out of the bushes by the Rugby Club.

'Get on.' I nodded at the saddle and she sat on it.

'But how are you . . . oh!'

I stepped over the crossbar and hopped up on to the pedals and got us moving before I lost my balance. 'Hold on.'

'Um . . . where?'

I twisted my head round. The unscarred half of her face was cherry red even under the streetlamps. My arse was wiggling around at her as I stood up on the pedals. 'Wherever you can grab! Before you fall off.'

She put her hands on my sides and went very quiet. I concentrated on the road. It was hard work up the hill to Strenton with the weight of two to keep balanced and my thighs ached. I got off the bike when we reached the village and pushed it with Jenna still on the seat. It started to drizzle and the light on the bike caught a stream of droplets in its beam.

'Was my bum so spectacular that it's struck you dumb?'

She shot me a filthy look. 'You are so full of yourself.'

'Your place.' I stopped the bike. She started to take my coat off. 'Give it back tomorrow – you'll get wet.'

She nodded and got off the bike. 'Thanks,' she said, shuffling and looking at the ground. 'For everything, I mean.'

'Yeah, well, if anyone else upsets you, you tell me and I'll smack their teeth down their throats for you. Watching an enemy bleed always makes you feel better.'

'You're very good at it, aren't you?'

'What? Sex? Yeah, I'm amazing!'

She snorted and slapped at me, but I dodged and she laughed. I realised I liked making her laugh. She probably didn't do it enough so it was like a little victory when I got her to.

'No, Ryan. Looking after people.'

She surprised me with that. Was I?

'Anyway, thank you,' she said abruptly and hurried off round the side of her house.

I waited until I heard their door open, and voices, then I wheeled my bike down the road towards the canal bridge. It was weird, but when I thought about it, I'd had a good time while I was with her.

I wasn't stupid. If I'd kissed her, she'd have liked it. Firstly, I knew how to make her like it. Secondly, she liked me that way, though she was too shy to show it, which was understandable. And cute too. I had a pang of regret that I hadn't gone for it. The idea of showing her how it was supposed to be done . . . it'd be fun: she'd start off thinking it was going to be like it was with that idiot, then it wouldn't be . . . and the surprise on her face when it wasn't . . .

But I couldn't. She was too young and it'd mess with her head. That was the last thing she needed. *Pity though because* . . . I imagined her little fingers curling at the back of my neck. *No, not going there.* She'd had enough shit to deal with without me and all mine. I wanted to see her again though, to hang out with her and talk because it'd been good talking to someone who didn't judge me. Someone who thought I was all right. Me. Not the act, but *me*.

It had definitely been the weirdest night.

19 – Jenna

Light filtered through the bedroom window and I rolled over and hugged my pillow. Sunday morning, no need to get up.

I smiled at the black canvas coat lying over the back of my dressing-table chair, remembering why it was there. That was a good reason to get up: I had to return it. But I lay still a little longer, recalling snippets from the night before. Ryan drying my face with his sleeve . . . hitting Ed . . . his arm round me . . . his grin . . . his bum on the bike on the way home, which really was gorgeous enough to strike me dumb.

I bounced up out of bed.

When I got downstairs, Mum had made breakfast and we sat around the kitchen table, eating.

'They have chocolate spread at Toby's house,' Charlie whined as he spread honey on his toast.

Dad turned over a page in The Times and fought to fold it so it didn't take over the table. 'Isn't Toby the lucky one!'

Charlie gave the honey jar a hard shove to send it sliding over the table to me.

Mum groaned. 'Charlie, pass it nicely.'

'What? She didn't drop it.'

Mum let it go and Charlie crunched through his toast as if he was racing to finish.

'Can I go on the PlayStation now?' he asked, already sliding off the chair. He got two luxurious hours of PlayStation time on Sundays. Mum nodded, seeming not to notice that he ran off upstairs with half a slice of toast still in his hand.

'Trumpet practice later though, don't forget!' she called after him belatedly as we heard his door bang shut.

I sipped coffee and munched toast, staring out of the kitchen window at the leaves turning red on the maple by the hedge. Was Ryan up yet or lying in? It was his day off. Perhaps he'd been up for hours making the most of it. Or maybe he was still tucked under the duvet, lolling the morning away because he could.

Eventually the silence around the table attracted my attention. Dad had put his paper down and he and Mum exchanged a significant glance.

'Did you have a good time last night?' Mum's forced cheeriness set me immediately on edge.

'Yes, great.'

'Did you meet any new people?'

'Some, yes. Beth's new boyfriend was there.'

Dad's eyebrows shot up. 'Beth has a boyfriend?'

'Yes, Dad. Beth has a boyfriend. We are both fourteen, you know. It's not unheard of.'

Mum interrupted before he could answer. 'Is he nice?'

'Yes, he's nice. Very nice.'

Dad set his jaw to his 'cutting to the chase' expression. 'Where did you get that coat you came home in?'

'I walked into town to get a burger because the food at the party was rubbish. It was cold so I borrowed a coat.'

'Whose is it?'

'It *was* cold, Clive,' Mum said.

'It's a boy's, Tanya. I'm only asking her which boy.'

'A friend's. He's a friend, that's all!' It wasn't a lie. Ryan said we were friends.

'So who is he?'

'Clive, she needs to have friends . . .'

'She needs to have friends we know about!'

'You knew all of them last time,' I couldn't stop myself from shrieking. 'What difference did it make? Do you think I'm stupid? Do you think I want to go through this again?'

'I think you're easily led,' he snapped back.

Oh, that again. The easily led thing. I wasn't. I never did anything I didn't want to. Only sometimes I didn't know whether I *did* want to do it unless I tried it. But that was my choice. I never told Dad that. We didn't talk that way to each other. I didn't talk that way to anyone now Lindz was gone.

Dad glared at me and I glared back until I threw my toast down on the plate and stormed upstairs. I sat on the bed and gathered Ryan's jacket into my hands while I shook with suppressed rage. The fabric smelled of cocoa butter from the skin lotion I'd put on last night, but I could still smell him through that.

Slowly I calmed down. Dad was not going to wreck last night. He couldn't take that away. Ryan wanted us to be friends. That was enough for me. Just being friends with someone who treated me as if I was normal again. Even if I did now have a Titanic sized crush on him. No need to be embarrassed about it so long as I kept it to myself. Perfectly normal. My own little secret.

I checked the clock. Time to get ready. I had a shower and went through my usual routine, except I paused once I was dressed to go through my make-up case. This was tricky – I didn't want to look like I was trying too hard. In the end, I flicked my eyelashes up with the curlers, gave them a faint stroke of mascara and put some coloured lip balm on. That'd have to do. Any more would be overkill for a casual Sunday morning.

Mum was preparing the roast for Sunday lunch, with Raggs following her round the kitchen hopefully. Dad tippy-tapped away on the computer keyboard in the study, probably more work for his stupid campaign group. Charlie was upstairs with the PlayStation, so nobody saw me slip out of the front door with Ryan's coat under my arm.

When I got to the boat I almost stopped and turned back — being here didn't seem like such a good idea now. Smoke was puffing out of the flue on the roof so they must be up. But how did I knock on the door of a boat? Would it be rude to step on to the deck? Should I just wait on the canal bank?

The lace curtain twitched at one of the windows and my stomach churned. What if his mum came out? What would I say? But when the door opened, Ryan's head popped out. 'Hey, saw you through the window.'

I hadn't expected the shiver that ran through me at the sight of him. 'I brought your coat back.'

He came out. I shook my head and had to laugh even though my mouth went dry at the same time — he was shirtless again. He was wearing combat trousers low on his hips with a hint of the waistband of his jersey boxers jutting above. I had to force myself not to stare.

He looked down at himself and grinned. 'Yeah, I know, I know. But it's baking in there. Mum's got the log burner on full blast. No dog?'

My eyes fixed on his stomach without my permission. I swallowed to try to find my voice. 'He's at home with Mum. She's cooking and he's doing cupboard love.'

He took the coat from me. 'Thanks for bringing it back. Got time to come in for a drink? No coffee though. We only have herbal tea.'

It was on the tip of my tongue to make an excuse, until I realised that wasn't an option. No matter how much I hated meeting strangers, I couldn't duck out of meeting his mum, not after what he'd told me last night or he'd think I was avoiding her for entirely the wrong reason. 'Have you got raspberry?'

'Probably. We've got everything.' He offered me his hand to help me on to the deck. His palm was rough against mine; I'd noticed that last night and realised now it must be from working at the boatyard.

His mum looked up in surprise as Ryan opened the door.

'Mum, this is Jenna. She's a friend from the village.'

I followed him down the steps into the boat. His mum jumped up, pushing away a table with piles of stones and crystals laid out in rows. Beads of sweat glinted on her forehead and upper lip.

'Come in, come in, sit down. Ryan, move that gear off the chair.' Her accent took me aback – it was one of those terribly posh, academic voices that women on TV arts shows have.

Ryan picked up an armful of small boxes and carried them off somewhere into the back of the boat. I perched on the edge of the wooden rocker he'd cleared. His mum didn't look much like him. She was tiny and covered in jewellery – silver and beads everywhere. There were even a few in her cloud of dyed curly hair, which was an impossible red colour. She didn't look like any mum I'd ever seen. None of my friends' mothers wore multicoloured vests with a peace symbol in the middle. Or some sort of baggy trousers in an ethnic print. But the look suited her. Her face was free from make-up in that scrubbed, Sunday morning way and from the lack of lines on her skin, I guessed she was younger than my mum.

'Take your coat off, poppet. It's sweltering in here. I'm drying some lacquered work.' She waved at some jewellery spread out on a rack beside the metal stove in the corner.

I slipped my jacket off and looked round. The boat was lined with pale wood planks. A small kitchen lay beyond the sitting area. I could see a washing machine and a fridge, which surprised me. The seats had bright patterned cushions and there were black curtains with gold stars hanging at the windows. A red, gold and green rag rug sat in the middle of the floor. It was so colourful compared to our house.

Ryan came back before his mum had a chance to say more. 'I'm putting the kettle on. Want some tea, Mum? And have we got any raspberry for Jenna?'

'Yes, in the blue toadstool tin. Nettle for me, please.'

He screwed his face up. Understandably, I thought.

'Raspberry is good in pregnancy,' his mum said to me. 'I drank it by the gallon when I was having Ryan. It opens up the cervix and makes the birth easier.'

I didn't know what to say. When I sneaked a look at Ryan, he was leaning his head on the kitchen cupboard, screwing his face up in a pained way. It made him look younger somehow, and crazy cute.

'What's nettle good for?' I managed in the end.

'Nettle is very cleansing and it's an excellent diuretic.' She paused, seeing I didn't understand. 'Makes you pee.'

A groan came from the kitchen.

Her hands fluttered as she talked and I wondered if this was normal for her or if she was ill at the moment. She reached out suddenly and touched my face. 'I can give you some cream for that.'

'*Mum!*' Ryan was beside us before I knew he'd moved.

She waved her hand dismissively. 'Go and make tea and let us talk.'

'Mum, leave it!'

'The kettle's boiling,' she said calmly and gave his leg a push.

'I'm sorry,' he mouthed, hovering beside us.

I smiled an 'it's OK' smile at him. I wasn't sure it was OK, but I didn't want him getting upset. Then a funny thought struck me. What if he brought Sadie home? Would his mum offer her de-orange-ing cream? I swallowed a giggle.

'This is better than you'll get from any doctor,' his mum said proudly. 'I'll fetch you some to take home. I make it myself.'

Ryan grabbed her arm as she passed the kitchen. 'Mum, leave it, please,' he growled.

She patted his hand. 'What a lovely girl,' she said, as she wandered off into the boat.

He brought the tea in and handed me a cheerful enamel mug with big painted flowers. 'Watch it. The tin gets hot and burns your mouth. Let it cool.' He cast a look behind. 'I'm so, so sorry about her.'

'Don't be. She's nice.' Which was true. Yes, she was weird compared to my mum and all the other mums I knew, but she'd looked straight at me and hadn't flinched, and I didn't think she'd been pre-warned either. Yet not a flicker. No pity in her eyes when she looked at my scars, but something else instead. Something I thought was called empathy. Like she understood. Like she noticed things others didn't.

She breezed back in with a glass jar. 'Let's try it.'

'Oh, I'm supposed to be careful what I put on . . .'

'Nothing here that'll do any harm, poppet.' She unscrewed the jar and Ryan jittered from foot to foot behind her. She scooped a blob of cream on to her middle finger. 'Only good stuff in here and lots of it. The colour comes from carrots, but there's land herbs and sea herbs in here too. This is a burn, isn't it?'

'Mum!'

'Oh, Ryan, sit down!' She smoothed the cream gently on to my cheek starting at the top of the scar tissue. 'He's such a fusser. This is grafted, yes? I expect the colour will fade with time. How does that feel?'

'Good,' I said, surprised because it really did.

She continued applying the cream down my face and neck. 'Scars are beautiful too, you know. They're a badge we wear for the world to show we've lived.' She tipped a finger under my chin and lifted it. 'And that we've survived. So they have a beauty all of their own.' She screwed the top back on the jar and gave it to me. 'Keep it.'

There were two possible options: she was crackers, or she had a point. It was certainly a different way of looking at things. Though there definitely wasn't ever going to be a time when catwalk models would slap a warm iron on their skin to fake having 'lived'.

Ryan had his eyes closed, like he wanted to sink through the floor and into the canal beneath. But I understood, because parents can be so *excruciating*. Mine certainly could.

I looked at his mug. 'What's yours?'

'Ginger. Wakes me up.' He glared at his mum as she rummaged in a box beside her chair, but she paid no attention to him. 'Are you hungry?'

'No, I've had breakfast and Mum'll have lunch ready when I get back. Honestly, sometimes I think all we do on Sundays is eat. I'm stuffed by bedtime.'

'You can't eat that much,' he said, looking me over. I wasn't sure whether to be pleased he didn't think I was fat or worried he thought I was too skinny.

'I do. I eat loads. But Mum's into organic and wholefoods so it's all healthy stuff.'

He nodded gloomily in sympathy.

'Very wise,' his mum answered, counting crystals out on to her lap. 'Food can be our medicine or our poison –'

'I'm going to show Jenna round the boat now!' Ryan said, jumping up. We stared up at him and he shrugged. 'She's never been on a narrowboat. Jenna, bring your tea.'

I scrambled up obediently. He'd already moved off, expecting me to follow. His mum smiled a slow, secret smile and said nothing.

The kitchen was clever, so much packed into a small space, even a baby range cooker. Behind the kitchen was the bathroom, again minute, but somehow a toilet, washbasin and shower all fitted in. I noticed a razor on the shelf above the basin. *So he shaves.*

He showed me his mum's bedroom next. The bedcover had a sunburst pattern of purple and black and chains of coloured crystals hung from the ceiling. Drawers and cupboards lined the wall at the foot of the bed, with more drawers beneath that.

'It's so smart, all this storage. I'd never have believed you could fit so much in a boat. What's it like living here?'

'Don't know really. I've never lived anywhere else. I'd rather have your kitchen than ours though.'

'No, yours is sweet.'

'And yours is big.'

'Big isn't always best.'

He turned to me, smirking. 'You sure about that?'

It took me a second to catch on. 'Shut up! You know I didn't mean that.' I was beginning to think embarrassing me amused him.

There was no crystal in his room and the walls held crammed bookshelves as well as drawers. His bed hadn't been made and the pillow still had a dent from where his head had been. He opened a drawer and grinned. 'I can put a T-shirt on if you're finding me distracting.'

'You are so full of yourself. How do you fit your head through doorways?'

He chuckled and flopped on to the bed without bothering with the T-shirt. I turned my back on him and examined his bookshelves.

'Are all these yours?'

'Mostly. I nicked a few from Mum.'

He had a strange mix of books – paperbacks of proper grown-up books, books on boat engines, a huge stack of dog-eared exercise books and old textbooks. Home school, I remembered.

I took a book from the top shelf. '*Slaughterhouse 5* – what's this about?' I asked, testing him.

'It's an anti-war book about the bombing of Dresden in the

Second World War. The guy can travel through time and meet aliens and –'

'OK, so you do read them.' I put the book back.

He laughed. 'No, I just read the covers and pretend.' He stretched his arms above his head and cracked his knuckles.

'Urgh! That's horrible.' I shuffled uncomfortably by the bookshelves, not sure what to do in such a confined space with him. He took up so much of the bed that if I sat on it I'd be touching him, and from that smirk, he knew he was unsettling me.

'Do you want to see the engine room? It's cramped and I have to wedge my bike in there, but you can stick your head around the door.'

Engines didn't interest me, but anything to get out of this room before I flushed bright scarlet did, so I agreed.

He jumped off the bed and led me to a door behind his bedroom. I looked in at some machinery I didn't understand and he put his head over my shoulder, pointing out . . . things. I couldn't concentrate on what he was saying . . . something about the engine . . . because he leaned against me, his arm brushing mine as he explained the mechanics of the boat. The smell of oil and diesel didn't cut out the smell of him, deodorant and ginger, warm and close.

He knew he was having that effect on me. I was sure of it. He was doing it deliberately to boost his ego, the big-headed pig.

'I'd better go. Lunch will be ready soon,' I said, abruptly bumping him out of the way.

'Thanks for bringing my coat back,' he said, following me back to the sitting area. I noticed how he flipped into edgy best behaviour the minute he was around his mum. It was so funny, seeing the childish side of him for a change.

She got up and pressed a necklace into my hands. Smooth shards of pink crystal intermingled with silver beads, and I realised she'd just made it. 'For you,' she said. 'Rose quartz. For healing inside and out. The more you wear it, the better it works.'

I gasped – it was beautiful. I knew it'd cost a lot in a shop. 'Oh, thank you, Mrs . . .' I stopped – I didn't know Ryan's second name.

'Karen, just call me Karen.'

I opened the catch and looped it round my neck. Ryan's hand brushed the back of my neck to lift my hair out of the way. My skin hummed at the contact.

'It's lovely,' I managed to say. 'Are you sure?'

'A friend of my baby is a friend of mine,' she said, and I caught a flash of Ryan's teasing eyes in hers, making them look similar for the first time.

He let out a loud huff of disgust behind me and stomped on to the deck to wait for me.

Karen laughed softly. 'He hates me calling him that, so sometimes I do it to annoy him. I can't stand men who take themselves too seriously so I'm not having him growing up like that.'

I thought of him lying in the horse muck and grinned back at her. 'I think it's working.'

She patted my cheek, the unscarred one this time. 'Drop by any time. You're welcome.'

Ryan was waiting on the bank and he handed me off the boat with a sheepish face. I pretended I hadn't noticed his mini-strop.

'If you walk the dog past here in the evening, call me. I'll come with you if you like.'

'Oh, it's getting a bit dark down here by that time.' I bit my lip, wanting to take him up on his offer, but not wanting to end up in the canal or lost in the willow copse. 'I normally stick to the lanes.'

'Doh!' He slapped his forehead. 'Of course. Have you got a mobile?' I fished in the pocket of my jacket and pulled mine out. He took it and punched a number into my contact list. 'There. Text me when you're going out and I'll meet you up at your gate.'

'You've got a mobile?'

'Jenna, I live on a boat not in the Outer Hebrides.'

I grinned. 'Sorry. Actually they probably have mobiles there too.'

He laughed and then looked at me hard. 'Are you still all right? About last night?'

And just when I'd talked myself into thinking he was a full-of-himself git, he had to go and pull that. I nodded, not able to meet his eyes, but not because I felt bad about stupid Ed.

'Good,' he said, ruffling my hair like Dad did to me and Charlie. 'His loss. Go on, and think of me when you're having roast dinner.' He made his comedy sad face.

But there was absolutely no danger of me not thinking of him.

Fifteen minutes later I skipped back into the kitchen, pretty sure that no one had noticed I'd been out. Mum looked at me suspiciously for a moment, but then said, 'Can you drain the carrots off? I'm nearly ready to serve.'

As I went to pick the pan up, the phone rang. I turned to answer it.

'Don't! Ignore it!'

'Why?'

'It's been going constantly for an hour. I'm surprised you haven't heard it. Nuisance calls. Drain the carrots, please.'

I took the pan off the hob, frowning. 'What do they say?'

'Nothing. It's silent. So don't answer it. It'll only encourage them. It's probably kids being stupid.'

Or Steven Carlisle and his friends.

Later we all pretended to watch the film on TV, except Charlie who really did watch it. Dad stared at the wall behind the TV, his face set hard. He'd unplugged the phone half an hour ago. Mum and I said nothing about it in silent agreement.

I looked out of the French windows. Beyond the garden, the fields and the copse ran the canal. I forgot about Steven Carlisle and disgusting Ed from last night and Dad's anger and Mum's worried face, and thought about Ryan.

Sometimes, I thought, a secret boyfriend, the kind you have only in your head, was the best kind. No worries over whether they liked you. In my imagination he'd always do and say the right thing. He'd think I was wonderful and perfect and beautiful and in my head it could never be awkward or embarrassing. He'd never make me uncomfortable or unhappy. He'd never break my heart.

I'd had several boyfriends like that in the last couple of years.

But now the boy in my head had Ryan's face. His voice. His smile.

It couldn't do any harm. It was only in my head and no one would ever know.

20 – Ryan

As I freewheeled down to the boatyard on Monday, Sadie walked out of the gates in her school uniform. I groaned quietly enough that she wouldn't hear me. She stopped behind the wall where her dad couldn't see her and waited for me to pull the bike up beside her.

'Hi,' I said. 'Did you get home OK Saturday?'

She dead-eyed me. 'Like you care.'

'You knew loads of people there. And your dad was picking you up.'

'Did your little troll get home OK?'

'Why are you so mean about her?'

She balled her hands into fists. 'Are you going to apologise to me?'

After what she said to Jenna? 'For what? Taking my friend home when she was upset?'

'I meant what I said about dumping you.'

'OK. I've got to go now or I'll be late for work.'

'You won't have a job if I tell my dad about you.'

I *knew* it – that's why she was here. 'Go ahead, but I don't think he'll be too pleased with you either.'

'What if I tell him you made me do stuff I didn't want to?'

I stared at her. 'Whatever, Sadie.'

Her eyes filled up as she realised I was never going to beg to get her back. She tried the waterworks instead. 'Are you sleeping with her?'

'What? No! She's my friend and she was upset and I was looking after her – she's only fourteen. You want to lie about me to your dad? You want to be that pathetic? Fine, get on with it. I'm going to work.'

I wheeled my bike through the gates away from her. When I parked it up, my hands were shaking. Would she go through with it or not? I wasn't sure what was worse – the thought of losing the job or Pete believing her. It mattered what he and Bill thought about me. It mattered badly.

21 – Jenna

Beth glowered at me when I walked into the form room. 'So? Are you going to tell me where you got to on Saturday? I was really worried and all you could do was send me two measly texts.'

'I was kind of busy.' I smiled apologetically.

'How do you think I felt? The club was buzzing with it after you'd gone.'

'Huh! I expect everyone's heard about it by now.'

Beth bit her lip. 'I think it has got round, Jen. Three people asked me about it at the lockers this morning. But really, everyone seems pretty disgusted with that guy.'

It crossed my mind I should be mad at Ryan. If he hadn't hit Ed, nobody would have known about it except those rugby morons. But I just couldn't be angry with him.

'How are you anyway?' Beth asked, scanning my face anxiously.

'Fine.'

She stared hard at me and waited, then sighed and gave up. 'OK, if you say so.' She grinned. 'Come on then, what's he like – Mr Knight in Shining Armour?'

'He's just a friend.'

'He must be a very good friend. He could have got his head kicked in.'

I laughed. 'I don't think he thought about that. He lost his temper.'

'Did you go home with him?'

'Yes, he lives near me.'

'Oh, that Sadie was so steaming. You should have heard her.'

'Serves her right. She doesn't deserve him.'

Beth's eyes widened. 'Ooh, you like him!'

I sniffed. 'So? Who wouldn't? Don't worry – he's boxed in the gorgeous but unattainable compartment in here.' I tapped my head with my finger.

'He is lush,' Beth agreed. 'What's his name?'

'Ryan.'

'Where did you meet him?'

'Walking the dog. A few times. Just got talking, you know.'

'Aww, he's a sweetie to stand up for you like that.'

I giggled – I doubted he'd like being called a sweetie. It didn't fit at all with his image of himself. I changed the subject and went on for a bit about how great Max was, which made Beth happy.

Later that afternoon, Mum drove me home from yet another hospital appointment. Normally I'd have been pleased to get out of double science, but not if it meant seeing the dermatologist to be examined and prodded.

'I think that went very well, don't you?' Mum said as we exited the car park.

'Yes.'

'You see, putting up with the mask – and I know how you hated it, darling – has all been worth it in the end. Dr Morrison was delighted, wasn't he?'

'Yes.'

She glanced over at me. 'The colour will fade. You heard what he said. Why don't you use the make-up more now? You did a fantastic job with it when you went out with Beth. It does cover the redness and I know that bothers you. You'll get used to using it in no time. Look how far you've come already.'

'Watch the road, Mum.'

She bit her lip. 'Sorry. Shall we stop in Whitmere to rent a DVD? Curl up in front of the fire and have a girly afternoon?'

'OK.'

'It's not that I think you need to hide your skin, but I do think it'll make you feel better. I know I feel like a raddled old hag if I don't put my make-up on. And remember before your accident how you were always nagging me to let you wear it?'

That was true. She was only trying to help, but I wasn't in the mood. Dr Morrison had made me look in the big mirror when he talked to me about my progress.

'I'm pleased with your neck,' he said, pointing. 'This is always a difficult area to get right. The skin tends to tighten and pucker here, but this is really quite smooth.' It didn't look smooth to me. 'There's no distortion dragging your facial features down — excellent. I think we made the right decision to remove the mask after six months. We're lucky you healed so well.' Six months was the minimum time, I knew. It could have been two years if things had gone worse for me. 'And you're keeping the massage up twice a day?' I nodded. 'Good, good. Make sure you do. We don't want to waste all that hard work.' He turned my head to examine my cheek in more detail. 'Very good result on the face too. And how are you in yourself? Your mum says you're back at school now and getting out and about again.'

'Yes.'

'How's that going?'

'OK.'

I willed him to put the mirror away. That's what Ryan saw when he looked at me. How did it not make him sick? It was all very well Ryan saying they were just scars. Perhaps he could look at them that way, but he hadn't had to kiss me. I bet he'd see it differently if he did.

'Jenna? Jenna?' Mum called me back to the present. 'What DVD do you fancy? Any ideas?'

'Something cheerful.' Please, something cheerful. 'A Disney film?' Baby stuff, like I used to watch when everything was OK. A fairy-tale world.

22 – Ryan

For the first time, I was glad to get out of the boatyard at the end of the day. My phone blooped a text message when I was halfway home – Jenna, waiting for me with the dog.

I dumped my bike in the paddock at the back of her house and met her by the front gate. Her eyes focused on my jaw.

'I didn't realise it was so bad.' She lifted her hand to my face and then let it drop back.

The bruises from where Steven Carlisle had hit me had really come up today and I had purple splodges over my chin. But he'd have a few too so I didn't care. 'I'm fine.'

She tutted. 'You always say you're fine.'

I liked how worried her eyes were as they scanned me for more injuries. I could've milked it for a bit of sympathy. Obviously she was quite prepared to dish that out, but a bash on the chin was nothing compared to having the skin burned off your face. I'd have been ashamed to play on a few bruises with her.

We set off, walking away from the village. The light was

fading so I skirted round her to walk on the outside in case of traffic.

'How was school?'

'Oh, OK,' she said, offhand. 'Everyone knew about Saturday, and that was . . . yeah . . . But I wasn't there long. I had a hospital appointment this afternoon so Mum picked me up at twelve. And then we slobbed out on the sofa afterwards and watched TV and ate junk.'

'Your mum let you eat junk?'

'Mmm. She bought crisps and dip and we toasted marshmallows for hot chocolate.'

I glared. 'If I get home to tofu tonight, I'm never forgiving you for telling me that.'

A car came by and we stepped up on to the verge until it passed.

'So what was the hospital visit for?'

'Oh, a check-up.' And there she was again – offhand.

'How did it go?'

'OK.'

I nudged her with my elbow.

She sighed. 'It was the dermatologist. And really, it went OK. He's pleased with how it's gone since the mask came off. I don't have to go back for a while now.'

'Hey, good result! You happy?'

'Suppose.' She hesitated. 'I wish the redness would fade quicker though. He said it could take up to two years.'

I wanted to say something really clever to make her feel better, but I couldn't think of a single thing. I grabbed her hand instead and gave it a squeeze. Sometimes it was easier for me to do something than find words.

'Me and Mum had a talk afterwards,' she said slowly, 'and I'm going to use the concealer make-up now. For school and for going to the shops and . . . oh, most of the time.'

'Don't you want to?'

'It's hard to explain. I want it to look better. But if I put the make-up on then I have to look at it myself. And then . . . oh, I don't know . . . then I have to accept that it's never going to go away. I can't pretend it's not there even though that doesn't work anyway. It doesn't make sense, I know.'

I should've ripped that Carlisle shit's throat out.

'Sorry,' she muttered. 'You don't want to hear all this.'

'Yes, I do or I wouldn't have asked.'

'Did you see Sadie today?' she asked in the least subtle 'I don't want to talk about this any more' change of subject ever.

'Yup.'

'And?'

'I'm dumped. Officially. So now I don't have to worry about getting sacked. Good result for both of us today.'

She looked doubtfully at me, but I gave her my best grin.

We walked round in a loop and she asked me about work and the boats until it got too dark and I dropped her back at home. 'Text me tomorrow?' I asked as I collected the bike.

'OK, and I'll bring you some marshmallows.'

I sniffed. 'Toasted?'

'But of course.' She grinned at me.

'That's all right then. You're forgiven.'

23 – Jenna

The following Saturday morning, I waved the car off as Mum and Dad took Charlie and his friend Toby paintballing.

'Have fun. Don't kill each other.'

Mum pulled a face at me. She wasn't sure she was going to enjoy this at all and I'd betrayed her by ducking out of it.

Twenty minutes later, there was a quiet knock on the back door, but when I opened it, no one was there. I stuck my head out and saw Ryan flattened against the wall. 'Have they gone?' he whispered.

I laughed. 'Come in.'

Raggs went mental at the sight of him and jumped into his arms. He'd discovered if he did that then Ryan would catch him so it was now my idiot mutt's favourite game. Ryan came through into the sitting room with an armful of slobbering ginger dog, but he lost all interest in playing with Raggs as soon as he saw the plasma TV screen on the wall. He looked like Charlie the first time we took him to Santa's Grotto when he was tiny. Ryan made some indeterminate drooling sound, the kind boys make over sports cars.

I poked him on the shoulder. 'The DVDs are in the cupboard. Pick something while I get the food. Here's the remote control.' I spoke quite slowly because his eyes were glazed over in techno-lust.

'Effphnargh,' he replied, or at least that's how it sounded. I tried not to laugh as I went to turn the chips over in the oven.

When I got back with a tray of drinks and bowls of snacks, I found him cross-legged on the sofa with his trainers kicked off, happily flicking through channels. 'You should've shouted me,' he said, waving at the tray, his eyes never leaving the screen. He didn't notice me leave to get the pizza and chips – he'd just discovered the sports channel.

He came to when I pushed a plate of food into his hands.

'Did you pick a film?'

He nodded eagerly, a chip already in his mouth, and hit the play button. 'I thought you might like this one too.'

The menu came up on the screen and I recognised the film. 'Two hot guys in this,' I said, settling back. 'What's not to like?'

He twisted round on the sofa to rest his feet on my knee and I eyed him. On one hand, I didn't mind as his feet didn't smell. On the other, was using me as a foot rest a step too far? If there was one thing I knew from having a little brother, it was that boys push their luck as far as they can. And Ryan, I knew by now, was sometimes just a big kid and a nightmare for doing that.

We'd been hanging around together for a couple of weeks now, since the Rugby Club incident, but it felt like a lot longer. He was the easiest person to talk to I'd ever met and he had some kind of sixth sense for when I was feeling down. A knack of dragging things out of me even if I didn't want to talk. And he was right – I always did feel better afterwards.

But that didn't make me his personal footstool. I made up my mind and shoved his feet off my lap. He chuckled and slid them back up to rest on the sofa next to me, knees crooked up to fit his legs on. A minute later, eyes glued to the screen, he slid his feet under my leg to keep his toes warm. It wasn't uncomfortable so I ignored him. He was as bad as Raggs, who'd crawl a leg at a time on to the sofa when we weren't looking.

When the film hit a slow scene, I seized my opportunity. I wanted to check something out with him, something I wasn't sure about myself. 'I'm going bowling tomorrow.'

'Who with?' He dipped a crisp into salsa and munched on it.

'Some people from school.'

He looked round in surprise. 'Oh, that's good.'

'Beth keeps moaning that I need to get out more, and you tell me I have to talk to people and give them a chance, so I've been trying to make more effort.'

'Good.' He gave me a smile that made my stomach molten.

'You know I told you everyone at school heard what happened at the Rugby Club? Well, some of the people in my year thought it was totally outrageous, according to Beth, and she says they've been making a big effort to talk to me because they feel bad about it.'

'Yeah?'

'So Matthew asked me to go bowling with his group this weekend, and . . . well . . . I said yes.' Had I done the right thing? I'd rather hang out with Ryan, but . . .

His eyebrows snapped together. 'Matthew? A guy asked you? On a date?'

I frowned too. A date? No. I'd known Matthew and his twin sister since primary school. He wasn't interested in me. He was one of those boys who had lots of girls as friends. I opened my mouth to tell Ryan that, but in a split second my brain wiring fired wrong and I had a moment of insanity. 'Oh, I didn't think of it like that. I suppose so.'

'How old is he? What's he like? Do you like him?'

I blinked at the volley of questions. 'Um, he's the same age as me. Er, he's all right. I've known him for years. And yes. Everyone likes him.'

'Do you fancy him though?'

When had this become an interrogation? I wished I hadn't said anything and I really regretted twisting the truth. 'I-I don't know. I haven't thought about it.'

'Well, you should,' he rapped back. 'You can't mess around wondering, if he tries it on with you. You need to know.'

'I-I don't think that's going to be an issue. We're going bowling with five other people on a Sunday afternoon.'

He grunted. 'If it was me and I wanted to, I'd find a way. So are you going to let him kiss you tomorrow?'

'Can we drop this, please?' I said, my face flaming.

'Or are you going to freak out because of last time and not having done it before?' His eyes were so hard – I didn't like how he was looking at me.

'Ryan, shut up. Just . . . just watch the film.'

He hit the pause button and folded his arms and stared at me. What on earth was wrong with him?

'Look, it's just bowling . . . I don't think –'

'Maybe we should make sure you do know what you're doing,' he said, tapping his fingers on his arms like a drumbeat. 'Yeah, maybe we should. That's not a bad idea at all.'

He wasn't making any sense. 'What are you talking about? And why're you snapping at me?'

'I'm not snapping,' he snapped. 'I'm thinking. No, I'm sure now. This is a good idea. Definitely.'

'What is?' I hadn't liked the look on his face before and I liked the smirk he wore now even less.

'Come here and I'll show you.' He beckoned me with his head.

Understanding began to dawn. 'Are you suggesting that . . .'

'Yeah, why not?' His grin spread. 'Just so there's no

embarrassment tomorrow. And I don't mind. I've kissed loads of girls.'

I didn't know whether I wanted to slap him or put my head under the cushion and hide. I compromised by glaring. 'Oh, that's so good of you! Offering yourself up as a sacrifice!'

That wiped the horrible grin off his face. He replaced it with an apologetic, wheedling look. 'Hell no, I didn't mean it like that. It came out wrong. All I meant was we're friends and I'll help you out so you don't go blaming yourself if he turns out to be useless.'

I stared back at him, trying to read his face. He didn't look as if he was winding me up. My pride was stung, but what girl isn't terrified of messing up her first proper kiss by not knowing what to do? Should I do it? Would he laugh at me if I got it wrong?

'Everyone needs a bit of practice at first,' he added encouragingly.

OK, so he wouldn't laugh. He never did if I was really worried or upset. But kissing him? I'd *die*. I'd give myself away. Lindz used to say boys gloated if they knew you liked them, though she'd never tried to hide her interest from Stephen, not like she did with the others.

Would Ryan gloat if he realised? Or maybe he'd run out of here so fast he'd leave skid marks in our gravel.

But then the temptation to try . . . to find out what it was like with him . . . I swallowed . . . my bones felt like they were made of plasticine and I couldn't get my eyes away from his mouth, which was still talking.

'See, if you get like this it proves you need to practise. You look like you're going to freak out now and it's only me.'

If it hadn't been me in this situation then I'd have laughed myself stupid. *Only him? Freak out? Yes, you idiot!*

He moved his legs and patted the seat beside him. 'Come on.'

Oh, what the . . . I didn't know how to get out of it now. If I said no, that'd look weird and he'd probably guess.

I shuffled up beside him. What if it was horrible and slobbery like last time? What should I do with my hands?

He didn't give me time to change my mind. He flashed me a quick grin. 'You're not facing the death squad. I'm quite good at it.' Then his face was so close to mine that I squeaked and stopped breathing.

I waited for him to lunge forward and squash my mouth. He didn't. He sort of brushed the side of my nose lightly with his and gave a huff of breath that sounded like a laugh. His hand touched my unscarred cheek and I wasn't sure what to make of that. His other hand ran lightly over my hair as he put his lips on mine in a feather kiss. 'You're supposed to breathe, you know.' He laughed and nudged his elbow in my ribs. I exhaled sharply and he sniggered, a particularly Ryan sound. Strangely that relaxed me, though it was *the* most infuriatingly smug noise.

'Better,' he said quietly. 'Now chill. It's really not that

difficult. Complete morons manage it all the time.'

His fingers moved gently over my cheek and it should've felt good, but all I could think about was that of course he hadn't touched the other side of my face.

Then he kissed me properly, tilting my head so my mouth fitted with his. He didn't force his tongue in; he kissed me slowly until I decided I wanted to put my arms round his neck. I didn't have the courage though and I pulled back. 'Am I doing this right?'

'Mmm,' he said, eyes closed. He tugged me closer again. 'Shut up. I'm not finished yet.'

I noticed how he didn't ask if he was doing it right for me – typical.

But he was. It felt more than right, but I was still too busy trying to work out how to do it back and not appear too enthusiastic at the same time. As this was supposed to be a lesson and nothing more.

Oh!

My hands knotted involuntarily in his hair as he slid his tongue into my mouth. And it wasn't a bit like last time. Not slobbery or like being attacked by a dish mop. I kissed him back, or at least I thought that's what I was doing.

He made a small noise and pulled his mouth away briefly. 'That's right,' he murmured, and then put his lips back to mine again.

Clearly he'd been right – that guy Ed was a drunken goon who didn't have a clue because this was nothing like how it had been with him. I stopped worrying about what to do and pretended that it was all real and not a lesson at all.

His hand slid back to my face, tilting it a little more.

I let out a gasp as his lips moved off mine to kiss up my right cheek. I flinched away and made a noise that should've been 'no', but wasn't anything that made sense.

He ignored me and his lips followed my face until he found it again. He held my head between his hands so I couldn't pull away while he kissed up my cheek, then down over my jaw and neck.

I couldn't feel much of it in my skin. The flames had done too much damage to the nerves and the whole area was numb like when a dentist's injection hasn't worn off properly. But I felt it everywhere else: in my stomach, in my head, in the cold place inside where the anger thing lived. *Why? Why is he doing this?*

'Ryan?' I mumbled, not knowing what to say, but having to say something before I burst or cried.

'Mmm, sshhh,' was all I got in return. He brought his lips back to kiss me on the mouth again. He wasn't as slow or as gentle this time, but that felt right too. And even better when he tightened his arms round me.

When he kissed me harder again, I wanted him to.

And then suddenly he pulled away and let me go. He flopped

back in the sofa, grabbed the bowl of tortilla chips and plopped it in his lap. 'There, you'll be fine now,' he said in a peculiar voice and he hit the play button on the remote.

The shock of him stopping, the sudden sound from the TV – it hit me like a bucket of ice water thrown over my head. I retreated back to my side of the sofa in panic. The set look on his face did nothing to help. What went wrong? Had he got grossed out?

He took a long breath in and relaxed a bit, though his mouth still looked tight. 'You don't have to scoot off over there like I'm a leper,' he said, and his voice was tight too. What was up with him?

'Come back here and watch the rest of the film.' He draped his arm over the back of the sofa and beckoned me. I shuffled over again. It was easier to do what he said than try to work out what was going on in his head and risk messing up. Plus I felt sort of small and cold since he'd let me go.

He gave me a one-armed bear hug and nodded at the TV. 'The special effects are good.'

'Er, yeah . . .' He made no sense at all.

'Think that scenery is CGI?'

'Um . . .'

'Want a crisp?'

'No, I'm full.' No way was I picking tortilla chips out of a bowl right over his groin.

'They're really good. Thanks for getting these. Do you want me to toast you a marshmallow?'

'No, I'm full.'

'Sorry, yeah.' He did that wheedling smile again. 'The pizza was great too. And the chips.'

If he was trying to make up for being weird, this was overkill. I watched the TV screen in silence. He sighed and munched another crisp.

'Jenna?'

'Yeah?'

'If this guy does try it on, you don't do it unless you want to. OK?'

'Uh-huh.'

'And you don't let him go further than . . . than we did. Not the first time. OK?'

'Uh-huh.'

'Unless you want to?'

I turned to look at him. He glared at me hard, as if it would be very bad if I did want to go further. Which was rich coming from him. 'I doubt it!'

'Hmm,' he said cryptically and watched the TV again. 'What time will you be back?'

'I don't know yet.'

'Text me.'

'OK, but will you shut up about it now? Please!'

He laughed and I felt him relax, though I hadn't realised he'd been tensed up before. 'Sorry! Just guys can be pushy and –'

'OK, now you are freaking me out.' I screwed my face up. 'You sound like my dad.'

He butted me with his shoulder and laughed again. 'Watch the film.'

Occasionally he stroked his thumb absently down my hair when the scary scenes were on. I wasn't sure he knew he was doing it as he was so absorbed with things killing each other on screen.

Then the truth hit me. He thought I was a little kid. Like when he made me eat those chips in the burger place. And that was why he offered to kiss me. That was why he kissed my face, just to make me feel better.

I sneaked a look at his profile to memorise its lines. I couldn't remember if Ed's lips had been soft – too busy trying to get away – but I'd always thought a boy's lips would be hard and raspy for some reason. Ryan's weren't. I got it now, why people liked kissing.

'I forgot to say before, is your neighbour a nutter?'

'Um, he's been a bit odd recently. Since Lindsay died.'

'Oh, of course, he's her dad!'

'Why?'

'When I came up the garden earlier, he was talking to a rose bush.'

'He keeps staring at that bush. I've seen him.'

'Maybe he planted it for her. Maybe he thinks he's talking to her.' Ryan shrugged. 'Takes time to get over stuff . . . Aww, that's gross! Hang on, I'll rewind so you can watch it.'

So he could watch it again, more like. I rolled my eyes as he sat wide-eyed while an alien's head was ripped off and blue gook spouted everywhere.

24 – Ryan

Later that evening, I lay sprawled on my bed, thinking about just what had got into my head that afternoon. If you could buy a big yellow Captain Stupid sticker then I should get one and wear it right in the middle of my forehead. Great idea – 'let's just kiss as practice', No big deal. Just make sure that she knew what she was doing when the knob who'd asked her out tried it on.

I ran through it in my head, trying to work out what had got into me. First off, when she told me – shock. She was *my* friend, not his. Next, was it a jerk like that git from the Rugby Club? Didn't sound that way though. Not from what she said about him. And then, yeah, my totally reasonable and genius idea. That was completely me being a good mate. That flash of 'he's not getting to do what I haven't' was only down to the surprise. I was just helping out.

But it all went a bit wrong.

It was fine at first. I concentrated on not rushing her, letting her get used to it, not freaking her out. It took me aback a bit that I liked it so much, but that was all right. For a while. Until she started to get the idea. Until I knew she was enjoying it. And that had a weird effect on me because . . . but I couldn't think about her like that. Off limits.

But then I didn't want to stop. I didn't normally have to hold back, but with Jenna I had to. And the longer I kissed her, the more difficult it got.

I did go further than I intended. Not too far, but I hadn't meant to get that into it. Plus when I kissed her face, she was shaking and she said my name like she was going to cry, and I sort of lost my head for a few minutes.

That wasn't how it had been with all the other girls I'd kissed. I couldn't grasp what the difference was exactly, but there definitely was one.

I banged my head on the pillow over and over. She must either think I was a total creep or a headcase. You don't go around volunteering to kiss your friends to show them how. And if you do, you shouldn't get off on it. If she kissed that guy tomorrow, I knew I'd want to rip his fingernails out and stick them in his eyeballs. But why? Because she was my friend and I didn't want some other guy pawing her? Right, and that was a really normal reaction.

I rolled on to my back and lay still for a while. Mum was in some kind of cleaning frenzy next door and I heard things clatter and crash through the wall. I wasn't in the mood to deal with her – I was having enough problems with myself.

Jenna texted from the bowling place to say she'd be home by seven so I texted back for her to meet me in the stable then.

I checked my watch. Five to seven. I'd been waiting there ages. She'd be officially late soon. My knee jogged up and down against the edge of the straw bale I was sitting on.

Minutes ticked by.

I checked my watch again.

Exactly seven and no sign of her.

My knee jogged faster.

At one minute past seven, a torch beam gleamed up at the far end of the field.

'You're late,' I muttered when she came into the loose box. I made room for her on my bale.

'We went for nachos afterwards.'

'Did you have a good time?'

She smiled. 'Yes.'

I waited.

And waited.

'Well?'

'God, you're in a bad mood! Well, nothing. We went bowling. We got nachos. End of.'

'Did he try –'

'Ryan, you might leap on girls the second you've met them, but not every boy does. No, he didn't.'

Perversely, I was angry with the kid in case she was disappointed he hadn't made a move. 'I don't leap on anyone who doesn't want me to.'

'No, I know. I'm sorry,' she said and I could see she meant it. 'But some people just want to be friends, or are shy, or –'

'Or weird,' I supplied helpfully. 'So did anything happen?'

'He bought me a Coke.'

'Ooh, slick!'

She gave me a dirty look. 'I thought it was nice. And he saved my seat for me when it was my turn to bowl.'

'He's a real player, isn't he?' Now I was mad at him for being interested in her and crap at it.

'Are you going to keep on being horrible?'

'No.' I sighed and tried to look like I wasn't going to be a git any longer. 'What else happened?'

'I'm not talking about it any more.'

'Did you want him to kiss you?'

'No. Now shut up. I'm sorry you wasted your time yesterday.'

I'm not. 'Never mind. It'll come in useful eventually.' Even I wanted to hit me for how I sounded. 'Sorry, I'm a bit stressed. Bad day.' Not that I wanted to get into that, but I needed to change the subject fast.

It worked. The urge to slap me vanished from her face. 'Oh? Why?' She shuffled closer on the bale.

I picked at a piece of straw, wishing I'd kept my mouth shut. 'Mum's not very well again.'

'What's she doing?'

'Can't sleep, cleaning everything, snappy and mean, and then . . . oh, the usual. It'll get worse for a few weeks until she hits her downer. Then she won't get out of bed for weeks.' Jenna did that thing where she put my hand between both of hers. I liked that. I liked the attention and I felt a sad bastard for admitting it. She had really soft hands, soft skin. 'But I don't know what to do this time because I'll be at work and I won't be able to stop her doing anything stupid. I should've thought of that, but I didn't.'

'Can I do anything to help? I get home from school earlier than you. I could sit with her until you get back.'

I wanted to bury my face in her neck when she said that. Hug her tight and hold on. But I didn't. 'No, she can be really spiteful when she's ill. I'm used to it. You're not.'

She sat up on her knees on the hay bale so she was taller than me and put both arms round me. I closed my eyes and leaned on her shoulder.

'I might not be able to come out much while she's like this. I ought to stay with her when I get home from work.'

'So text me if you think she's up to visitors and I'll come round and see you.'

I looped my arms round her waist so she'd sit there with me

for a while longer. We watched Raggs rolling in the loose straw and scratching himself. I wished she'd kiss me out of sympathy so I could find out if yesterday was a fluke, but she didn't.

Mum was out when I went back to the boat. I got tired of sitting around waiting for her to get back and my head hurt so I went to bed. She hadn't gone off like this for a long time, but it wasn't the first time. I thought things had changed. Obviously not.

I started thinking about Jenna again. That maybe I only wanted her because she was off-limits. That's how it is with what you can't have – you want it all the more for it being taboo. Jenna was doing exactly what she should: going out with some kid her own age who was probably as clueless as her, who her parents would like, who'd still be here in six months time.

For fuck's sake . . . I didn't want to move on. I liked it here – the job, hanging out with her. I couldn't stop the smile curling at my mouth – I loved how she looked at me, like I was smart and knew stuff she didn't, like I had all the answers and could make everything better. I tried to stop loving it because it didn't help, but the feeling was always there when I saw those things in her face.

I wish she was here now. I wish she was older. I wish we never had to leave.

What if I left and she got all hung up about her scar again? Perhaps it bothered me less because I'd never known her without it, but she was my friend so she didn't look ugly to me.

Girls always got way too worked up about how they looked. Most of them looked fine. But get their clothes off and they all got flappy about whether they were fat and all that crap. Drove me nuts because I wouldn't be there if I didn't like how they looked. But like with Sadie – the bra was padded, but so what? Other bits of her were great. Though with Sadie, it sure wasn't her personality. Jenna didn't have big tits, not at all, but small could be good too. She had the cutest bum in those jodhpurs, and hair you wanted to bury your face in and stroke all the time.

I had to stop thinking like this. I wished Cole was here to help me get my head straight.

Maybe it was a good thing I wouldn't see so much of Jenna for a while. It didn't feel good though. It felt empty and achy inside, especially at the thought she might hook up with this guy while I was busy with Mum.

As if on cue, I heard the door crash open. Mum was laughing. So was another voice, a male one. I heard her saying something, then him replying. She wasn't drunk. He was. She was worse than drunk. High. High on whatever ate up her head. They stumbled into her bedroom. I put the pillow over my head to drown their noise out. She was never quiet when she was like this.

25 – Jenna

The following weekend, I went out with the people from school again. We decided to go and see a film on Friday night. The nearest cinema was fifteen miles away at an out of town shopping complex. Beth's mum was recruited to drive us there and pick us up in her MPV so we all squashed in together.

When we got there, the cinema foyer was packed and I fought the urge to run for it. Beth glanced at me anxiously and I made myself remember what Ryan had said.

'So what if people stare. Let them. Ignore it.'

'But . . .'

'But nothing. Forget them. They don't matter. People are sheep. They stare at anything they haven't seen before. If someone off the telly walked in, they'd stare. Doesn't mean anything.' He grinned. *'Stare back – they'll soon stop.'*

Matthew, his sister Katie and I went for the drinks and popcorn. The girl at the counter flinched when I gave her the order so I pretended I was Ryan and raised an eyebrow and looked her back full in the face. She turned away quickly, but when she handed me the drinks she acted like I was just any other person in the queue.

'It's just a surprise to people. Let them get used to it. Don't overreact.'

Of course, I'd also had the warning about Matthew trying it on.

'Remember, if you don't want to then you don't –'

'Yes, I heard you the first ten times.'

In the dark of the cinema, no one could see my face and I started to feel normal again. The way I used to last year when I was out with friends. That feeling didn't go away when we went for pizza afterwards and I realised Ryan might be right. The more I relaxed, the easier the others were around me and their eyes didn't slide away from my scars as much. He wasn't right about Matthew though. Katie kept on teasing him about how he fancied Chloe in the year below, but wasn't getting anywhere. I wondered at why I wasn't disappointed about that. Why I had to stop a grin of relief. The truth was I'd rather have Ryan in my head than a real boyfriend right now. Beth wouldn't be impressed if I told her that. She'd say I was hiding away again. But Ryan hadn't kissed her, so what did she know?

I went round to the boat for a while when I got home. Ryan looked relieved to see me. Karen was all smiles and gushing with talk, but she made me dizzy with her jumping up and fiddling with things for no reason. She walked in and out of the kitchen, sitting down then going out to move tins of tea about, turning the kettle on and off, babbling away the whole time. Even when Ryan was talking to me, he was watching her and his eyes were red with tiredness.

I couldn't stay long. I had to get home before Dad freaked at how late I was. Ryan walked me up to the house, his torch lighting the way up the towpath and along the lanes. When we got to the gate, I felt so bad for him that I reached up and hugged him.

'You look shattered.'

'Yeah,' he said with a sigh. 'She's been driving me crazy tonight. I'd better get back. I'm going to try to get her to go to bed. Bad day at work too.'

'Why?'

'Sadie told her dad about that fight at the Rugby Club. She made me sound like a total psycho. Pete had a right go at me.'

'Why did she do that?' I asked, brimming with indignation.

He sighed again. 'Revenge. It could've been worse, but I don't know why she waited so long to do it.'

'Maybe she thought she could get back with you and now she's realised it won't happen.'

'Yeah, maybe. She does keep showing up at the yard, but I stay out of her way.'

'She's such a bitch. Are you in trouble?'

'No, Pete's OK about it now. He went off at me about being

a dumb-ass and giving the place a bad name. And giving myself one. But then Bill made me tell them why I did it. And Pete said he'd have done the same. Sorry, I know you hate people knowing what happened.'

'It's all right. As long as it got you out of trouble. Look, Mum and Dad are out with Charlie at his Swim Club thing tomorrow. I'll come round again for an hour if you like?'

He hugged me tighter and nodded. But he didn't make a dumb joke or tease.

He waited until I got to the front door and then the torch beam headed back down the lane.

26 – Ryan

The next week seemed to go in a flash. When I got in from work on Friday evening, I could hear Mum singing in the bathroom. I checked my phone, but there was no text from Jenna. Mustn't be back from the supermarket yet. Maybe she'd call later. Maybe we could do something after work tomorrow. Just me and her doing some regular stuff.

Mum breezed out of the bathroom wrapped in a towel. Her eyes had a glassy look. I knew what that meant.

'You going out?' I asked before she disappeared into the bedroom.

'Yes,' she replied and shut the door on me.

I stamped back to the rocking chair and sat down to wait.

She emerged an hour later, face painted and reeking of some scented oil.

'Where are you going?'

'Into town. The bus goes in fifteen minutes.'

'To a pub?'

'Yes, Ryan, to a pub.'

The look she gave me warned me to shut up, but I didn't.

'To pick up another guy, I guess.'

'What's it to you?' Her voice hitched in anger. 'What I do is none of your business. No man controls me and I'm not having my kid trying to start that.'

'What if you meet some weirdo? There's nutters out there. You can't keep doing this, Mum. It's dangerous.'

'That's the argument men have used to keep their women controlled for years. For centuries. "You're weaker than us. You need us to protect you. Get back in your place, where you're no threat to our primitive ideas of masculinity." Haven't I taught you anything?' Her hands waved wildly, another 'back off' sign.

'What's wrong with being worried about you getting attacked?' I didn't mean to sound as aggressive as I did, but I was tired. She'd kept me awake most of last night pacing up and down the boat and banging things about.

She laughed. 'Well, if you are *so* concerned about my safety, you can come along and sit in the corner and follow me home. And if I haven't been attacked by then, you can take yourself off to bed and mind your own fucking business.'

'You're serious? You expect me to sit there while you pick up some guy?'

She stormed forward and shoved me. 'Why not? If all you care about is me being safe. Bullshit! You're trying to control me. My God, Ryan, I tried with you, I really tried, but you're just like all the rest. You're such a disappointment to me. My great big failure. My —'

'Mum, you're not well. I'm supposed to tell you when that happens. You know I am. We agreed.'

'Oh, I'm mad, am I now? Because I want to go out and get laid?' I jerked back from her and her lip curled in disgust. 'Can't stand to hear that? It's about keeping me in my place, isn't it? I can see it written all over you.'

'No! You're my mum and . . . and . . . mums don't talk to their kids like that. It's just . . . not right . . .'

'Not right? Women have the right to control their own sexuality —'

'Mum, really, you're not well. You've not been sleeping and you know what that means.'

'So I'll sleep better after I've had sex!' She giggled and it made me feel sick to hear that when her face was red with anger.

'You did this to Cole. When you got ill. Shouting at him, blaming him for things, saying he didn't respect you.'

'Oh, Cole, always bloody Cole. Did you have some little fantasy that he was your replacement father and we were some ridiculous stereotyped family? Let me tell you about families, Ryan, the kind you want. They're all white and crisp-washed cotton sheets on the outside, but when you look inside, they're dirty and stained and stinking.'

'He was good to you. And he put up with loads from you. He loved you.'

She opened her arms. 'Do you see him here? I don't. He was no different from the rest. A lying bastard who ran out when he got what he wanted.'

'You drove him away!'

'I loved him, you stupid little shit!'

I felt like the bottom of the boat had opened beneath my feet and I was falling through it. Drowning in the water beneath. Never . . . she'd never said that before . . . never come close to admitting it . . . I'd never known . . .

She shoved me again, knocking me backwards. 'And he's not coming back so you'd better get over it. He doesn't love me. And he doesn't love you. All lies. All bloody lies. Did you hear me? He didn't love you. You're nothing to him. He was only nice to you to keep me sweet. So yeah, Ryan, I use them! I use them before they use me. Now get out!' She shoved me again towards the door. 'Get out! Get out! I can't stand to look at you!' She picked up the work table and hurled it down by my feet. The leg snapped off and caught me on the kneecap. 'Get out, you hateful –'

I ran. I couldn't stand to hear any more. She wouldn't stop, not in this mood. And what she'd said about Cole . . . had she told him she loved him, and he'd still left? I ran so fast down the towpath, stumbling in the dark, then down the lanes, that I made myself sick. I fell into the verge unable to run any further and vomited bile until I could breathe again.

Not going home. Not back to that. I can't.

I lay there with my face pressed to the wet grass, thinking of the day Cole left. That final row before he went, the bad one.

'Why do you stay?' I'd asked him when Mum was out of earshot.

'You really want to know? She's good in bed, that's why.' I looked away. 'Sorry, kiddo. Shouldn't have said that to you. It's just, well, Karen's sometimes hard to be with.'

I nodded and stared out of the window. He'd be moving on before long. I knew the signs.

Oh well, he'd lasted longer than the rest.

I still cried the day he walked out though, face in the pillow so Mum wouldn't see if she came in.

I felt in my pocket. My wallet was there and I had enough money to get hammered and that's what I wanted to do. Anything to get her words and her face out of my head.

I walked into the centre of the village. The shop was still open and I went in and picked up a bottle of vodka. The woman at the till looked me over. 'How old are you?'

'Nineteen.' I slammed the bottle on the counter almost hard enough to break it.

She let me pay. She was scared being alone in the shop with

me and locked the door as soon as I left. I didn't care.

I started to walk back down the lane, but I'd only gone a few steps when someone tackled me from behind. I went crashing into the verge. As I rolled to fight back, I saw a flash of pale face – Steven Carlisle. Great. Just what I needed. He drove his fist into my face and I felt a ring tear into my cheek. I blocked his next blow and twisted under him to get away. As I scrambled up, he got to his feet too and came at me, swinging. I charged him and took him down. We fell back over a low hedge and landed in a front garden. Inside the house, a dog barked.

We wrestled, grabbing at each other's arms, no words, just silent rage. Hate.

He tried to get a hand on my throat and I brought my knee up sharp between his legs. He let out a strangled yell and fell back.

Behind us, a door opened and the light washed into the front garden. A woman screamed.

'Stop that, stop that now or I'll call the police!' And then calling back into the house, 'George, come quickly!'

Carlisle staggered up and ran, half doubled over, back the way he'd come. No, he wouldn't stick around to be picked up by the police. I had no desire to be dragged off to the station by them either . . . or taken home. I leapt up and hurdled the hedge before George, whoever he was, got there. I saw the glint of my vodka bottle on the grass opposite and picked it up as I legged it the opposite way down the lane.

When I was clear, I stopped and took a long swig before I walked on.

There was only one place I could think of to go and I headed there, drinking the vodka down fast.

27 – Jenna

I was watching TV when I heard the car on the drive. Dad slammed the front door and marched into the kitchen. Mum cast me a worried glance and went after him. The fridge door opened with a creak. Ice chinked in a glass, followed by the slosh, slosh of liquid being poured to angry, hissed voices.

I caught the odd word.

'Bloody Carlisle kid,' and 'more damage,' and 'lying swine'.

I turned the TV up to drown them out. When would Dad learn? His stupid action group only brought more grief.

After a while, they came in and sat down. I waited just long enough for it not to seem I was leaving because of them and then I made my exit. Dad could rant in peace with me gone.

I went into the kitchen and let Raggs out of the back door. 'Go be clean, boy.' I checked my phone again, but Ryan still hadn't texted me. Then I rooted in the larder to see if we had any hot chocolate. Raggs still hadn't come back when I'd finished drinking it so I put down the magazine I was flicking through and went to call him.

'Raggs! Come on! Bedtime!'

No response. No bark or pattering of paws coming back up the grass. I took the torch off the hook by the door and stomped out to look for him. As I got further down the garden, I heard him whine and speeded up. 'Raggs, are you OK?' But it was an excited whine, not a hurt one.

I located him by the paddock gate, hopping up and down on his hind legs. 'What are you doing?' He looked up at me and whined again and scrabbled his paws at the gate. 'Is something there?' I backed away, but he kept whimpering and scratching at the wood.

I opened the gate and let him through, tracking him with the beam of the torch. He tore down to the loose box where Scrabble and Ollie were shut up for the night. I jogged after him, worried that one of them was ill. But when I got there, he was around the back, at the door of the feed store, where I met Ryan sometimes.

Ryan?

Raggs was excited enough for that.

I opened the door quietly, holding the dog back with my foot, and pulled the light string. The bulb lit and I saw a figure on the floor.

Ryan looked up, his eyes blinking groggily in the sudden light. I winced at the bruising on his face and the cut along his left cheekbone.

'What're you doing here?'

'Sorry.' His speech was slurred and he propped himself up

on his elbow with difficulty. 'Needed somewhere to crash.'

'Are you drunk?' I shut the door, leaving Raggs scratching in frustration outside.

He didn't answer and lay down again, hugging his knees up to his chest.

I sighed. 'What happened?'

'Had a fight with Mum.'

'Your mum hit you?' I dropped to my knees beside him.

'No, no,' he mumbled. 'This happened after. No, she went off on me and stuff got said . . .'

'Who hit you then?'

'Carlisle.'

'Steven? What happened?'

'Went to the shop. He ambushed me. Had a scuffle.' He looked up at me, his eyes struggling to focus. 'Can I stay here tonight?'

I sat down properly and put a hand on his shoulder. 'You can't sleep in here. It's too cold. You're freezing now and it's not eleven yet.'

'You got any horse blankets?'

'Don't be mad! They stink. I'll get you a blanket from the house if . . .'

I froze as he shuffled up to me and put his head in my lap. He threw his arm over my knees and buried his face against my legs. I wasn't sure what to do for a minute, but then I started to stroke his hair. I couldn't help myself. 'Are you OK?'

He nodded, but kept his face hidden. Was he crying? If he was, he didn't want me to see. I curled over so I could put my arm round him and he pressed his face tighter against my legs.

'I'll bring a few blankets down here. Do you want me to stay with you for a while?' Leaving him in this state couldn't be sensible. He nodded again. He was definitely trashed. There was no way he'd have wanted me to risk staying, or admitted it if he did, when he was sober. 'OK. I'll go and get them.'

'You will come back, won't you?'

I had difficulty making his words out. What the hell had his mum said to make him freak like this? 'Yes, I'll come back.' I carried on stroking his hair until I got too cold and I realised he'd fallen asleep. 'Ryan, wake up.' He grunted and held my legs tighter. I prodded him hard on the shoulder. 'Ryan, move. I need to get those blankets.'

He rolled over, grumbling something unintelligible.

I grabbed Raggs and ran up to the house as fast as I could in the dark, praying Mum and Dad hadn't noticed I'd been gone so long. Raggs struggled in my arms, wanting to get back to Ryan, but I held him tight.

I called into the sitting room on my way upstairs. 'I'm just making a drink and then I'm going to bed.'

I grabbed a couple of blankets and a pillow and pulled on a thick sweatshirt. I needed another pillow, but I couldn't carry it so I gave up and hurried back downstairs. People on TV always drank coffee to sober up so I made some for Ryan and packed some food into a carrier bag with the flask.

'Night!' I called loudly as I went back to the stairs.

'Goodnight,' they shouted back over the noise of the TV.

I settled Raggs in his basket with a biscuit and slipped out of the back door, pocketing the spare key as I went. Mum might notice if the torch was missing so I had to stumble down the garden in the dark.

'Are you awake?' I whispered before I turned the light on.

'Yeah.'

I pulled the cord and he sat up, slumping over his knees. I dropped the bedding beside him and poured some coffee. 'Drink this.'

'Didn't think you were coming back. You've been gone ages.' He didn't sound like the usual Ryan – all cross and whiny. I didn't think he'd have let me see him this upset if he wasn't so wasted.

'How much have you had to drink?' I sat down beside him and got the food out. 'And are you hungry?'

'Bottle of vodka. Most of it, all of it, not sure. And I'm starving.' He picked up a piece of quiche and devoured it.

'Are you going to tell me what happened?'

'Had a row. Had a fight. Got smashed. Came here,' he mumbled between mouthfuls.

I poured more coffee for him. 'What did your mum say to you?'

He shook his head. 'Doesn't matter. She's ill and she doesn't understand what she's doing.'

'So why are you here and not at home?'

'Because she won't be on her own tonight and I'm sick of hearing it and I've had enough!' He stopped and sucked a deep breath in. His hands curled on the straw, knuckles straining. 'I've fucking had enough and I can't take any more from her tonight.'

I'd never seen Ryan like this before. His face looked scary under the harsh light of the bulb with the bruises making alien shadows. The reality of what it must be like to have to deal with Karen when she was ill struck me hard, but he didn't want to talk about it so I changed the subject.

'Did Steven hurt you?'

'Not really. And he got back what he gave.'

He finished the quiche and started on a ham roll while I spread one of the blankets out on the straw. I hesitated with the second, trying to decide how I could arrange this with only one pillow. That turned out to be a mistake because immediately he finished eating, he lay down on the blanket and pulled the other over him.

'Can you put the light out? It's hurting my eyes.'

I pulled the cord and wondered what to do next. Maybe I

should sit up and let him sleep. But it was cold. The ponies whickered softly in the box next door and I could smell their sweet hay breath through the slats.

'Can't you see to come back?'

'Just letting my eyes readjust.' I inched back over until my foot made contact with something. 'Is that you?'

'Yeah.' He reached up, tugged me down and flipped the blanket back to let me in.

Not a good idea, but it looked like I was stuck with it. It'd be fine – plenty of room . . .

I sat down, but as soon as my bum hit the ground, he pulled me towards him. I stiffened.

'I'm not going to do anything I shouldn't,' he snapped, and I wasn't sure if he was hurt or angry.

I groaned inside. Whatever I did was going to be wrong while he was like this. 'Um, I was going to sleep over there . . . but if you want me to sleep here . . . er . . .'

Silence. Prickly, jagged silence. And then he turned away from me. 'Sleep where you fucking want.'

'Are you always this foul when you're drunk?'

More silence.

He rolled back. 'No,' he said in a crushed voice. 'Sorry.' He tugged my arm lightly. 'Please. I-I don't want to be on my own tonight. I won't do anything.'

I couldn't believe he'd said that. Not Mr I'm Fine. It hit me worse than him crying, him admitting that. I slid down next to him because what else could I do?

'I didn't think you would. What makes you think I think you want to?'

'Eh?' I could hear his confusion.

'Nothing. Never mind.'

I felt awkward next to him, like a spider dropped into a puddle, limbs struggling to work out what to do. He didn't have that problem though, even drunk. His arms fitted round me so easily he obviously hadn't had to think about that. Or how to pull my head to his shoulder so he could rest his cheek on my hair. He just knew.

I gathered enough courage to put my arm over his side and he sighed, a contented noise.

'I would,' he said into the silence several minutes later.

My breath hitched. 'You would what?'

'I would want to. But I won't.'

That was the vodka talking. 'You really are smashed, aren't you?'

'Yes, but it doesn't make any difference. I would and I won't sober too.'

It took me a second to unpick that sentence. 'Why?' I didn't know how I managed to force that question out.

'I like you,' he said very quietly into the darkness.

'Oh.' I didn't expect that. 'So . . . why won't you?'

I felt him smile against my hair. 'Because I like you.'

I really didn't expect that, not from him.

The silence this time wasn't prickly. It felt charged, like air after heavy rain.

'Do you like me?' he asked in the same quiet voice.

I stepped off the edge of a cliff into space. 'Yes.'

He held me tighter. 'Do you like me enough to respect me and not do stuff to me while I'm asleep?'

I laughed, and the tension flooded away. 'I think I can control myself.'

'Good,' he said seriously. 'Cos if you're going to do stuff to me, I want to remember it.'

I was so relieved he'd started to sound like himself again that I wriggled my head up on an impulse and kissed the first part of his face I found. It turned out to be his chin.

'Aww, wow!' he whispered. 'Do that again.'

I reached up again to the same spot, embarrassed now he was expecting it. But he'd shifted in the dark and my lips met his. His hand slid behind my head so I couldn't pull away.

It was even better than the first time because I wasn't worrying about how to do it. I just melted into it.

'I'm glad you're here,' he mumbled against my cheek eventually.

'Are you feeling better now?'

'Way better.' He kissed me again.

'Ryan, you do mean this? You've not had a brain meltdown?' I held him off with my palms on his chest. 'Only . . .'

He huffed a breath, exasperated. 'What part of "I like you" are you not understanding? Shut up and kiss me.'

'You are so rude sometimes . . . mmph –'

He'd got fed up with waiting and I didn't get to argue for a few minutes. Then his head flopped back on the pillow and his eyes closed. 'Don't go anywhere . . .' he mumbled.

I curled into him and his breathing slowed.

I lay awake listening to the silence and his breathing, and that of the horses next door. I wanted to stay awake all night to remember this.

28 – Ryan

Somebody was pounding a pneumatic drill inside my head. I prised my eyes open to tell them to stop.

And then I remembered.

The daylight hurt like hell, but I smiled. Jenna was asleep next to me, with her head tucked into my shoulder.

But I shouldn't have let her stay. She'd get in major trouble if her parents found out. Hard to be sorry – she looked so cute asleep. To hell with it – maybe I could talk Mum into sticking around here. Maybe this time we wouldn't have to move on.

I checked my watch. Seven o'clock. We had to get moving. Her parents could be up. I shook her shoulder gently.

'Wake up.'

She moaned in protest and turned her face into my shirt. I kissed her hair.

'Jenna, wake up.'

She jerked back, opening sleepy eyes to study me carefully. If she had a thought bubble coming out of her head, it would've said 'Have you changed your mind?' so clearly that I wanted to laugh.

I ignored the pain in my head and the hangover churn of my

stomach and squeezed her. 'Morning. God, I wish I had a toothbrush.'

She rubbed her eyes. 'Why?'

'Cos my mouth feels like a pub carpet so I can only do this.' I kissed the top of her hair again.

She blushed. 'How do you feel?'

'Awful,' I groaned. 'I need water and paracetamol. But listen, you've got to get home before they know you've been out. I shouldn't have asked you to stay. And I've got to go to work.'

She looked disappointed, but she scrambled up while I hauled myself to my feet. She folded the blankets and picked up the pillow. I staggered out into the light and closed the loose box door behind her. She looked up at me hesitantly and I hugged her round the armful of bedding. 'Can I text you later? When I get back from work.' I felt her smile.

'Yes.'

'See you later,' I whispered in her ear and kissed it. Then I headed home.

When I reached the boat, I tried to sneak in as quietly as I could, but Mum was sitting in the rocker opposite the door, her head slumped down and purple rings under her eyes.

She jumped up as soon as she heard me. 'Where've you been? Look at the state of you.' She burst into tears and threw her arms round me. 'I thought you'd run away.'

'Sorry.'

'Have you been drinking? Where were you?'

'I slept in Jenna's stable.'

She touched my face. 'You've been fighting.'

'It's OK. Just some local dick last night. I'm OK.'

'Don't you ever, ever do that to me again. I don't know what I'd do without you. I've been sitting here all night, terrified you wouldn't come back.'

I let her try to straighten my hair. Normally I wouldn't have, but I figured I owed it. 'I always come back.'

Her mascara was running down her cheeks in black tracks. 'One day, you won't. One day, I'll go too far. You'll leave me too, and I wouldn't blame you.'

That was as close as she got to saying 'sorry'. She never used that word. It wasn't something she could bring herself to say. But this was her version of it and I understood that. I hugged her harder. 'You say stuff you don't mean sometimes. I know that.'

She leaned on me like a dead weight and sighed. 'Don't forget that, Ryan, please. Ignore the words when I'm like that and remember I love you. The words fly away as soon as I've said them. The love never goes.'

She made me screw my face up when she said things like that, but it was just her way and you had to wince and take it.

I made her some tea before I left for work. When I got out on to the towpath, I saw two cars parked up at the bridge. As I got closer, a man in uniform hurried off the bridge towards me and I realised they were police cars. I froze as he came over. Two cars? That was overkill to move me and Mum on, surely?

'Where you going, son?'

'Up to the road. I'm going to work.'

'You'll have to go round another way, I'm afraid. We're about to tape this area off.'

'Oh, OK.' So they weren't here to move us. 'Why?'

'Can't say at the moment. It's a crime scene.'

'Oh! Hey, look, my mum's back there in our boat.' This was more important than covering up that we were moored without a permit. 'Is she safe there?'

He looked down the canal towards the boat. 'Oh, right. Might be better if you went home then, lad. We'll need to come and ask you some questions later. You could be witnesses.'

'Witnesses to what?'

'We've found a body.'

29 – Jenna

I crept back in through the back door. Raggs pattered over and I shushed him. He didn't seem in a rush to go out so I sent him back to his basket with a biscuit and slunk up the stairs on tiptoe to crawl under the duvet. I was asleep the moment I shut my eyes.

I felt like I'd slept for ages, but when I cracked an eye open at the clock, it was only quarter to ten. I went for a shower so I didn't smell of stables and padded downstairs in my bathrobe to find something for breakfast.

Mum and Dad were in the kitchen at the table. Charlie was nowhere to be seen. Dad's face was grey and worn. Mum had her hands folded on the table; they were shaking.

'What's wrong?'

She took a deep breath. 'Mary just called.' I frowned at her in confusion and then realised she meant our vet's wife who was a friend of hers. 'Ted is in a terrible state. He was called out to see a sick horse this morning and he found a body by the canal on his way to the call.'

'What?' My skin went cold.

30 – Ryan

Mum looked surprised to see me back so soon. 'I thought you were going to work.'

'I've just rung them to explain. Look out of the window.'

She lifted the net curtain and peered out. 'Where?'

'Up towards the bridge.'

She craned her neck. 'Police? What's going on?'

'They've found a body. The policeman said to come home. They're coming to interview us in case we're witnesses.'

She dropped the curtain and stared at me, mouth open. 'Whose body?'

'I don't know. They wouldn't let me up there.'

Her face paled. 'Sit down.'

I sat in the rocker, puzzled, and watched her pace up and down plucking at her sleeves with restless fingers.

'Where were you last night?'

'I told you. Over in Jenna's stable.'

'You didn't get those bruises in a stable. Or are you going to tell me the horse kicked you?'

I put my hand up to the cut on my face, remembering

how the policeman's eyes had hovered there.

'What happened, Ryan? And tell me properly.'

'I went to the village shop and bought a bottle of vodka.'

'And they sold it to you? Didn't they ask for ID?'

'Um, yeah . . . but . . . I was a bit arsey with the woman so she sold it to me anyway.'

Mum passed a hand over her face. 'Oh Christ! Then what?'

'I got jumped by this guy from the village.'

'What guy?'

'Just a lad. He's been giving me some hassle over hanging out with Jenna. He's a knob. So we had a fight.'

She gripped the back of the chair. 'Did anyone see you?'

'A woman came out and yelled at us and he ran off. I don't think she saw us properly. It was dark. Then I drank the vodka on the way to Jenna's and crashed out in the stable.'

'That's it?'

'That's it, Mum, honest. Why're you looking so worried?'

She sank her head into her hands. 'They've found a body. Your face is cut up and we're strangers here. Travellers. You know what the police are like about that. You know that and you still ask me such a stupid question.'

'Just because I had a fight, it doesn't mean I murdered someone. Who says it was murder anyway? It could be an accident.'

'It doesn't matter. You've scared a woman. You had a fight.

They'll be here, sticking their noses in.' She took a deep breath. 'Right, you tell them you went to buy the vodka for me and then you came straight home. Don't mention the fight. If they ask about your face, you fell off your bike. After you got back from the shop, you were here on the boat with me all night. We didn't hear or see anything.'

'Don't you think you're going a bit over the top? It's probably nothing –'

She crossed the space between us in two paces and slapped my face with a crack. 'Over the top? Don't you realise how much trouble this could bring us? Sometimes, Ryan, you are so naïve. If they can blame us for anything, they will.' She stared at the patch on my face where her hand had left a stinging hot imprint. 'Go to your room! Just go!'

I swallowed to stop myself saying anything back to her. She'd never hit me before. And the last time she sent me to my room, I was nine. But I got up and went. There's a time you argue and a time you don't.

This was all so stupid. Probably someone had fallen drunk into the canal. Or tried to top themselves. Mum was paranoid, part of her being ill again. But then my mind flicked back to how the policeman had looked at my face . . .

If I hadn't been here on the boat all night, I had no alibi because if Jenna's parents found out where she was . . .

I sat on the bed and sent her a text.

<Need 2 talk. Call me when u can>

I waited, but there was no reply. Either she was asleep or she wasn't on her own. I lay down and watched the screen and waited and tried to ignore the unease that was suddenly bubbling through me.

31 – Jenna

'A body?' My legs folded under me and I grabbed at a chair.

'Yes.' Mum looked down at her hands. 'Steven Carlisle.'

The rush of relief nearly made me faint. Not Ryan. Not Karen.

Then it hit me. Steven. 'How . . . did he . . .?'

'Ted said his head had been beaten in,' she said bleakly. 'They think it's murder.'

My first thought was, *Good*!

The second was, *I shouldn't be thinking that*. Followed by, *But it's all over now*. A cycle had been broken. I'd never have to see Steven again. Never have to avoid him or see him with another girl, showing how he didn't care what he'd done to my best friend. Dad could stop his stupid campaign and we could go back to some sort of normal. Maybe I wouldn't even mind my face so much now because it felt like justice had finally been done.

I knew I should feel some regret, some pity for him. But right then I didn't feel anything other than release.

Slowly, as I looked from Mum to Dad, I began to realise that they weren't feeling the same way. Nor were they upset at another life snuffed out, or sorry for his parents, or anything like that. They were scared.

Dad twisted his fingers in his palms. 'The police may come round later. They may want to talk to us.' He sounded as if it was a struggle to keep his voice steady.

I groped through a fog towards something I couldn't quite see. Something dangerous was lurking just out of sight. 'Why?'

Mum took hold of my hand. 'Your dad stopped off to see David Morris before he came home last night. When he came out, manure was smeared all over the car. Over the windscreen, the windows, even stuffed up the exhaust.'

The hairs on the back of my neck stood up as I saw Dad's knuckles turn white and strained. Manure . . . David Morris . . . Charlotte's dad lived on the other side of the village to us, and Dad would only be over there for something to do with his campaign group. And Steven Carlisle would know that too . . .

'Cow manure. Probably from the heifers in the field next to David's house. David and your dad cleaned it off before he drove home. He stopped in the village to put the latest newsletters in the postbox, and Steven was sitting outside with some others. When your dad went past, Steven mooed at him, and his friends laughed and joined in. It was obvious he'd messed the car up. There was a row and Dad threatened him with the police. Steven spat in his face and your dad lost his temper and pushed him over.'

'I didn't have to push him hard. He was drunk. He fell off the kerb and into the gutter,' Dad said.

I turned to him. 'Is Mum trying to tell me you killed him? That he hit his head when you pushed him?' I could hear myself saying the words, but inside I screamed that it couldn't be true. Dad could never . . . never . . . not even Steven. My dad got faint at the sight of blood. He'd never so much as smacked Charlie or me once, no matter how badly we'd behaved when we were little.

Mum gripped my hand harder. 'Of course not. He was fine when your dad drove off. On his feet and yelling. But the police are bound to want to question Dad. They . . . they may want to take him to the station. We don't know.'

'But it's a possibility,' Dad said.

'You didn't do it,' I said. A statement rather than a question because my dad . . . No, just no.

He took hold of my other hand. 'God knows, Jenna, I've wanted him dead, for him to have died in that crash so many times, but —'

'Clive! Don't say things like that.' Mum's eyes widened with fear. 'Jenna, you mustn't tell the police your dad said that.'

I snatched my hand from hers. 'Don't be stupid, Mum. I'm not an idiot.'

'I know you're not, but I'm so worried I can't think straight.' She clutched her head as if it hurt. 'And what are we going to tell

Charlie? He mustn't know. He's too young.'

Dad pulled my hand closer. 'I don't want you going out alone. Or Charlie. If that boy was murdered then whoever did it could still be in the area and . . .'

But I stopped listening. The force of the thought that hit me was so hard I nearly cried out. Dad wasn't the only one who'd had a fight with Steven last night. What if the police found out about that?

No . . . no . . . no . . .

I got up, knocking the chair over.

'I feel a bit sick. I'm going to lie down.'

And I ran out.

Mum fussed after me as far as the stairs. 'It's the shock. Do you want me to come and sit with you?'

I shook my head and fled.

The ceiling whirled above me as I lay on my bed.

Ryan said he had a fight with Steven . . . and he was so upset. I'd never seen him like that before. He couldn't have though. I hadn't known him that long, but even so . . .

What if he'd hit Steven and he'd fallen and cracked his skull? Maybe Ryan had run off and didn't even realise Steven was dead. He'd been drunk. Had he done it and not known? But he'd seemed more cut up about his mum than the fight with Steven. Then again, if he couldn't remember . . .

I reached for the phone beside my bed. One missed text message.

I didn't know if I could speak to him right now. I didn't know what to say.

I held the phone tight and stared up at spinning black spots on the ceiling. He couldn't have killed Steven. How could I even think it? But someone had.

32 – Ryan

I heard the rap on the door and then Mum answering it.

Low male voices. Authoritative.

They were here then.

The phone rang, making me jump, and I dropped it on the floor before I could answer it.

'Ryan?'

'Yes. Listen, something's happened. The police found a body.'

'I know. Do you know who it was?' Jenna sounded odd. Odd enough to make me tense up.

'No.'

'Steven Carlisle.'

'Oh fuck . . .'

'Ryan . . .' And she stopped. The pause was a question that made a chill run down my back. Not accusing – not that. More tentative.

'It wasn't me.' Oh Christ, please believe, it wasn't me.

Her silence went on, freezing into my bones until the marrow tingled. And then, 'You were drunk . . .'

'No! No, I swear! I told you what happened. He was fine. He ran off and he was fine.'

Another pause.

'Maybe you just didn't notice . . . ?'

'No. I came straight to yours, and yes, I blacked out then, but that was when I went to sleep.'

I heard her breathe out. 'OK.'

'Do you believe me?'

'Yes.' She said it with absolute conviction.

The relief squeezed me so hard it made my eyes sting. 'Jenna, I've got to go. The police just arrived. The body was found near here. Mum says to tell them I was with her. I don't want to get you in trouble.'

'It's OK, don't worry. Call me when they're gone. It'll be fine.' I knew from her voice she thought I was scared.

'You promise you believe me?'

'I promise. Go, before they get suspicious. Call me straight after. Don't worry about my parents. Just call.'

Someone knocked on my door and I flipped the phone shut. Mum pushed the door open. A policeman stood behind her.

'Sorry, I'm coming,' I said, scrambling up. 'I was just going to call work.'

The policeman hovered over Mum, a fluorescent-jacketed giant. 'Where do you work?'

'The marina in Whitmere.'

His face relaxed a bit. 'With Bill?'

'Yeah?'

He smiled. 'He's my uncle. He said they'd taken a new lad on last time I went for a pint with him. Come through and answer some questions for us.'

The other policeman stood up when we came in. He was the one who asked the questions. Bill's nephew made notes in a pad.

'Were you here on the boat yesterday evening?'

'Yes,' Mum said. 'All night. Oh wait, Ryan went to the shop in the village for me before it closed. But he got back before seven.'

'Must have done,' I added. 'It closes at half six.'

'Did either of you go outside again at any point in the evening? See or hear anything?'

'No, I was up quite late, but Ryan went to bed early because he had to be up at seven. He works Saturday mornings.'

I nodded in agreement.

The policeman passed over a picture. 'Do you know this boy?'

Mum looked blank. 'No. I don't know anyone round here other than a few people in the town who stock my jewellery.'

'I know him.' I passed the picture back. There was no point hiding it. They'd know soon enough if I lied. 'Well, not know him exactly, but I know who he is. His name's Steven Carlisle. He lives somewhere round here.'

'Right, had any dealings with him?'

'I had an argument with him at the Rugby Club party the other Saturday. We ended up in a scuffle. He mouthed off at me over this girl I know and I gave him some grief back. Wasn't much.'

'What did he say to you?'

'Just stuff about me being a traveller, and he was rude about my friend. It was weeks ago. Haven't seen him since.'

Mum glared. 'You never told me that.'

'Nothing worth telling. Wasn't a big deal.'

'This friend,' the policeman said, 'who is she?'

Shit! 'Jenna Reed. He —'

The two men exchanged a glance. 'I take it you know about the circumstances there?' the second asked.

'Yeah and I couldn't believe he was so harsh about her, not after that.'

'Is she your girlfriend?'

I paused. How did I answer this one? 'Yes,' I said in the end. 'She wasn't then, but she is now. Only she hasn't told her parents yet. It's only really recent. I mean, we've been friends for a while, but she's younger than me and it isn't anything heavy. Just . . . er . . . we like each other, you know.'

I had a feeling Bill's nephew was trying not to laugh, but that was better than him thinking I was a psycho killer.

'He didn't tell me that either,' Mum said, fixing me with a death glare. 'Jenna comes round often. Lovely girl.'

'Was sort of waiting for the right time,' I mumbled.

'I can't see why you thought you needed a right time. You know I like her.'

'I was waiting for her to tell her mum,' I mumbled again. 'Just thought it'd be more polite.'

The policeman started up the questions again. 'Do you know if Jenna had any contact with Carlisle recently?'

'No, she avoids him. Mostly if she's out in the village, she's with me. I go with her when she takes her dog for a walk. She doesn't go out much.' I waved at my face. 'People staring upsets her.'

They both nodded sympathetically.

'So why're you asking about Carlisle? What's he done now?'

'It's his body.'

Mum clapped her hand over her mouth.

I shrank back in the chair, hoping my shock looked genuine. 'What happened?'

'We can't say much at present. The forensics team are there now. But we are treating his death as suspicious.'

'Shit! Oh, sorry, it's just . . . I didn't expect that. I mean, I didn't like the guy myself, but who'd want to . . . to kill him?' I leaned forward. 'Look, I know you're not allowed to say much but my mum's here on her own all day and –'

'Don't worry about your mum – our lads will be swarming all over this place for days. It's probably the safest place she could be.'

'Could you tell them she's on her own here? You know, if they see anyone strange round the boat . . .'

'We'll have a word. Don't worry.'

'Thanks.' I rubbed my face to get some feeling back in it. It was numb from the shock. Real shock. I mean, murder? I'd assumed he'd been pissed and fallen in the canal or something. I'd never thought anyone had actually done him in.

'What happened to you?' The policeman smiled and pointed at my cheek. I wasn't fooled by him trying to slip that one in casually.

I faked a touch of shame. 'Came off my bike last night. Hit a pothole in the dark and got smacked in the face by the handlebars.'

He quirked his eyebrows at me. 'Too busy thinking about the girlfriend?'

I laughed sheepishly. 'Yeah.'

He chuckled, with that 'I remember when I was young' look adults always get when you talk about girls and stuff.

They took my statement and then they left. As soon as they were safely clear, Mum rounded on me.

'Well, you deserve an Oscar for that! You knew it was that boy, didn't you?'

'Yeah, Jenna called to tell me, but I thought it was an accident.'

'Huh! You even had me convinced with what you spouted — worrying about me with a murderer on the loose.'

'Hey, I meant that. I am.'

234

She glared at me again, and then came to sit on the arm of my chair. 'Oh, stop looking so hurt. I hate it when you do that. You make me feel like I should call the NSPCC and report myself for abuse.' She stroked my face. 'I'm sorry I hit you before. I was scared for you.'

'I didn't do it, Mum.'

'I know that. I know my own son.'

I leaned my head on her. 'Mum?'

'Yes.'

'I'm scared as well.'

She put her arm round me. 'I know that too.'

33 – Jenna

My phone rang and I jumped to answer it. Ryan's voice was urgent.

'Jenna? I'm at the stable. Can you meet me?'

'I don't know. I'll try. Give me a few minutes. If I can't, I'll call you back.'

Mum was still at the kitchen table when I went down.

'Where's Dad?'

'On the phone to the police. I sent Charlie to play upstairs. He knows something's wrong, but I don't want him overhearing anything. How are you feeling?'

'Oh, OK now. You were right – it was the shock. Listen, nobody's been over to the horses. I'll nip down and see to them.'

A frown line creased her forehead. 'Maybe I should come with you.'

'No, you stay with Dad. I'll take Raggs. It's broad daylight and if there's anyone around he'll bark. I'll take my phone and I'm only in the next field.'

'I don't know . . .'

'I won't be long. And Dad might need you. We can't leave

the ponies any longer or Ollie will eat his way through the hedge. I'll be fine. Nothing's going to happen to me in the paddock.'

'OK,' she said reluctantly, 'but be quick.'

I flew down the garden with Raggs racing beside me. When I clanged the latch on the gate shut, Ryan's head appeared round the side of the stable. I ran down to him. 'Are you all right? Are you . . . oof!'

He hugged me so hard he squeezed the breath out of me, and I hugged him back while Raggs washed his trainers with an eager tongue.

I wriggled loose. 'I haven't got long. Mum's in a flap. How'd it go?'

He kissed my nose and released me. 'The police came round to see if we heard anything. Mum covered for me, but she told me not to say about the fight so I didn't. I told them I fell off my bike.'

'Did they believe you?'

'I think so. Hard to tell.'

'They have to suspect everyone. It's their job. I remember how they were when they questioned me after the accident.'

'There's something else,' he said, searching my face. 'I had to tell them you're my girlfriend. They asked if I knew Carlisle. I didn't tell them about everything, but . . . oh, it's too long a story. I'm sorry. I don't want to get you in trouble, but I couldn't get out of it.'

His face was pale and the bruises stood out all the more starkly on his face because of that. I put my arms round his waist again. 'Am I your girlfriend?'

He looked down at me, puzzled.

'Only you haven't actually told me that yet.' I dredged up a grin to relieve the tension I could feel in his muscles. 'Or asked me.'

He laughed and tugged my head closer. 'Yes, you are.'

'And I don't get a say in that?'

'No, I decided for you.'

I thumped him gently on the chest. 'Big-head!'

He rested his chin on my hair. 'I was going to ask if you'd come to the cinema with me tomorrow, but I don't suppose you'll be allowed now.'

'Will you buy me popcorn?'

'Yup.' I felt him grin. 'Might even take you for a pizza.'

'We're going then. Leave the explaining to me. Call for me at . . . oh, what time?'

'Eleven. We can get lunch before the film.'

'OK, eleven. At my back door. What're we seeing?'

'It's a surprise. But you want me to meet you at your house? What –'

'I said I'd sort it.'

'OK if you're sure . . . oh no!'

I jerked up to look at him. 'What is it?'

238

He smirked. 'Just this.' And he kissed me. Properly.

'You're evil,' I said when I pulled away several minutes later. 'Urgh – I haven't got much longer and I've got to feed the horses. Can you give me a hand?'

'What do you do with them?'

'Tip a bag of pony nuts in the feeder.'

'Leave them to me. I'll do it in a bit. We're not wasting valuable time messing around with horse feed.' He looked down at his feet. 'That mutt of yours is chewing my laces now.'

'Raggs, stop it!'

As usual, Raggs ignored me.

'So well trained,' he murmured, tucking his head down for another kiss.

When we walked back up to the gate, he held my hand. 'You do believe me? I know I hit him, but –'

I put my finger on his lips, but worried hazel eyes continued to ask. 'I know. Yes, I believe you.'

I felt guilty for even considering it was a possibility. But surely he couldn't have been so drunk that he'd kill someone without knowing it.

I bent to scoop Raggs up under my arm and then tugged Ryan's head down for a last kiss. 'See you tomorrow!' And I ran back up the garden before Mum came looking for me.

*

I was upstairs sorting the laundry for Mum when the doorbell rang. Peeking out of the window, I could see a police car on the drive. Charlie's bedroom door was still closed and the noise of his PlayStation echoed through it so he wouldn't have heard the bell. I heard Dad take them into the study and then I scuttled downstairs with the washing under my arm. Mum was in the kitchen at the table, twisting her rings round on her fingers.

'Just drop it in the utilty room,' she said. 'They want to talk to us too.'

I got rid of the washing and sat with her at the table. The house was strangely quiet, but for the ticking of the clock on the wall, and I couldn't hear a sound from the study.

It must have been half an hour before two police officers came out. Mum got up without a word and showed them through to the sitting room and I was left to wait alone. I sat staring at the study door, hoping Dad would come out, but he didn't.

They didn't take as long with Mum and when they'd finished, she brought them through to the kitchen.

The policewoman smiled at me. 'I'm DC Evans, Jenna, and this is my colleague, DC Plummer. Just a few questions. It won't take long. Nothing to worry about.'

'OK.'

'Now yesterday, can you tell us everything you did from the time you left school?'

'Yeah, sure.' I could handle this. The number of times I'd had to go through interrogations after the accident, all the questions, every insignificant detail. 'Um, I got the bus home so I arrived here around half four. Mum and I went to the supermarket with my little brother. We had tea there – Charlie likes the fish and chips in the café.'

The PC smiled. 'Sounds like my son. What time did you get back from the supermarket?'

'About half six or seven. Charlie and I had some homework, then we watched TV for a while. Charlie went to bed just before ten. Dad came in not long after.'

'Would you happen to know an exact time?'

'About five or ten past ten. Definitely no later because we had BBC1 on and the news had just started.'

'And did you see your dad when he came in?'

'He went in the kitchen for a few minutes to talk to Mum and get a drink. Then he came to watch TV. I stayed up for a while, but then I went to bed.'

'And your dad was still watching TV?'

'Yes.'

'And what time was that?'

'Around half eleven.'

'It was after eleven?'

'Yes.'

'And you're sure?'

241

'Yes, positive.'

She nodded. 'What was your dad wearing when he came home?'

'His work suit. Um, the navy pinstripe one. Oh and a pink shirt. I remember that because I always tell him it looks stupid with that suit, but he never listens to me.'

They both smiled. 'One final question,' the man said. 'Did you notice anything unusual about his appearance?'

He didn't come home spattered in blood if that's what you're getting at! 'No, nothing. Just normal.'

DC Evans got up and turned to Mum. 'I think we're done here now. No need to speak to your son at this stage as he was in bed when your husband got home, although we may need to talk to him later depending on the forensics result. Thanks for your co-operation. There's just the matter of Mr Reed's clothing . . .'

'Yes, I'll get it for you now,' Mum said.

I bristled. 'Why?' They were treating him like a suspect, but he hadn't done anything wrong.

'Routine,' the man said. 'Helps us to eliminate your dad from our enquiries.'

Mum went upstairs with them and they came down shortly after with Dad's clothes in a clear plastic bag. She called Dad out of the study and the detectives exchanged a few words of thanks with him before they left.

It felt like the house sighed with relief as their car crunched away on the gravel. Dad leaned against the study door with a face that'd aged ten years in a day.

'I'm hungry.' Charlie stood at the top of the stairs, kicking the skirting board.

Mum gasped. 'Oh darling, I'm sorry. Jenna will make you a snack, won't you, Jen?'

I was dispatched to the kitchen with him while she and Dad retreated behind the study door to talk.

I made a toasted sandwich while my brother sat on the table swinging his legs. His mouth pursed as he watched me. He looked like a mini version of Dad when he did that.

'What's going on, Jen?'

'Grown-up stuff. Do you want tomato on this?'

'No. I want to know.'

'Well, you can't.' I put his sandwich under the grill and folded my arms.

'If you don't tell me, I'll tell Dad you were out all night.' He smirked as he saw me flinch. 'So you'd better.'

'I-I wasn't.'

'Yes, you were. I saw you come back.'

My pulse beat faster. 'You're lying.'

'Oh, am I? Ha! I don't think so. I woke up early this morning. I had a bad dream so I came down to see if there were any biscuits. Raggs wanted to go out so I let him. Then he wouldn't come and I had to fetch him.'

He was bluffing. He had to be.

'He was trying to get into the paddock. I had to drag him back.'

But maybe he wasn't – I remembered Raggs hadn't wanted to go for a pee when I got in.

'When I was going back to bed, I saw you coming up the garden.' He gave me a triumphant glare. 'See!'

'Charlie, shut up! You can't tell Dad. You can't.'

He grinned. 'Better tell me what's going on then or I'll tell them about that boy you meet.'

'What boy? There's no boy. Don't be stupid.'

'So who was that you were kissing by the gate? A ghost?' He screwed his face up. 'Eww! It's disgusting. I could see you from my window. You were all over each other.'

'We were not!'

He punched the air. 'I win! You admitted it.'

'You horrible little brat!'

He sniggered. 'Yeah. So tell me . . .'

I scowled. I'd have to tell him something. He'd hear about Steven Carlisle at school, but I was keeping Dad out of it.

34 – Ryan

On Sunday morning, I crept up Jenna's garden and hovered outside the back door. It felt weird going so openly to the house, but it was quiet, no sign of her parents. I knocked softly.

Jenna opened it and peeked round to find me standing against the wall. 'Come in.'

Raggs leapt straight at me of course. I stooped and fussed his ears as we went inside. It wasn't until I straightened up that I saw the woman at the table. I knew who she was before Jenna spoke. They had the same shape faces, the same noses. And her mum looked as shocked as I felt.

'Mum, this is Ryan.'

'Hello,' Mrs Reed said faintly.

I mumbled something that was supposed to be good morning.

Jenna smiled, all innocent. 'Mum doesn't think it's safe waiting around at bus stops, especially with the Sunday service being so unreliable, so she's going to drive us to the cinema.'

That look was wasted on me. I could just imagine what she'd done – 'Mum, I'm going to the cinema with a friend.' Didn't tell her it was a boy, didn't tell her it was me.

Fair play to Mrs Reed, she rallied and smiled. 'Yes, and you'll be there much quicker by car so you've time for a drink if you'd like one, Ryan. Tea? Coffee? Oh, and do sit down.'

'Um, coffee, please.'

'I'll make it,' Jenna said. She went to put the kettle on as I sank into a chair.

'Have you two been friends long?' her mum asked.

'A couple of months.' Well, that was when I'd first met her. A couple of months sounded better, like we'd known each other longer. Say something . . . think of something reassuring . . . my mind's a blank.

'Oh!' She didn't manage to hide the blink of surprise, but followed up with one of those 'that's nice' smiles. 'Are you at the same school?'

'No, I . . .'

'Ryan works at the marina in Whitmere,' Jenna said from across the kitchen.

Her mum gave me another of those smiles, more forced this time. 'Is that where you live, Ryan?'

'Um, no, I, er . . . live in Strenton at the moment.'

Her eyebrows shot up and I looked at Jenna. Help! What should I say?

'Ryan lives on a boat on the canal with his mum. She makes this incredible jewellery. I bet you've seen it – it's in all the craft shops in Whitmere. She made that pink necklace of mine.'

'A boat? Oh, that's unusual.' Her smile became so fixed, it was nearly a grimace. She and Jenna locked eyes as the kettle bubbled to a boil. 'The necklace . . . yes, it's lovely. Your mum must be very clever.'

It was my turn to do the grimace-smile.

Jenna made the coffee and we watched her to cover the silence. She brought the mugs over, grinning as if we were all the best of friends.

'So where did you two meet?' Mrs Reed asked Jenna, giving up on her attempt to get me to talk.

'Walking the dog. Ryan was washing the boat windows.' She giggled. 'Raggs knocked his bucket in the canal.'

'That dog!'

Say something, stupid. 'He just wanted to say hello. He didn't mean any harm. He got excited.'

'Yes, he does tend to.'

Jenna's mum sipped her coffee. I could see she was trying to figure out if we were just friends, or more. Jenna, the evil little witch, put her hand over mine and squeezed.

Mrs Reed's face didn't flicker, but I could almost see the cogs in her brain whirring at warp speed.

She put her mug down. 'What film are you going to see?'

'Ah, er, it's sort of a surprise,' I said.

Wrong move – her eyes got a hint of ice in them.

'It's a PG,' I added quickly. 'It's the one she keeps going on about — *Touchdown Angels*.'

Jenna bounced in the chair. 'Brilliant! I told you, Mum, Beth went to see it with Max last week and she said it was great.' She looked at me. 'Ryan, are you sure? You'll hate it. He's as bad as Charlie, Mum — likes those things with heads being ripped off and monsters and —'

'It's OK, I'll live.' I looked at her mum. I could've been wrong, but I thought she'd thawed slightly.

'Have you got enough pocket money left? I can give you an advance,' she said to Jenna.

'Oh no,' I cut in. 'I'm paying. I asked her.'

'But aren't you going for lunch too?'

'Yeah, but it's fine. I've got enough from my wages.'

'Is your boat anywhere near the bridge, Ryan?' Mrs Reed asked, suddenly changing the subject. I nodded. 'I can't believe what's happened. That's a terrible business.'

'Yeah, it happened quite near our mooring. The police are still up there, which is good because my mum's on her own. I hope they get the guy soon.'

She shivered. 'This has always been such a safe place to live and now . . . I don't know. I heard his head was caved in, that it was beaten repeatedly on the bridge wall until he was dead. How could anyone do that? I can't take it in.' Mrs Reed looked at her watch. 'I'll pop up and let my husband know we're going. He's having a lie in – not feeling too well. You two finish your coffee.'

The second she was out of the kitchen, I glowered at Jenna. 'I can't believe you did that!'

'What?' She gave me the big blue eyes, all wide and clueless.

'You know exactly what.'

She giggled. 'Look, it was going to come out after you told the police. You know what it's like round here.'

'You didn't have to do it like this.'

'She was more likely to be all right about it once she'd met you. It worked.'

'No, it didn't. She doesn't like me.'

Jenna stopped grinning and leaned over to give me a quick hug. 'She does. She's surprised, that's all.'

'She doesn't. She thinks I'm . . . I'm . . .'

'Rubbish! Mum doesn't think like that. She just worries way too much since the accident. She'll be completely fine when she gets to know you.' I obviously didn't look convinced. 'OK, if you don't hear shouting in about one second then she hasn't told Dad about you, which means she's more than halfway to liking you.'

'Oh great, so now your dad is about to boot me out of the house.'

Jenna listened. 'I don't think so. It's very quiet up there.'

Feet sounded on the stairs and Jenna's mum returned. 'Ready?'

I stood up. 'Yes. Thanks for driving us.'

'No problem.' She smiled at me.

'Told you,' Jenna whispered as we left.

Mrs Reed kept up the Spanish Inquisition all the way to the cinema.

'How old are you, Ryan?'

'Sixteen.'

'Oh, I thought you were older.' She smiled at me in the mirror. 'I expect that's because you're tall. You'll just have left school then.'

'Um . . .'

Jenna rescued me. 'He didn't go to school. His mum taught him at home.'

'Really? I watched a documentary on the home school movement a couple of weeks ago. It's very big in America apparently.'

Jenna smirked at me. 'Ryan's mum's a vegan.'

'Oh!' Her mother's face lit up and I got interrogated on vegan lifestyles for the next fifteen minutes.

We stopped at a garage to fill up with petrol and Jenna was sent inside to pay. While she was gone, her mum glanced at me in the mirror and said, 'This is the first time in months I haven't seen her nervous about going out in public.'

I got the feeling the maternal ice caps had melted a bit more.

Jenna's mum dropped us outside the cinema and we waved

to her as she drove off. I felt like an idiot doing that, but I thought it's what I should do. As soon as the car was out of sight, I put my arm round Jenna and slumped on her shoulder in relief.

She laughed and shook her head. 'Didn't you dare do that in front of Mum? Wuss!'

'Shut up, I've not forgiven you yet for pulling that stunt on me.'

She wound her arm round my waist. 'Where are we eating?'

I looked round. 'Frankie and Benny's?'

I hid a grin as we walked over because she chattered away at me, still so full of it over wrong-footing me with her mum that she forgot to notice if anyone was staring at her. Like the only person she noticed was me.

She liked the film; I didn't. But I held her hand all the way through it, cringing to think what Cole would have said if he could see me. When I was thirteen, he'd come home with a bunch of red roses for Mum. She glowed when he gave them to her and I laughed and made retching noises. Cole shoved me on the head and said, 'You wait until you meet a girl you like. You won't laugh then.'

Turned out he was right.

35 – Jenna

School on Monday was foul. Everywhere I went, people stopped me to talk about the murder. Word had got round fast and I couldn't get down a corridor without being mobbed. Stupid questions, stupid gossip. Beth and I hung out in the library at lunchtime where they couldn't hassle me.

I was glad to get home again, though the village was still bustling with policemen doing door-to-door enquiries. The school bus dropped me and Charlie off, but as we got to the fork in the road, I took the lane towards the canal instead of home.

'Where are you going?' Charlie called, and then I heard his feet scampering behind. 'Jen? Hey, Jen!'

I kept walking. 'I want to see where it happened. I don't know why, but it's something I have to do.'

'I'll come with you.'

'No, go home.'

'I'll come with you,' he said firmly.

I looked down at my little brother, treading determinedly beside me, his face set into a protective expression. Charlie could be so unpredictable. He wasn't a great talker, unless it was about football, and most of the time he was just an obnoxious, accident-prone little brat. But he had those other moments, like when I was in hospital and he brought me a pot of hyacinths he'd bought with his pocket money. I thought it must have been Mum's idea, but she was as surprised as I was.

I slowed down as we got to the bridge. Blue and white crime-scene tape stretched across the lane blocking it. A police car was parked over the bridge on the other side of the tape and a man in uniform was standing in the road. He eyed us as we approached, but made no move towards us.

There were marks on the tarmac where the body had been. A chill crept over my skin as what had happened finally felt real. I'd hated Steven Carlisle for so long, but now . . . now, as I pictured his body lying there . . . the hate sizzled and burned away. It left a hollow behind it, an empty space where all that feeling had been.

What had gone so wrong? It all used to be easy and peaceful here, then one night, one stupid mistake, and we were all still paying for it. Not just me, all of us, and our families. The chill crept deeper and I shivered.

Charlie tugged at my arm. 'Come on, Jen. Let's go home.'

I looked a moment longer and I realised part of me was sorry Steven was dead. Maybe part of him had been sorry about everything too. Yes, maybe he had been sorry about Lindsay, but he couldn't show it, like I couldn't show strangers how much them staring at me hurt, and Ryan couldn't show how he sometimes hated being the grown-up for his mum. Maybe Steven wasn't really that different to us. Maybe he hid feelings too. Strange how that was easier to see with him dead.

Dad's car was on the drive when we got to the house. I frowned – why was he home so early?

There was no sign of him or Mum as I unlocked the front door. Charlie spilled past me into the hall, dumping football kit, trumpet case and school bag on to the floor.

The study door was closed. He went to turn the handle, but I seized his wrist and pulled him back.

'Ow! Cow!' he squealed, rubbing his arm. He glared at me as if I'd betrayed him for his support at the bridge.

Mum opened the door. She started to speak, then stopped and frowned at Charlie. He took a step back.

'What did you just call your sister?'

'She hurt my wrist.'

'You do not use language like that in this house, young man. Take your things up to your room now and get on with your homework.'

Charlie gawped, but even he could see the lines of strain on her face and the red rims of her eyes. Her mascara was blotched on her cheek where it'd run and she'd wiped it away.

My brother picked up his kit and went upstairs with dragging feet.

I waited until he'd gone.

'Mum?'

'Dad was called into the police station from work. They needed him to give a DNA sample and make an official statement. He's only just got home.' Exhaustion oozed from every word.

'Is he OK?'

'He's . . . he'll be fine. He's in here. Just needs a little while to himself. Have you got homework?'

'Yes.'

'Go and do it, there's a good girl. I'll . . . I'll call you when dinner's ready.'

She turned and went back into the study and closed the door in my face.

After a moment, I heard her crying.

36 – Ryan

Jenna took some convincing about going to the Bonfire Night thing in Whitmere. She didn't think she should be out watching explosions when it was all imploding at home. I talked her round in the end by telling her we should take Charlie along – the kid needed to get out too. It sounded like it was Stress City in her house. As her dad didn't know about us yet, and Charlie had threatened to tell, I thought keeping him sweet was a good idea. When we got there, he hooked up with some kid he knew and Jenna let him go as long as he didn't wander too far. He muttered something about not staying here and watching us slobbering on each other, then slouched off. I'd been ten – I got it.

We watched a firework explode into red and gold and silver sparks, lighting up the Mere and the faces of the crowd. There was a bang and then another starburst, this time blue and purple.

Jenna wriggled against me.

'You cold?' I whispered.

'A bit.'

I unzipped my jacket and pulled it as far round her as I could, then I rested my chin on the top of her head.

A series of loud cracks: one, two, three . . . and a fizzing fountain of white against black sky . . .

'Brilliant fireworks,' the girl next to me said.

I smiled and nodded – it was Jenna's friend, Beth, the girl from the Rugby Club, so it was sort of important to make a good impression. Jenna said I didn't have to double-date if I didn't want to, but I could see she did and her mum was happier if there was a group of us. It was only twelve days since the murder and she was still shaky about Jenna and Charlie being out after dark.

'There'll be a second display later,' Max said. 'After they've lit the bonfire and burned the Guy. They save the best ones for last.'

'Great.'

Now Beth's boyfriend was more of a problem. Mostly when I came across lads my own age, they were travellers or townies. I knew how to talk to travellers, and the townies generally wanted to kick my head in, but Max didn't and I had no idea how to get along with him.

I realised he was watching me out of the corner of his eye and I hunched closer round Jenna. A few seconds later, I noticed him move closer to Beth, holding her tighter. Interesting.

Next time I saw him watching us, I slid my hands down to

rest on Jenna's tummy and pull her back against me. She skewed her head round to look at me and I kissed her scrunched nose.

Sure enough, I saw Max's hands drift lower and he gave Beth a squeeze.

I sniggered, remembering he was younger than me. He didn't know how much he could get away with – thought he'd try copying me. Maybe I should take him aside and give him the benefit of my experience.

The temptation to turn this into a competition was irresistible. I tilted my head and kissed Jenna's neck, down and then up again, and nuzzled her jaw.

His move.

Max stared fixedly at the fireworks shooting over the Mere. He was obviously not brave enough to try that one! Eventually he hugged Beth harder and gave her a quick peck on the ear.

Nowhere near! I win!

'Will you behave?' Jenna murmured.

'What?' I whispered back.

'I know what you're doing. Stop showing off.'

I chuckled and she trod on my foot.

A bit later, Max and I went to the food van to get the girls jacket potatoes and Cokes while they saved us a spot in front of the bonfire. Max shuffled from foot to foot as we waited in line.

'So, er, you and Jenna, that's . . . er . . . well, it's great.'

I dead-eyed him. 'Yeah.'

'I mean, she's great. Um, not that I know her that well. But Beth talks about her all the time and she obviously is great if Beth likes her because . . . er . . .'

'Yeah.' Dumb-ass.

He squirmed under my glare. 'Um, Beth cares a lot about her.'

'Right.'

He took a deep breath. 'So, not that this is any of my business, but like I said Beth cares a lot about her and . . . um, she'd hate to see her get hurt.' He stood up a bit straighter, but he was still half a head shorter than me. 'And so would I.'

I stared down at him. He held my gaze though I could tell he wanted to look away. 'Yeah, join the club.'

He let his breath out and smiled. 'Oh, great. Oh, look I'm sorry. I promised Beth that I'd . . . well . . . um . . .'

'Check me out?'

He made to take a step back and stopped himself. 'Um, I guess. Er, sorry . . .'

I let him wriggle a bit longer and then laughed and shoved him, but not hard. 'No worries. I'd do it if she was my girlfriend's mate.'

'You would?' Max sighed in relief.

I grinned at him. I liked him better for that. He was all right. 'Yeah. Hey, what do those two want on their spuds? I forgot to ask.'

'Get 'em tuna. And Diet Coke.' Max said, rolling his eyes. 'Beth thinks she's fat.'

'You know how to fix that? Next time you see a picture of one of those supermodels, you know, the bag of bones ones, just sniff and say "Too thin" and look all *ewww*! Then get real huggy with Beth.'

'You think?' He smiled cautiously.

'No, I know. Trust me.'

His smile widened. 'OK, I will. Thanks.'

I waved to Charlie as we got to the front of the queue and he trotted over. 'What do you want on yours?'

'Beans and sausages. And a Coke, please.'

I passed them down to him when the guy behind the counter served up. 'Having a good time?'

He looked at me like I was an alien life form. Probably thought I was – he had seen me kissing his sister. 'Yes.'

Were little kids supposed to be this hard to talk to? I looked at Max.

'Did you think the fireworks were exciting?' Max asked. Even I knew that was a mistake. He was ten, not three.

Charlie snorted. 'Seen better.' He turned and headed back to his friend.

Max glared at him. 'Isn't he supposed to think we're cool or something at his age?'

'He's a brat,' said Jenna, materialising by my shoulder and

taking her food. 'And girls are icky, so that makes you two dorks.'

I could live with her brat brother thinking I was a dork because she looked like she was having a good time. The worry crease between her eyebrows had disappeared, and she was laughing as Beth pulled a face at Charlie's back.

The forensics tests had to be back soon. It'd been over a week. Then her dad would stop shutting himself in his study and her mum would stop stressing, and Jenna could concentrate on me. I laughed at myself – sad or what? But yeah, I liked having all her attention.

37 – Jenna

A few days after Bonfire Night, I got something else beside Dad's tests to worry about. We were in the village shop. Mum was at the till paying for a sauce mix.

'Having fish tonight, Tanya?' Mrs Crombie asked.

'Yes, I forgot to buy some last time I was at the supermarket so I've had to rush down here. Honestly, it's coming to something when you daren't send one of the kids out in broad daylight.'

'I know. Terrible business. Mrs Carlisle was in here the other day. She looks a wreck, poor thing. You can't imagine anyone local doing something so terrible. I said as much to the police.'

I glanced over at Mum from the magazine rack where I was browsing. Her face blanked as Mrs Crombie gabbled on.

'They'll have been round to yours, with their questions? They were here ages. I thought they were never going. I don't think there's a family in the village they didn't interrogate us about. It's awful – doesn't feel right to talk about neighbours in that way, but I suppose you have to when something like this happens.' She hesitated. 'Asked a lot of questions about your Clive, they did.'

'Oh,' Mum said stiffly.

Mrs Crombie's gossip sensors homed in on Mum's shuttered face. 'They grilled my Derek too. He was out walking the dog around the time it happened. He told them in no uncertain terms that the Carlisles are respected customers.' She stopped, her voice faltering a little. 'I mean, you know he was never keen on me being involved in the action group, Tanya. Not that he doesn't support the principle or . . . but, well, he doesn't like upsetting customers.' She gave Mum an apologetic smile. 'You know, they even asked us about poor John Norman.'

Mum frowned. 'About John? Why?'

'They didn't say. Just asked if we knew anything about his movements on the night Steven died.'

Mum's face clouded in anger. 'Hasn't that poor man had enough to deal with? He never goes out now. Why would they want to know about him?'

'That's what I said. I took a box of groceries around for him that day once I closed the shop. He was in his pyjamas and robe when he answered the door. I don't think he bothers getting dressed a lot of the time since Lindsay died.'

'No, well, he's not been himself at all since he lost her.'

Mrs Crombie nodded as she scanned the sauce through the till. 'It's a terrible thing, they say, to lose a child. You can understand him not being the man he was. That's why I was glad my Derek noticed the lights were on in John's sitting room when he took the dog out.'

'That was lucky,' Mum said flatly. I wondered what Mr Crombie had said about seeing or not seeing Dad. Mum wouldn't ask, but I could tell she was worried too.

'Yes, and when Derek was on his way back, he saw John through the glass in the front door, shutting up the house for the night. If he hadn't, I bet they'd have questioned that poor soul within an inch of his life too.'

I wondered if Mr Crombie had caught nosiness from his wife.

'And then they started on about David Morris. Pestering and pestering. When your Clive left his place, it seems David had a stroll down to the Green Man for a quick half before closing.' She paused for breath to take the money Mum was proffering. 'Thanks. And can you believe this? They've only had him down the station to do one of those DNA tests on him because he was walking back before closing time. I never in all my days heard the like. Can't even walk around your own village without being accused of all kinds.'

Nosy old bat! She'd heard something about Dad. I was sure of it. And now she was testing Mum out.

Mum picked the parsley sauce off the counter, ready to make her escape, but Mrs Crombie leapt in again before she could make a dash for it. 'Anyway, I said to those police, if you ask me, it should be that boy they're looking for.'

'What boy?' Mum asked, out of politeness for her eyes were on the door.

'The one who was in here throwing his weight about that night. Never seen him before. Buying alcohol, Tanya. Aggressive, he was. He scared me, I don't mind telling you –'

'Mum?' I tugged her sleeve hard, wishing I had psychic powers and could bring the shelf above Mrs Crombie's head crashing down on her. 'Can we go now?' I practically dragged Mum from the store before she realised who the old witch was talking about.

38 – Ryan

By three o'clock on Saturday afternoon, the Winter Market in the town square swarmed with shoppers carrying packed bags of early Christmas presents. From what I'd heard, every market from now to mid-December would be just as busy. People came from miles. The sweet, musky smell of chestnuts roasting on a brazier made my mouth water. I scouted the sea of faces looking for Jenna. Meet her by the clock tower in the square, she'd said, but if I saw her on the way, I'd run up behind her and make her jump.

I heard the disturbance ahead before I saw it. A voice carrying over all the other babble. It turned my blood to ice.

'You! Come on! You! You want to buy this . . . Why're you pretending you can't hear me? Look at me! I'm not invisible. Here, you can see me, can't you?'

The crowd ahead of me began to disperse. People moved away in that small town way, where making a scene is a crime equivalent to murder. In a few seconds the row I was in was all but empty. The shoppers moved on to other stalls. Their eyes appeared to be fixed on the goods for sale, but they were secretly watching the spectacle.

Seeing the mad woman in the market screaming at no one, at everyone. Seeing my mum.

'So I'm invisible, am I? Well, to hell with you! To hell with all of you and your poxy lives.'

Everyone watched and didn't watch with their special brand of English embarrassment, as she scooped up handfuls of beads and bracelets.

'Who will buy? Who will buy?' she sang out, in some tune she'd told me was from a musical. She used to sing it to me when I was a kid, sitting me on her knee and singing it in my ear just for me.

She hadn't seen me. The hairs on the back of my neck prickled up with shame and I slid behind the nearest stall for cover.

She whirled around in a dance to the music in her head, spreading her arms and looking up at the sky. Beads scattered from her hands to rattle on the cobbles.

'None of you are free,' she shouted. 'All afraid to be yourselves.'

I knew I had to stop her, but I couldn't move. Just couldn't. Rooted there.

Then I saw a familiar figure trotting towards her and I caught my breath.

'Karen! Hey, Karen!'

Mum turned.

Jenna rushed up to her. 'Hi! I didn't realise you were over here. I've been wandering around for ages. Are you packing up? I'll buy you a coffee. There's a great café over there. I'm starving. I bet you are too. Shall we go?'

Mum's arms, still outstretched stiffly, went slowly round Jenna as she woke from wherever it was she'd been. 'Oh hello, sweetie.'

'I'll help you pack up,' Jenna said. 'We can beat the rush if we go now. Oh, they have organic cakes – I'm sure the banana nut brownie is vegan. I bet you'll like that.' Jenna chirped at her as if nothing weird was going on. As if Mum was just any normal person she knew. She grabbed Mum's hand and tugged her back to the stall. 'Let's put these away.' She handed Mum a box. Slowly, dazed, Mum began to gather her things.

Jenna continued to chatter. 'This yellow crystal necklace is beautiful, Karen. Are you going to make more of those?'

Gradually the people around me began to move on and talk again, quietly at first, eyes still warily on the crazy, but then louder – back to normal.

My hands were shaking and a ball that felt like granite was lodged in my throat. Because Jenna, Jenna who hated people staring at her, Jenna had done that.

I made my legs move.

I went over to join them, picked up a box and piled stuff into it. I couldn't speak.

We packed up without a word. Mum looked like she wasn't really there, like she didn't know I was either. Jenna stacked the boxes and I picked them up, with my chin on top to balance them. She linked her arm through Mum's. 'OK, coffee shop, my treat!' she said. I trailed behind them.

We sat at a table by the window and Mum stared out through the glass into the street. The woman at the till came over and took our order. While we waited, Jenna linked her little finger round mine on the table.

I knew then that she'd seen me hiding. I couldn't look at her. I kept my eyes fixed on a rose on the PVC tablecloth. My skin burned up.

She leaned over and kissed my cheek and whispered in my ear. 'It's OK.'

I shook all over with the effort it took me not to lose control and howl like a baby as Jenna took my hand off the table and cuddled it on her lap between hers.

That's when I knew I loved her.

39 – Jenna

Karen crumbled pieces of brownie in restless fingers as she watched the market packing up through the window of the café. Ryan's hand slowly stopped shaking.

'Come home with us for a while?' he asked in a low voice.

I got my phone out and called Mum. 'Hi, it's me,' I said, too cheerful for the silence on either side of me. 'I'll be back later than I said. I'm going round to Ryan's . . . Yes, he'll walk me home. Don't worry.'

'Stay for tea,' he mumbled.

'I'll have tea round at his. Yes, love you too.'

I closed the phone.

'Seen enough, have you?' Karen shouted at the window.

Ryan's hand clenched again. The man outside the café looked away and hurried on.

Karen subsided and watched the streetlamps twinking on along the road. 'Winter's coming,' she said. 'The Solstice is on its way, and the world hibernates like a slumbering dragon beneath the hills waiting to be woken.'

I glanced at Ryan.

'It's a legend,' he said in a flat voice, staring down at his muffin.

'But it'll be Christmas soon, Karen. I love Christmas, don't you?'

Her forefinger stabbed the crumbs around the plate. 'When I was small, we used to have the biggest Christmas tree in the village. My sisters and I would sit in the hall and gaze in the dark at the fairy lights. I thought there was no more beautiful sight than that. Magical. On the last Sunday before Christmas, the church choir would go from house to house. They'd come to us last and sing carols under our tree. My mother would bring out mulled wine and mince pies for them. We'd stand together and listen, our arms round each other. A quintet. Like the perfect family.'

Ryan pulled his hand out of mine and rubbed his forehead in slow, tired circles. I looked from one to the other.

'Will you be visiting them at Christmas, your parents?' I tried to sound upbeat, but I'd hoped Ryan would be around at Christmas.

She laughed, tinkly harsh. 'We weren't the perfect family.'

'I've never met them,' Ryan said, getting up. 'We should go. Catch the next bus.'

Back on the boat, Karen insisted on cooking a proper meal. Afterwards, Ryan cleared the plates away, and then took my hand and pulled me off to his room. Karen ignored us. She sat with her eyes shut, clutching a crystal as she chanted something under her breath.

'I'm sorry,' he said as soon as he closed the door.

'What for?'

'Everything. Her. Being a coward in the market. You having to do all that. It should've been me.'

'But it's been you before, hasn't it?'

His breath juddered heavy through his chest into me. 'Yes.'

'So this time it didn't have to be.'

He pulled my face up – a flash of anger in his as he kissed me. It wasn't me he was mad at though. He led me back towards the bed with his mouth still pressed hard to mine. I wound my arms round his neck.

He lay half across me and his hand crept under my top, circling on my side for a while, then travelling further. It cupped my breast – I sucked my breath in at the sensation of his fingers there.

He pulled his fingers away and his mouth broke free of mine. 'Sorry.'

'No, it's OK. Really.'

'Sure?'

'Yes.'

The angry light had gone from his eyes and something else was there – I didn't recognise it, but it made the pit of my stomach wobble.

He kissed me again and I felt his hand on my breast a second time, stroking, sending sweet shivers through me. I snatched at some courage and sneaked my hands under his T-shirt to touch his back. My own daring made me breathless. So did the way he shifted against me at the contact.

He'd think I was so stupid if he knew how brave I felt to even do this.

His lips moved down my neck and his hand stilled. He tucked his face against me so I could barely catch his words. 'Love you.'

I froze. I could hear his heartbeat against mine, suspended between the minute when my world was one thing and some far ahead future minute when it would become another.

I breathed.

He took his hand away and rested it on my waist, skin on skin. 'It's all right,' he murmured. 'You don't have to say it back.'

'Yes, I do. Because it's true.' I leaned my mouth to his ear and whispered.

He uncurled and pulled my face into his shoulder. Rough — like he couldn't wait for it to be there and wouldn't let go when it was.

He held me.

Slowly, slow as a marble falling through treacle, the seconds moved again.

He breathed.

I breathed.

He let out a laugh and loosened his grip. 'I was scared shitless of saying that to you.'

I wriggled my arm free so I could hug it round him. 'Have you ever said that to anyone before? A girl, I mean.'

'No,' he said, half scornful, half embarrassed. 'Have you?'

I rolled back so I could see his face. 'What do you think?'

He gave me a triumphant grin. If it were possible to win an Olympic Gold for smuggest expression, he'd have got it without a contest then.

'Do you have to do that?'

'What?'

'Gloat.'

'Yes.'

I had to laugh.

He shut me up by kissing me.

When he stopped, I gathered my nerve to ask, 'Why?'

'Fishing for compliments?' I opened my mouth to deny it, but he tapped my jaw closed with his finger. 'I just do.' He stroked his thumb over my scarred cheek. 'All of you.'

Beth said Max told her she was beautiful. He sent her love songs by email, ones he said made him think of her. I wouldn't have exchanged Ryan's monosyllables for that.

I groaned and butted my head on him. 'I suppose I'll have to take you home to meet Dad soon.'

'Bloody hell, woman, I'm not asking you to marry me!'

I snorted. 'What makes you think I'd say yes if you did?'

He tickled my ribs. 'You're crazy about me.'

I sat up and tried to frown and look disgusted while he laughed up at me. 'Is there some disease you caught that makes your ego so big?'

'You look really hot when you're cross with me, do you know that?'

I made a pathetic attempt at slapping him and gave up to cuddle down next to him again. 'Dad's going to go mental though.'

'Suppose I'll be skewered with a garden fork when he finds out.'

'Probably. Might deflate your ego so it could be a good thing.'

'You're supposed to say "No, I'll protect you" and stuff like that.'

'Are you mad? He pays my pocket money.' I twizzled the ends of the leather cord on his wrist between my fingers. 'Seriously though, I don't know what to do. I've never seen Dad so stressed. He's not sleeping and he looks awful.'

'The DNA tests can't be much longer and then he'll be in the clear. But you know what I think about why they haven't got anyone for it? It could be anyone. That dickhead had a big mouth. Maybe he pissed off someone a lot harder than him.'

'But killing him? And the way they did it . . .'

He held me tighter. 'There's psychos everywhere you go.

You just don't expect them in a place like this, I guess.' He jerked his head round to look at the clock. 'Shit! Have you seen the time? I'd better take you home. I don't want to make your mum mad with me. She's all that'll stand between me and that garden fork.'

'In a minute. I want to ask you something.'

'The answer's yes.'

'What? You don't know the question yet.'

'Yes, I do. It's am I fantastic in bed.'

I debated suffocating him with the pillow, but it was getting late and I did need to get back. 'Is your mum going to be OK? Are you?'

His grin faded. 'Yeah. I told you, she's not dangerous. Just acts a bit crazy sometimes. She comes down quickly from it. Real fast. Her downers are worse than the highs and they last longer.'

'What happens then?'

He shrugged. 'She . . . stops. Everything. Doesn't get up some days, unless I make her. Lies in bed and stares at the wall. Cries. Stares some more.'

'How long does that last?'

'It varies. A few weeks usually for the really bad part. Lasted a few months once.'

I didn't know what to say. Stupidly, I rubbed his arm as if that could help. He nuzzled my hair as if it did.

The walk home was over too quickly. I didn't want to leave

him so soon. He gave me a last long kiss and said 'I meant it,' gruffly in my ear. Then he jogged off down the lane.

Mum raised an eyebrow at me when I sat on the sofa beside her. She glanced meaningfully at the clock.

'Where's Dad?'

'I asked him to take Charlie and his friends bowling. He needed to get out and do something normal and you can't brood with a pack of ten-year-old boys in tow.'

'Oh, nice. Good.'

'It is good, considering the time you've come home.'

'I was thinking I should bring Ryan to meet Dad soon, but I don't want to stress him more.'

She frowned. 'It might be better if you did. It'll give him something else to think about. But please warn the poor boy this time. I thought I was going to have to resuscitate him when you sprang me on him.'

'Oh, I knew he'd be nervous if I told him.'

'Why is he nervous about meeting us?'

'The boat, Mum. People have attitude about it.'

'Really? I thought he was a very polite boy. And quite shy, in fact.'

'Mum, he is so not shy.'

She watched me as I tried not to giggle. The more I tried, the more serious she looked. 'Jenna, do we need to have a private talk?'

'No, Mum, we do not!'

Honestly, parents! Why did they think teenagers did nothing but have sex? I blamed the TV.

40 – Ryan

The next day, we walked up the hill above the village and sat on the exposed roots of the oak tree at its brow. Strenton spread out below us, Sunday-peaceful like a picture postcard. I cuddled Jenna close to keep her warm, and leaned my back against the tree trunk.

'It looks so calm down there,' she said. 'Like it used to.'

'Mmm.'

'Sometimes I think you can feel the fear in the air as if everyone's waiting for a psycho to pounce whenever they set foot outside.'

I twisted a strand of her hair round my finger. 'I didn't think your mum was going to let you come out today.'

'Me neither.'

'Do they still think it's someone from outside the area? The village lot, I mean.'

She nodded. 'It can't be someone local. It just can't. I mean . . . we'd know. Surely?'

'I don't know. Maybe. I guess.'

We watched a couple of birds soar above us and flap off to

perch on a hawthorn tree in the field hedgerow. Raggs ran out of energy and flopped down.

A leaf drifted down and landed on us. She picked it up. It curled over at the edges, dry and yellow. Jenna twirled it in woollen-gloved fingers.

'If we lay here long enough, do you think the rest of the leaves would cover us like a duvet?'

I looked up at the bare branches. 'Not enough left.'

'When I was little, Mum used to read me a story about fairies and they sewed leaves together to make coverlets for beds made from twigs.'

'Were they cute fairies?'

'Yes, why?'

'My mum used to tell me stories about fairies too. Except hers were called the Fey. Beautiful women who'd lure men into the hills and suck out their sanity, leaving them empty shells to wander lost in the wilderness.'

'Eww!'

I grinned. 'She's always had issues with female oppression in fairy tales. I was really shocked when I found out Snow White had a wicked stepmother. In her version, it was a capitalist stepfather.'

'Was there a prince or did Snow White set up a hippy commune with the dwarves?'

'Nah, she sold the dwarves into slavery and ran off with their money.'

Jenna frowned at me. 'Surely Karen wouldn't . . .' Then she laughed and thumped me. 'Liar!'

We kissed for a while until we got hungry and stopped to eat the picnic her mum had made us. Raggs gobbled scraps of sandwich and grapes from our fingers.

Jenna brushed the crumbs away and checked her watch. 'I need to get back. I want you to come and meet Dad.'

'Uh . . . I don't know . . .'

'He won't really chase you with a fork, you big baby.'

'I am not a big baby!'

She jumped up and held her hand out. 'Prove it then.'

I walked down the hill beside her, humming the funeral march while she pretended she wasn't laughing at me.

When she pulled me in through the back door and shouted, 'Dad,' the man who came into the kitchen was just what I'd imagined: a typical big house village guy, tallish, wearing cords and a checked shirt. He frowned at the sight of me.

'Dad, this is Ryan.'

Jenna still had hold of my hand and her father's shoulders tensed.

I let go of her and held my hand out to him. 'Hello.'

We shook. I hoped my palm wasn't sweaty because the back of my neck was.

'Hello,' he said.

If we lived in an age when it was OK to threaten your

daughter's boyfriend with a shotgun and run him from the house, I reckoned he'd have been reaching for his right now judging by that clenched jaw.

'We've been for a walk, but Mum told us not to be long,' Jenna said, dropping her mother right in it without a qualm. 'Is anything on TV?'

Mrs Reed appeared in the doorway, led by the scent of danger. 'Hi, Ryan. Thanks for looking after her. You didn't see any strangers about, did you?'

'Didn't see anyone at all.'

'Are you staying for a while?'

Jenna jumped in. 'Can we watch some TV?'

'Of course. You go through. I'll make some hot chocolate. Would you like one, Ryan?'

'Yes, please,' I said and scuttled after Jenna.

I caught an angry voice before we were halfway across the hall. 'Who the hell is that, Tanya?'

'It's her boyfriend. Now be reasonable and keep your voice down. She's brought him home to meet you. We'll talk about it later.'

Jenna closed the sitting room door behind us. 'Leave him to Mum,' she whispered and turned the TV on.

I'd no idea what Jenna's mum could have said to him back there, but when they came in with a tray of hot chocolate, Mr Reed wore a different face. Charlie came clattering down the stairs when he was shouted for and made a dive for the remote control. He wanted cartoons on. His mother tutted and said he was rude so he asked me if I minded. I said I didn't and that was true. I'd never got to watch that stuff at his age so I had catching up to do.

We watched the TV until some girl stuff came on and he started to fidget. 'Do you play football?' he asked. 'Want a game?' I nodded and he scrambled up. 'I'll have Dad in goal. You can have Jenna. She's useless.'

'I bet she's not,' I said. She probably was, but you can't say that. It made Charlie smile anyway, though I saw her dad roll his eyes.

I helped Charlie set up the goals and we had a kickabout for half an hour. Then I decided I ought to be getting back to Mum.

When I left, Jenna's dad even let her walk down to the gate with me. I saw him shift uncomfortably in the chair as we went out, but he didn't say anything to stop her.

'He'll come around,' she said with a grin as she kissed me goodbye.

41 – Jenna

On Monday, Mum picked me up from school at lunchtime as planned. I threw my school bag on the back seat and flopped into the front with her. 'We've got time for lunch,' she said. 'Your appointment isn't until half two.'

'Oh good,' I said, trying to smile back. This wasn't something I was looking forward to, but neither were split ends and my hair definitely needed a trim.

'You're sure now? Lorna did say if you can't face it that she'll come to the house again.'

'No, it'll be OK,' I said, hoping it would be. Maybe it would today, on a quiet day. Skipping school to get a haircut on Monday afternoon wasn't something Mum would ever have sanctioned last year. But that was last year.

We had lunch at the Lemon Tree Café. 'Is Dad going mental about Ryan?' I asked, wanting to talk to take my mind off the ordeal coming up.

'Mostly not.' Mum sipped her coffee. 'He's taking it quite well.'

I sniffed. 'You mean it only took you an hour to calm him down and not two.'

'Something like that,' she said with a laugh. 'You have to understand it's difficult for him. You'll always be his little girl and it's hard for him to see you growing up.'

'Huh! Charlie is going to have it so much easier than me. It's not fair.'

Mum shuddered. 'Don't. I dread the time when Charlie gets interested in girls.'

I had a hard time picturing my baby brother grown up and with a girl at all. 'Don't worry, he'll never get a girlfriend. He won't be interested unless she looks like a football.'

'I think he might grow out of that, Jenna,' Mum said.

'OK, place your bet. I think he'll be . . . ooh, nineteen before he manages to persuade some poor girl to go out with him. What about you?'

'Fifteen,' she said gloomily. 'Right before his GCSEs. Bound to be.'

I laughed and changed the subject. 'What do you think of Ryan?' I'd been dying to ask her this, but putting it off too. It all depended on her answer.

She thought for a moment. 'I've only met him a couple of times, of course, but . . .'

I put my fork down and waited with bated breath.

'He's quite grown up for his age, I think. Vey nice manners.

But one thing does surprise me — that he's working and not going to college. He seems bright . . .'

'I don't think he's thought about it.'

'I don't understand that. From what you've said, his mother is obviously an educated woman. I can't understand her not encouraging him to go.' She studied me for a second. 'He's a very attractive boy too.'

I just managed to stop a smirk. 'Is he? I hadn't noticed.'

Mum rolled her eyes. 'Yes, I'm sure you hadn't. Anyway, there's something I wanted to ask you. Perhaps this is the right time . . . As I said, he does seems more mature than most boys his age. He isn't . . . oh, how can I put it . . . he doesn't expect you to . . . um . . .'

'Mum, for God's sake! No, he isn't pushing me into anything.'

'You can't blame me for asking. He is older than you.'

'Yes, I know.'

'Is it something you've talked about?'

I felt my face heat. 'No. We've only been going out properly for a few weeks. Before we were just friends.'

'Only if you were thinking about it, I'd like to think you'd talk to me about it. OK?'

'Yes, OK, OK, but . . . it hasn't . . . I mean, I don't feel ready . . .' Not that I hadn't thought about it, but as something way, way ahead, all blurry and hazy and scary. One step that was too huge and too fast and impossible to imagine doing for real.

'Perhaps he knows you're not ready. Maybe he respects that.'

I thought about it. 'Yes, I guess so. He's funny like that – good at knowing things without having to be told.' I paused and gathered my nerve. 'But . . . he's been out with quite a lot of girls before me . . . you know, girls who're older. Sometimes I sort of worry about that because . . . oh, I don't know . . .'

'Does he know you haven't had a boyfriend before? Did he know that before he asked you out?'

I chuckled. 'Yes. Actually one time when I was going out with some of the people from school, he thought it was a date – which it really wasn't. He gave me a lecture about not going too far. He sounded like Dad!'

'Now that I wish I'd seen,' Mum said with a smile. 'There you are then – he doesn't mind. Don't create problems that don't exist. You know your granny's favourite saying . . .'

'"I've worried over many things and most of them have never happened,"' I chorused with her. I stuck my tongue out. 'And that applies just as much to you fussing over Charlie.'

She shook her head despairingly. 'There's an exception to every rule and that exception is called Charlie. I only have to turn my back for a second and he's broken something or cut himself. Trouble follows that child like a rat after the Pied Piper.' She checked her watch. 'Oh, eat up. We need to get over to Lorna's.'

*

The doorbell jingled, announcing our arrival in the salon. I shuffled in behind Mum and breathed with relief at the sight of the empty chairs. But then I gulped – empty chairs laid out in front of a row of . . . mirrors.

Mum gave me a quick hug as Lorna hurried over with a black nylon robe.

She ushered me to a chair. 'What's it to be? A trim or a new look?'

I looked in the mirror, focusing on her face and not mine. 'A trim. Keep the length, but maybe some long layers?'

She lifted my hair and fiddled with it. 'How about a few around your face? Shape it up and update it a little. Something like that.' She pointed to a picture on the wall.

I wanted to ask Mum if she thought that would suit me, but I didn't have the courage in case the thought flashed through Lorna's head that it would take more than a few layers to make me look good. Instead I agreed so I could get to the safety of the washbasin where I couldn't see my reflection.

Once Lorna started to cut my hair, I had an excuse to keep my eyes closed to stop the snipped strands falling into them. Being here with all this reflective glass reminded me too much of the day I'd got home from the hospital. When I'd gone upstairs to clean my teeth before bed, when I took off my mask and turned to the basin . . . when I saw my reflection in the mirror . . .

. . . the mass of puckered, angry skin stretched down from

below my eye to the base of my neck, the new graft still knitting into place, raw-looking and ragged . . .

. . . hideous. Which was when I broke the mirror.

'I'm just going to blow the hair off your nose,' Lorna said, breaking into my thoughts. I felt a quick blast of warm air on my face from the dryer. 'All done. I'll dry it off now.'

There was no excuse to keep my eyes shut any longer so I searched for another memory to give me the courage to open them.

I found one from a few days ago. One that still made me smile. Ryan tucking my hair behind my ears, holding my chin and staring at me. 'What're you doing?' I'd asked him.

'Deciding which bit to kiss first.' He said it as if he was trying to choose between chocolate fudge cake and cookie dough ice-cream. 'I have to start somewhere, but I want it all at once. Hmm, let's pick . . . here!' He pounced on me, making a smacking noise with his lips at the top of my right cheekbone where the scarring started.

If he was here now, he'd prod and tickle me until I opened my eyes, I knew that, so I sucked a quick breath in and looked in the mirror.

My reflection wasn't as bad as in those early days. The scar tissue had faded and flattened with the pressure mask and with time. I looked . . . human, I suppose. Scarred but human. I could almost hear his smug voice saying, 'Told you so.'

*

Mum let me stay quiet on the way back to the car. She was probably happy I'd got through it without losing the plot and she didn't expect more of me. But as we got close to the car park, I surprised us both.

I stopped outside the kitchen and bathroom showroom at the head of the alley. 'Mum, do you think they have steam-proof mirrors for sale there?' She stared at me. 'Only I need a new one.'

Her face lit up.

It was while we were in the shop that she got the call. She answered her mobile and listened for a moment before bursting into tears.

'Mum? Mum, what's wrong?' Was it an accident? Dad? Charlie?

She put her arms round me. 'Nothing's wrong, darling. It's your dad. The tests are back. He's in the clear.'

42 – Ryan

The phone vibrated in my pocket.

'Can I answer it?'

At the nod, I flipped it open.

<Tests came back. Not Dad>

I know . . .

I closed the phone.

'Was that your mum?'

'My girlfriend.'

'Are you sure your mum will be back soon?'

'I think so, but I told you, I didn't know she was going out.'
I clamped my hands together while he watched me. His colleague
stared out of the window.

The door opened with a clatter and Mum ran down the steps.
She stopped short at the sight of the two strange men.

'Who're you?'

'Police, Mrs Gordon.' They got their badges out.

'What do you want?' Her face snapped into her 'I fought the
law and the law ain't never gonna win' look.

'We were waiting for you. We need your son to come

to the station and give a DNA sample.'

She opened her mouth to rant about civil liberties and the police state so I leapt up and went to her. 'It's to eliminate me from their enquiries. They're asking a few people.'

The shorter of the detectives nodded. 'That's right. If he wasn't involved then there's no need to be concerned. Just part of the investigation. If you can come along now, we'll give you a lift back when it's done.'

How much of my DNA could Carlisle have had on him from that fight? But if I didn't say yes then they'd suspect me. I tried to glance at Mum for help when they weren't looking, desperate for her to know what to do because I didn't have a clue.

They sat us in the back of the police car. I'd have felt sorry for them if I hadn't been busy trying to stop shaking – Mum looked ferocious and was attempting to bore holes in the back of their heads with her eyes. She gripped my hand tightly while I stared out of the window.

They took us to a room at the station and left us there. A woman came in and babbled on at us like she was reading from a script . . . something about fingerprints and how long they kept the DNA on record and did I consent. All I could think was just shut up and do it and let me out of here. My heart banged faster, my skin flamed, and every nerve told every muscle in my body to get up and run.

Mum glared laser blasts of hate at the woman. 'He's only doing this, you fascist bitch, because he wants to. If it was up to me, you wouldn't get anything –'

'Mum, don't. Leave it, please. I want to get this over with.'

The woman inked my fingers and took my prints while Mum ranted at her. 'I know what you're doing here. Trying to soften him up by sending a female officer in. Well, it won't work on me. You should be ashamed –'

'Mum, drop it.'

The woman asked me to open my mouth to take the swab and she stuck something like a giant cotton bud in there. I felt her scrape it against my cheek.

'You wouldn't be doing this if we weren't travellers,' Mum muttered. 'You lot love to persecute us. Find a minority to pick on and you're right in there.'

I gave up trying to get her to stop. At least she wasn't shouting now.

The woman stepped back. 'Thank you. That's me finished. You can go now.'

Mum grabbed my hand and dragged me out, slamming the door behind us. The policemen who'd picked us up materialised as we came out. 'Go to hell!' Mum snapped, but she shoved me into the patrol car all the same when they offered us a lift back.

As soon as we were home, I reached for my phone. There

was only one person I wanted to see now. Someone who wouldn't rant and rage all night. Someone who would just be there for me when I needed her.

43 – Jenna

Ryan didn't text me until quite late that night. It was nearly eight o'clock when I finally got a message saying he'd been held up and was it too late to come round. He was at the door in fifteen minutes.

Straight away, I knew something was wrong. He was pale and jumpy, his fingers drumming on the tablecloth as Mum made him a cup of tea.

'Your hair looks nice,' he said softly. 'It suits you.' I was pleased he'd noticed, especially as he was in such an odd mood.

'If you two want to watch some TV, go through,' Mum said. 'Charlie's upstairs doing his homework and Dad's helping him. I'll be busy in here for a while.'

Sometimes my mum was the best.

But even on our own, Ryan was quiet. I shut the door and snuggled next to him on the sofa. 'You're not annoyed with me for dragging you here yesterday to meet Dad, are you?'

He came back from wherever he'd been with a jump. 'No, don't be dumb. Did he give you a hard time when I'd gone?'

'Um, not too bad. It's not personal – he'd be like that

whoever it was. He doesn't even like me talking about Beth and Max. He forgets we're out of primary school.'

Ryan didn't laugh or make a joke. That worried me.

'He's cheered up a lot since he got the news about the DNA test. The feeling of being suspected – it really got to him.'

He didn't answer.

'What's up?'

'Bad day. Just knackered.'

'Oh. Do you want to go soon then?'

'Do you want me to go?'

'No, of course not. But do you?'

He slumped further down the sofa, pulling me with him. 'Nah, I just feel like watching some TV with you.'

'OK.' I smiled and gave him the remote control. 'You choose.'

But the sense of unease wouldn't go away.

44 – Ryan

The atmosphere in the area was totally different since the murder. You couldn't miss the posters with appeals for information in Strenton and Whitmere. They were strapped to lamp posts, propped on boards by the road, in shop windows.

Pete and Bill had been talking about it at work.

'What's your nephew said?' Pete asked.

Bill shrugged. 'He's not allowed to say much, but they've got no one for it so they'll step it up now the forensics are back. They'll be all over that village until they get their man, I reckon.'

'Like flies around shit,' Mum said sourly when I told her. She was still livid about me being taken to the station. And I still felt sick over it, not that they'd treated me badly because they hadn't. But I had no idea what those tests would show up and every time I thought about it, panic set in. I kept trying to squash that down, but it wouldn't go away.

I couldn't tell Jenna. Not after she'd been through the weeks of waiting with her dad. She thought me being moody was down to Mum's illness and I let her think it. I couldn't dump more on her.

And Mum . . . well, the high was fading. She had clouded eyes like someone had died. When she went to bed early on Tuesday night, I told her I loved her.

'You don't,' she said and she walked off without looking at me.

45 – Jenna

'Dinner's in the oven,' Mum called. 'When's Ryan coming round?'

I walked through to the kitchen. 'About ten minutes.'

'I don't know how long we'll be. It depends on the queues. Some of those parents talk for hours, no consideration.' She grinned at me. 'Still, I don't suppose you'll mind.'

No, I definitely wouldn't.

Charlie slouched in behind me. 'Do I have to go? It's not compulsory.'

Dad followed him, with Charlie's coat in his hand. 'It's your Parents' Evening. You need to hear what your teachers have to say. Is it going to be disappointing?'

My brother stuck his lip out and shrugged. I nudged him and snuck him a sympathy biscuit from the jar.

Raggs ran past us barking and bouncing before we heard the knock on the back door. His tail flailed wildly.

Mum laughed. 'I think Ryan's here.'

*

Ryan was quiet again. I talked determinedly while we ate, hoping to cheer him up, but he seemed content to listen and not contribute much. 'Great chicken,' was all I got out of him unprompted.

'Come upstairs. I want to show you something,' I said once I'd cleared the plates.

When we got to my room, he looked around with an interest more like his usual self. 'Nice room,' he said, touching the cream wallpaper. 'I thought girls had hundreds of teddies in their bedrooms.'

I picked up Barney, my scruffy black bear, and hugged him to my chest. 'No, just the one. He's too special to have rivals. I've had him since I was born.'

Ryan shook his head. 'That's wasted on him. Give it to someone who'll appreciate it.'

I laughed and put Barney back on the chair. 'Come here then.'

He folded his arms round me, but I couldn't help feeling I was hugging him more than the other way round.

'I suppose if you don't cheat on the bear, you might not cheat on me either,' he said out of the blue.

'Of course I won't. What is wrong with you?'

'Nothing. It was supposed to be a joke. It didn't come out right. What did you want to show me? No, don't go . . .' He hung on to me tighter. 'Tell me.'

'It can wait.' Karen must still be bad. It must be awful being a boy sometimes. If I was down and I wanted a cuddle, it was OK for me to ask. Boys didn't find that so easy. He had to be the grown-up at home when she ill and he wasn't really that much older than me. If he wanted some TLC when he got the chance, I could understand that.

After a few minutes, he let me go. 'Go on, what is it?'

I pushed him to the bed. 'Sit down.' I rummaged in the back of the wardrobe. 'I've never shown this to anyone since . . .'

He patted the bed when I emerged with a box. 'Come on.'

I sat next to him and took out the hated plastic mask. 'I don't know what to do with it. I couldn't burn it because Mum said it might give off toxic fumes. I can't throw it in the bin because it'll never rot away and I can't stand to think of it on a waste dump where someone might see it. I want it destroyed so there's nothing left, but I don't know how.'

He took the mask from me and turned it in his hands. 'You had to wear this for six months?'

'Yes, twenty-three hours a day. I could take it off to wash and that was about it. It drove me crazy. It was hot and uncomfortable, it dug in and it made me look like a freak. It made me feel inhuman. I wouldn't go anywhere, and that's when Mum and Dad got me Raggs, to encourage me to go out. I'd take him to the paddock to throw his ball, but nowhere else. It took two months for me to get that far.' I closed my eyes briefly at the memory. 'I'm crap, aren't I?'

He shook his head and held the mask up to my face. 'Show me.'

'I don't want to.'

'It's still you underneath.' He fitted the mask carefully against my face. I didn't pull away, but I didn't help him either.

He leaned back and took a long look, then he smiled. 'It's just a mask. Something to make you better, nothing more. It's good you don't need to wear it now though.'

I nodded and pulled away.

He shook his head. 'You think I said that because it puts me off. You're so dumb sometimes.'

'Oh, thanks!'

He grabbed my face in his hands. 'I said it because it'd get in the way when I want to kiss you.' He tipped me suddenly back on to the bed. I squeaked as his elbow dug in my arm. 'Shit, sorry, did I hurt you?'

'Yes, kiss it better.'

He brushed his lips across my mouth. 'Stupid bear can't do this, can it?'

I suppose we forgot the time, lying on my bed kissing, and stopping to look at each other, then kissing some more. He stroked my face and I traced my finger along his eyebrows. I'd always wanted to do that. They fascinated me – thick and straight on the top with only the faintest of arches. Now winter was here, his tan had faded and the blond lights in his hair were darkening back to the colour beneath. He caught my fingertips and kissed them and smiled.

Crash!

My bedroom door rebounded off the wall.

I jerked up.

Dad stood in the doorway.

'You, out!' he shouted at Ryan, his hands clenched white.

'Dad!'

'Get out before I throw you out!'

'It was my fault, not hers,' Ryan said, on his way to the door while I screamed at my father. 'Don't be mad at her. It was me.'

'Oh, I'm bloody sure it was. Now get out of my house.'

'Sorry,' he said to Dad, and then to me, 'Sorry.'

I heard Mum's voice on the stairs. 'What on earth is going on?' And then Ryan's feet on the stairs going down.

Dad slammed the door on me and I ran after him to wrench it open.

Mum was on the other side about to come in. I all but cannoned into her.

'Has he gone?'

'Yes. Jenna, what were you thinking of? You know you're not allowed to have a boy up in your bedroom.'

'You never said that.'

'I didn't think I needed to!'

'We weren't doing anything. Dad just assumed. But we weren't.'

She sighed. 'Well, good luck convincing him of that. I think you'd better let him cool down before you try. Really, how can you expect us to trust you when you go and do this?'

'But we weren't doing anything!'

'Stop shouting. That's not going to improve your father's mood.' She came in and sat down on my bed. 'Honestly, the time I've spent talking him round, telling him to give you a chance and that you're ready to behave responsibly. And now I wonder if I'm the one who was taken in all along.'

'Oh, shut up, Mum! I told you, nothing happened. Ryan's down because his mum's ill and –'

'His mum's ill? What's wrong with her?'

'She has this thing called bipolar and –' I broke off as her eyes widened in alarm. 'What?'

'Jenna, perhaps . . . well, I hate to say it because it's not the poor woman's fault . . . but I'm not sure I want you going round there if she is . . . unwell. People with that condition, well, they can be dangerous. I know it's an extreme case, but not so long ago I read an article in the paper where someone with that problem had stopped taking their medication, gone on the rampage and killed four people in a shopping centre –' She stopped suddenly and put her hand to her mouth. 'Oh! No! What if she was the one . . . Oh my God!'

'Don't be so stupid, Mum. She's about five foot one. As if she could have beaten Steven Carlisle's head in.'

'But if she got in a rage, she could be stronger than you think. It's the adrenalin –'

'This is completely stupid and over the top!'

Mum compressed her lips. 'Well, perhaps so, but I think you need to calm down. I'll go downstairs. But I mean it, you are not to go round there again until we've discussed this properly. I'll need to meet her before I feel comfortable about you being there. I feel very sorry for her, but you're my daughter and it's my job to keep you safe.'

'And a fantastic job you've done of that!' I screamed as she hurried downstairs. 'Yeah, go and tell him the latest so he can rant about it too.'

I looked for something to throw, but there was only Barney. I burst into tears instead.

Stop it, you stupid, snivelling cow. Pull yourself together. How must he feel, thrown out like that? Do something.

I dried my face on my sleeve and crept down to the kitchen to find my phone – no messages. I typed a text quickly.

<Sorry. Luv u xxx>

He must have been waiting because almost immediately, one came back.

<R u OK?>

<Yes. R u?>

<Yes. Call u 2mo>

I sent one last text where I filled the screen with Xs. When I looked up, Charlie was standing at the door, grinning. 'You are in so much trouble.'

'Shut up!'

He sauntered into the kitchen. 'You'd better be nice to me, or else. You can start by making me a milkshake.'

'Make it yourself.'

He stuck his tongue out. 'If you don't, I'll tell Dad how you stayed out all night with him and then –'

He stopped at the sight of my face. Charlie turned . . . and looked up at Dad standing in the doorway behind him.

'Charlie, go upstairs.'

My brother shot me a 'sorry' with his eyes before he slunk out past Dad.

Dad's face was white. 'Well?' he said, as though it killed him to speak to me.

'Ch-Charlie got it wrong –'

'Yes, you would say that.'

I gritted my teeth. 'He did. Look, I went to meet Ryan one morning before he went to work and Charlie saw me coming back, that's all.'

'Am I expected to believe that?'

'Ask his mum then! She'll tell you – he was with her.' Because she would, wouldn't she? She'd already lied to the police about where he was that night.

'She's hardly reliable from what your mother's just told me.' A muscle twitched in his jaw.

'She's depressed, not a psycho!'

'I'm going to say this once, Jenna, and I mean it – you are not to see that boy again. You are not to go near him or his mother. I am not having it.' He turned on his heel and strode back to the sitting room.

I stormed after him. 'You believe what you want. But you are not stopping me from seeing Ryan. You've got no right!'

He sat on the sofa and stared at the muted TV screen. I waited for a moment. Mum ignored me. Then I stamped upstairs so they wouldn't see me cry.

46 – Ryan

The boat was in darkness when I got back on Thursday night. I opened Mum's bedroom door cautiously.

'Mum, do you want a cup of tea?'

'No.'

'Are you feeling bad?'

'Leave me alone.'

'Want some dinner?'

'No.'

I gave up. I'd try harder if she wasn't up tomorrow, but for now I couldn't cope with much more.

I went up to the loose box and hung around outside until Jenna came to see to the ponies. Her face lit up when she saw me in the torch beam and she flung her arms round me.

'I can't be long. Dad'll be home from work soon.'

'What happened?'

I heard her anger in the darkness. 'I'm not supposed to see you any more. But they can't stop me and I told them that.'

It was only what I'd expected all along. 'Maybe we shouldn't for a few days. Let it die down.'

'Don't you want to see me any more?' she asked in a small voice. 'I wouldn't blame you after the way Dad treated you.'

I put my chin on her head. 'No, it's not that. I don't want you getting grief and anyway, Mum's not good. I should be there now.' And it was getting harder and harder not to tell Jenna I was in trouble and scared.

47 – Jenna

The house crackled with the static of unspoken anger as we sat in silence over dinner. Halfway through the meal, Charlie dropped his cutlery on to the plate with a clatter and burst into tears, something he hadn't done for years, not since he broke his arm falling out of a tree.

Mum immediately scooped him on to her knee, as if he was still that little boy. Normally he'd have wriggled free, but not tonight. 'What's wrong, darling?'

'Everything,' he wailed. 'Everything's horrible. Dad's always angry and you're weird. And nobody will tell me what's going on and I know something is. And now Jen hates me too, and it's all my fault. But I didn't mean to tell and she won't listen and –' He broke off, hiccuping as he tried to breathe through his sobs.

Mum glared at me.

'The only person at fault here is your sister,' Dad said. 'And frankly her behaviour at the moment doesn't give us any reason to think she's responsible enough to be believed.'

In my head I stood up and screamed at him and threw my plate across the kitchen to shatter against the wall. I stopped myself just in time. He wouldn't believe me any better for that.

I put my cutlery down quietly. 'We weren't doing anything. I took him upstairs because . . . because I wanted to show him my mask. And yes, we kissed, but that's all.'

'You are so naïve,' Dad snapped. 'He's a sixteen-year-old boy. In your bedroom. What do you think would've happened next?'

'Nothing.'

'I know teenage boys, Jenna. I was one. They're all after the same thing.'

Mum lifted her eyebrows. 'Do we have to have this conversation in front of Charlie? And I think you're doing that boy a disservice, Clive. It's not as if we have any reason to think ill of him. After all, he obviously doesn't care about her . . . her . . .' She looked at me and stopped, her cheeks flushing.

'Or he thinks he can take advantage of her because she's vulnerable!'

That did it.

I threw the plate.

48 – Ryan

At eleven thirty on Friday morning, a police car pulled up at the boatyard. Two men in uniform got out.

They walked towards me. The older spoke. 'Ryan Gordon?'

I nodded.

'We'd like you to come with us to the station in connection with the death of Steven Carlisle.'

The spanner dropped from my hand. 'Are you arresting me?'

'No, we'd like you to come voluntarily and answer some questions.'

I hadn't heard Bill hurry over, didn't know he was beside me until I felt his hand on my shoulder. 'Hang on a minute, he's only sixteen. Doesn't he have to have someone with him?'

'We've been trying to get hold of his mother. We need him to tell us where she is.'

'She's at home,' I said, every part of me numb.

'There's no answer. We've tried there already.'

'She's in bed. She's ill.'

The man frowned. 'Is she too ill to come down the station? If so, we'll need someone else to act as an appropriate adult for you. Is your dad around or another relative? Otherwise we'll have to call Social Services.'

Pete marched over too. 'What's going on?'

'They want to take him in for questioning over that murder,' Bill told him.

Pete screwed up his face, incredulous. 'What? Him? You're barking up the wrong tree, mate. Stop arsing about and get out there and find who really did it, because I'm telling you it's not Ryan.'

'Look, lads,' Bill said. 'Two boys having a bit of a scrap is one thing. Doing someone in is another.'

'Just some questions, sir. Just following our orders,' the policeman replied.

Pete stepped between me and the two officers. 'Ryan, you got someone you can call? Someone you want me to call for you? Do you want me to come with you?'

'There . . . is someone . . . maybe,' I said slowly. 'I don't know. Can I try?'

'Go on,' the policeman said, stepping away to give me space.

I pulled the phone out of my pocket, fumbled, and nearly dropped it. Bill's hand tightened on my shoulder. I found the number in my contacts and hit the ring button.

It rang and rang.

What if it wasn't the right number any more?

What if he was tied up and couldn't answer?

What if he didn't want to?

The ringing went on forever.

Please, please pick up . . .

Finally, a voice spoke in my ear. Surprised. Worried.
'Hello? Ryan?'

'Cole, I need . . . I'm . . . Cole, I'm in a mess . . .'

49 – Jenna

I texted Ryan at lunchtime in the cafeteria. No answer.

'What if he's getting fed up with me and I'm too much effort?' I stared at the phone trying to make it ring, message, do anything but sit there in my hand ignoring me.

'Maybe he's busy. He is at work.' Beth split her chocolate cake in half and pushed a piece over to me. 'Here, you have some. I can't eat it all.'

'But it's his break now.'

'Something could've come up.'

'You don't understand. He's been weird all week. And then there's that stuff with Dad.' I shoved the cake away. 'What if he's met someone else?'

'That's mad, Jen. He likes you a lot. It's dead obvious.' The chocolate cake headed my way again and she pulled a face at me. 'And not eating that isn't going to change anything.'

'But there's something he's not telling me. I thought it's because his mum isn't well, but it's more than that, I'm sure of it. Why won't he tell me?'

'Have you asked him?'

'I don't want to come over as clingy and desperate.' I sighed. 'I am being clingy and desperate, aren't I?'

Beth laughed. 'Just a bit.'

50 – Ryan

My phone vibrated and I snatched it up.

Please don't let this be Cole saying he can't make it after all.

It wasn't.

'My girlfriend,' I told the policewoman who'd been left to mind me.

'Do you want to answer it?'

'No, not now.'

I put the phone away and looked around the waiting room for the two hundredth time. Nothing much to see. Plain walls with a few posters about advice lines. I'd read them so many times now I could practically remember the phone numbers by heart. The room was bigger than any of ours on the boat, but it still felt like a cell.

'Shouldn't be long now,' the policewoman said, glancing at her watch. 'Do you want another drink?'

I shook my head. 'Can I go to the toilet, please?' My bladder had begged me to ask for the last hour – nerves getting to it – but I didn't know if it was allowed.

'Of course.'

She got up to escort me and I felt like a fool – they'd hardly leave me to wet the floor.

Back in the waiting room, another fifteen minutes ticked by until the door opened and a policeman waved Cole in.

My eyes smarted in relief at the sight of him – big, hairy, leather-clad, his presence filling the room. I scrambled up, knocking the table aside.

'Come here, kiddo,' he said and he grabbed me in a Cole bear-hug. 'Bloody hell, Ryan, you've grown again. You'll be taller than me soon, you great long streak of piss.' He laughed with his 'fuck authority' belly chuckle and I held on to him tighter.

I didn't ever want to be bigger than him.

'I want a few minutes with him first,' he said to the woman. 'And get us a coffee, love, will you? Have you got the duty solicitor on call? He's not doing this without one.'

She answered something or other, but I didn't listen. Cole would look after everything now. My head was on his shoulder and I breathed in the smell of leather and safety.

'I picked Karen up on the way. She's outside. Had to get her in case they needed her consent to let me sit in with you. Plus I knew she'd want me to. Do you want to see her?'

'I can't. Not now. Is she all right?'

'Yeah, course she is. She's Karen. She's fuming. Left her

giving the desk sergeant full blast about persecution of children and minorities.'

'Nooo . . .' I groaned.

He laughed again and rocked me hard, staggering me from one foot to the other. 'Stop worrying. Let her rant. It'll take her mind off flapping over you.'

'She's not well.'

'Yeah, I could tell. But she's up and at 'em now. Snapped right out of her black dog, she has. Let them deal with it. You're her kid – they expect her to give them grief.'

I pulled back from Cole, though I didn't want to. I wanted to stay where I was – safe. 'I didn't do it.'

He mussed my hair. 'I know that, you stupid bastard.'

'I did have a fight with him though. My DNA might be on him. I think they've got the results back.'

'Yeah, so Karen told me.' He gripped my face between dinner plate hands. 'Now listen – you tell them everything. You tell them it was your mum who said you should keep quiet. You tell them she's ill. You tell them all that, you hear? Exactly what's wrong with her. Whatever it takes. You get me, Ryan? You don't know what they know so all you've got is what really did happen that night.'

But Jenna . . . I couldn't tell them that . . .

I realised there was something I hadn't said to him. 'Thanks, Cole. For coming. I didn't know . . . I didn't . . .'

'No need for that.' He butted his head on mine. 'Now focus, we've got to get you out of here.'

The solicitor turned up not long after Cole arrived. 'Ryan Gordon?' He held his hand out. 'I'm James Gregson.'

'I didn't do it,' I said immediately, then I realised I was supposed to shake hands with him. 'Oh, sorry.'

'He definitely didn't do it,' Cole said. 'Now tell him what to say to get him out of here.'

'Well, um . . . now, it doesn't quite —'

'Christ!' Cole sighed and slumped into a chair. 'Just explain his rights to him.'

Gregson briefed me. I didn't really understand it, but Cole did. Then two detectives turned up, both guys in their thirties. They introduced themselves and sat down opposite me.

I nodded at them, my mouth dry when they asked if I was ready.

'Can you tell us in your own words what happened on the night Steven Carlisle was killed?'

'I got home from work. Me and Mum had a row and I took off to the shop in the village. I bought some vodka and Carlisle jumped me when I came out. We had a fight and some woman from a cottage came and yelled at us. Carlisle ran off and I went the other way.'

'And this was around what time?'

'Half six-ish.'

'Go on.'

'I didn't want to go home because my mum was mad at me so I headed over to my girlfriend's. I drank the vodka on the way over to hers. I let myself into the feed store next to where she stables her horses. It was cold and I was feeling dizzy from the booze so I pulled some straw out of a bale and crashed out on it. I didn't wake up until next morning and I stayed there until it got light.'

'So the last time you saw Carlisle was around half-six?'

'Yes.'

'Why did he attack you?'

'He doesn't like me.'

The detective doing the questioning stared at me, his eyes unreadable. 'Why?'

'Because I'm a traveller. Because I'm seeing Jenna and he's got an attitude over her dad running that campaign.' I remembered Cole's words about being straight with them. 'Because I decked some guy he knows when he did something really shitty to my girlfriend.'

He consulted his notebook. 'This would be the incident at Whitmere Rugby Club?'

'Yeah.'

'Take us through that.'

I went over it all again: how I'd decked Ed, then how Carlisle came after me, how he threatened me when the guy from the club split us up.

'Did you take his threats seriously?'

'No, I just thought he was a bigmouth showing off in front of his mates. You get used to it when you're a traveller. And I didn't see him again until that night in Strenton.'

'Did you kill Steven Carlisle?' the second detective broke in, catching me off guard.

'No!' I swallowed and tried to stay calm. 'No. The last time I saw him, he was alive and running off. I swear.'

But they didn't believe me. I could see it in their faces.

51 – Jenna

I sat cross-legged with my back against the boat door. Half-five, and a sliver of moon stood out from behind the clouds over the willow trees. It lit the water beneath silvery grey. The rest of the canal bank lay in darkness.

I pulled my coat tighter round my body and hugged my knees to my chest.

He should have been back by now. And where was Karen?

A fox screeched from the willow copse, setting my teeth on edge.

Mum and Dad would know I'd snuck out by now. They were supposed to be going out for dinner. They probably wouldn't now.

My phone rang – Dad.

'I'm fine,' I said over him yelling. 'I'll be back later. Leave me alone.' I snapped the phone shut and set it to silent. He called again and this time I blocked the call.

I leaned my head on the door and waited.

The clouds moved and covered over the moon.

In the distance, I heard an engine thrumming through the

night, a motorbike, a big one. It halted on the bridge for a minute and roared off again.

I tucked my hands into my sleeves to defrost my fingers.

Feet crunched on gravel. I turned the torch on and flashed it to the towpath.

Ryan blinked as the light hit his eyes.

'Where've you been?' I jumped up, knees stiff, to go to him, but he got to me first. His arms went round me and I could feel he was shaking. 'What's happened?'

'Tell you in a minute,' he said, hunching down so he could bury his face in my neck.

It's not another girl. It's OK. I rubbed his back. 'Can I come in?'

He let me go. 'Yeah, sorry. Sorry, you're freezing. I'll get the fire going and put the kettle on.' He fished in his pocket and pulled out a key.

I let him get the woodburner going and brew the tea in silence. He put the mugs on the table and tugged me on to his knee, hanging on to me as if he needed to do that to hold it together.

'What's up?' I whispered.

'Got taken in for questioning by the police.'

'Why?' I sat up straight.

'Carlisle.'

'But —'

'They took my DNA on Monday. It's back.'

'Why didn't you tell me? And it can't be back already. Dad's took weeks.'

'I didn't want to worry you. And it took ages with your dad because they had to do the forensics on the body. Matching mine up was quicker. The solicitor reckons they might've asked it to be rushed through.'

'But how can your DNA be . . .?' I stopped as understanding dawned.

'The fight. They've got me on him.'

'But –'

He stared up at me with pleading eyes. 'I didn't kill him.'

'I know.' I kissed his face. Again and again, scattering them over his skin. He sat and let me as if he was drugged. 'They've let you go though, so it's OK now.'

He shook his head. 'I don't know. It might not be.'

'What did you tell them?'

'The truth. About the fight and crashing in your stable. They didn't seem surprised. I think they knew I wasn't with Mum. She went out a few times to look for me that night. Maybe someone saw her and they found that out. They've been questioning lots of people.'

'But you've got an alibi.'

'No, I haven't.'

'Ryan, you did tell them you were with me?'

'No.'

'Ryan!'

'It doesn't matter. I could've done it before you found me.'

'No, they questioned us, don't forget – it happened later. Tell them.'

'You don't know that for sure and your dad is going ape with you already.'

'So what? Don't be stupid. This is a murder. My dad having a strop is nothing compared to this.'

The door opened and Karen came down the steps followed by a man carrying a couple of bike helmets under his arm.

'You got the fire going. Nice one,' the stranger said and he flopped into a chair by the stove, stretching out heavy booted legs. 'Jesus, Karen, have you got any whisky? I could do with one.' He nodded at me. 'All right?'

I'd seen men like him before. Crowds of them gathered in the summer outside the pubs around Whitmere. They'd rip down the roads on their bikes, overtaking cars in a sudden explosion of noise that made my dad jump and swear when they passed us.

'This is Cole,' Ryan said, stroking my arm.

Oh! I looked past the hair and tattoos and found a friendly pair of eyes looking back at me. He winked. 'Don't need him to tell me who you are.'

Karen passed him a mug of whisky and faced us. Her mouth

opened, ready to launch at Ryan. Cole grabbed her hand. 'Not now, Kaz. Leave him. He's had enough.'

To my surprise, she backed off and sat down in the empty chair beside Cole. 'Hello, Jenna,' was all she said.

It was awkward sitting on Ryan's knee in front of them, though they didn't seem to care. Maybe he felt my tension because he nudged me and said, 'I'll walk you home.'

Out on the towpath, he draped an arm round my shoulders. 'They need some space to talk. Is it all right if we walk back slowly?'

'Yeah, of course. If anything happens tomorrow, you will phone me, won't you? Or get your mum to. Please, Ryan.'

He squeezed my arm. 'OK.'

'What's with Cole being here? Are they back together?'

'No. I called him. I had to have an adult in the interview with me. Cole . . . well, Cole isn't fazed by stuff like that. I needed someone who wouldn't freak out.'

'Was it horrible?'

He didn't answer straight away. 'A bit,' he said finally.

'I wish it was me and not you.'

'Don't be stupid.'

'But I do.'

'Well, I don't.' He stopped and kissed me. 'I don't want you involved in any of this.'

I'd always thought Ryan was tougher than me. I knew then

that wasn't always true. I knew it wouldn't bother me to sit through questions and accusations as much as it did him. What I had to walk around with every day was worse than that. But then I had a dad who'd get me the best legal help money could buy, and a village of people behind me who wouldn't believe I'd done it, and friends. He had no proper address, a sick mum and a biker who'd walked out on them once before. Oh, and me.

Not much to take on the criminal justice system with.

'Maybe they're investigating other people too,' I said.

'Maybe.'

He held me extra tight when he said goodnight. 'Love you,' he whispered before he trotted off. He didn't wait for me to say it back.

My reception inside the house was as warm as a January blizzard. Dad stood up as soon as I walked in and Mum refused to look at me.

'Go straight upstairs to your room and stay there. You're grounded. And you can leave your phone here.'

'No,' I said, forcing my voice to stay calm. 'I'll go to bed, but you're not having my phone.'

'You will do as I tell you! I am not having a fourteen-year-old dictating to me under my own roof.'

Charlie whimpered on the sofa for us to stop, but nobody paid him any attention.

'I said no. I had to go out. The police took Ryan in for questioning. I needed to see if he was OK, so you are not having my phone.'

Dad slammed his hand on the table behind the sofa. 'He's in for questioning? Jenna, what kind of people are you associating with? A suspected murderer? Have you gone completely mad?'

'Are you a murderer? They questioned you. He didn't do it, you stupid, fucking idiot!'

So much for keeping my cool. Mum leapt up from the chair and shoved me to the door. 'Get upstairs now. You've done enough for one night.'

I slammed the door on the pair of them.

When I got upstairs, I hid the phone inside my pillowcase in case one of them sneaked in and tried to take it. After I undressed, I lay in the dark fuming. I'd been all prepared to feel bad about spoiling their night out, but not now.

A lot later, I heard a quiet knock at the door. A voice whispered, 'Jen, can I come in?'

Charlie.

He padded over to the bed and crawled under the covers like he used to do when he was younger and had a nightmare. 'Is Ryan in trouble?' He sounded snuffly as if he'd been crying again.

'I don't know. Maybe.'

'You really like him, don't you?'

'Yes.'

'I think he's OK too.'

'That's only because he took you to the fireworks and played football with you.'

'I still think it though.'

'Charlie, what's this about?'

'I didn't know the police suspected Dad.'

'You didn't need to know. It's all over now anyway. They know it wasn't him.'

'You should've told me though, Jen. You should!' His voice hitched.

'Why?'

He didn't answer and tugged at the duvet cover with rough little fingers.

'Charlie, do you want something? Only I'm not really in the mood to talk about this.'

'Is he nice to you?'

'Ryan? Of course he is.'

'How?'

'What?' What's up with him?

'How is he nice?'

'Um, he makes me laugh when I'm fed up. And he talks to me about . . . about stuff that bothers me. He doesn't let me get upset over what people think or say or how they look at me.' I stopped – there were other things, but nothing I'd share with Charlie. 'He's just really nice to be around.'

'Oh, OK . . . I'm going to go to bed now.' He wriggled out from under my covers and paused. 'If I'd done something really bad, would you still love me?'

What? Charlie never said things like that. 'Of course I would. Why?'

'Nothing. Just wondered.' He went out and closed the door quietly behind him.

I felt guilty then, in a way I hadn't over Mum and Dad. All the upset in the house must be getting to him. I should try harder to be nice. Sleep didn't come easily that night.

I woke the next morning to something shaking by my ear. By the time I remembered and reached inside the pillowcase, I had missed the call.

Ryan's number.

'Shit!'

I hit CallBack.

A man answered. 'Hello?'

'Where's Ryan?'

'Is that Jenna? I just called you. It's Cole.'

Panic exploded inside me. 'What's happened?'

'They arrested him this morning. We're down at the station now. He wanted me to tell you – said he'd promised.'

52 – Ryan

What are you supposed to think about when you're waiting in a police interview room? Everything in my head was a tangled mess.

Cole was outside trying to calm Mum down while we waited for the solicitor to arrive. I could hear her yelling from a distance.

Please don't let them think she's mad and cart her off.

Are they going to charge me? Will they lock me up?

Mum, stop screaming, it's not helping. Cole, shut her up before she gets in trouble.

Is Jenna upset? Will she think I've done it now?

This isn't happening, it's not real. It's not real. It is not real.

I swallowed to make the empty, sick feeling go away. I repeated words in my head like Mum with one of her meditation mantras, willing the world to be what she wanted it to be. Make it stop. Make it stop. Make it stop.

A different policewoman to yesterday stuck her head round the door. This one was older, about Mum's age.

'Have you had breakfast?'

'No, I –'

'Bacon and egg roll all right? And a coffee?'

I nodded. I didn't want it, but I did want her to go away.

They'd arrested me at eight o'clock. Must have thought we'd skip off if they didn't get there early. As if you could make a run for it on a narrowboat. Mum had tried to hit one of them and Cole had to hold her back.

She seemed to have stopped screaming. Maybe he'd managed to calm her down.

The policewoman sat with me when she brought my breakfast in. 'Eat it,' she said, as I picked at the roll. 'You won't get anything else until lunchtime and you have to be in a fit state for questioning.'

I took a small bite, chewing slowly, and attempted not to gag.

'Try to manage half,' she said more gently.

I wanted to tell her I didn't kill anyone, but there was no point. Probably everyone said that.

The solicitor arrived eventually, bringing Cole in with him.

'Is Mum OK?'

'Yeah, stop worrying. She's in the waiting room. She's calm now. They'll come and get me if she goes off on one again.' Cole sat in the chair next to me. 'Right, now listen to this guy while he explains how this is different to yesterday.'

I tried to concentrate on the solicitor's words, but the voice in my head was still saying: make it stop make it stop make it stop.

It was the same detectives who came to interview me. Like yesterday, one did most of the talking and the other sat back and watched me. Looking for guilt, I thought.

I went through my story again, but this time they asked me questions for the tape. Why did I hit the lad at the Rugby Club? What did Carlisle say to me after that? Why had they found my blood in the grooves of his ring? Why hadn't I gone home? Why did I lie about being home?

I told them everything like Cole wanted me to.

'Mum was trying to protect me. She knew it looked bad. But I didn't do it.'

They made no comment and moved on. Had I known Carlisle would be on the bridge? Had we arranged to meet there to fight? Was it coincidence or had I followed him there, waiting until the car picked his friends up before I attacked him? What were my motives for attacking him?

On and on and on.

I kept saying I didn't do it, I wasn't there, but they wouldn't stop asking.

After what seemed like hours, another detective came in and called the quiet one out. We waited a few minutes in silence until he came back.

'We have to take a break. There's something we need to look into. I'll get an officer to bring you some tea.'

*

Over an hour passed, in which Cole bobbed in and out between me and Mum, before they came back and started the questions again.

'When you went to the Reeds' stable, you said you were alone there all night. Is that true?'

'Yes.'

This is serious shit. You have to tell them.

I can't do that to her.

This is not a game. You have to.

'Nobody came to the stable while you were there?'

'No.'

Tell them, you idiot.

The detective sat forward. 'I'd like to remind you that you are under caution. Look, Ryan, we need to know exactly what happened. You're all we've got for this right now. If we get it wrong, there's someone still out there who could hurt another person. Maybe this time he could hurt someone you care about. Your girlfriend lives round there. What if she was next?'

Mr Gregson coughed. 'I don't think this line of questioning –'

'Right, right.' He sighed. 'I'll make it easier for you, Ryan. We've just taken a statement from Miss Reed. She tells us she was with you in the stable on the night in question. Is that true?'

A lump formed in my throat. Why did she do that?

'Mr Gregson, can you explain to your client the severity of

the offence he is under arrest for? I'm not sure he's quite understanding.'

'Shut up and give him a minute,' Cole snapped. He shifted his hand from the back of my chair to make slow circles on my shoulder.

The clock on the wall ticked as they all waited.

'Were you and Miss Reed in the stable together on the night Steven Carlisle died?' the detective asked.

I nodded slowly.

'I need you to say it for the tape, Ryan.'

'Yes.'

'Why did you tell us earlier that you were alone?'

'I didn't want Jenna to get in trouble with her parents.'

The policeman rocked back in his chair and made an exasperated sound.

'My client is a juvenile,' Gregson reminded him. 'I think he's just demonstrated that his failure to disclose absolute events stems more from that than a desire to withhold evidence.'

The detective rubbed his head. 'Yeah, OK. Ryan, look, we need to go through all this again now. After you had the fight with Carlisle . . . give it to me again, the real version this time.'

Cole kept his hand on my back.

'I walked over to Jenna's. Slowly. I was drinking the vodka. I stopped to sit down a few times. It started to go to my head.'

'You finished the bottle?'

336

'More or less. It might've had a tiny bit left in the bottom. I chucked it in a hedge.'

'Where?'

'Must've been somewhere on the road down to Jenna's. Barker's Lane, I think it's called.'

'OK, go on.'

'I went to the stable and let myself in the feed store because I was cold.'

'Did you have a coat with you?'

'No. I-I didn't stop to pick one up when I left. I just wanted to get away. Um . . . then I crashed out. I woke up when Jenna came in and turned the light on.'

'Tell me what happened then.'

'She sat with me for a while. I was quite out of it. She asked me if I wanted her to stay and I said yes. I know that was wrong, but I was smashed and I didn't think . . .'

'And?'

'I . . . was . . . upset. Over some things Mum said. I-I didn't want to be on my own.'

'And what exactly did your mother say?'

'Is that really relevant?' Gregson said. 'It is clearly distressing to my client and –'

'Your client is under arrest for murder. I'd say anything that distresses him is highly relevant,' the detective retorted. 'We need to understand his state of mind at this point.'

'Mum's not well. She doesn't mean what she says when she's like that.'

'Ryan, we're not here to judge your mother but to establish who killed a young man. Please answer the question.'

I stared at a scratch on the table. 'She said I was a disappointment to her and she went on for a bit about how all men are bastards. She said she was going out to get . . . to get laid and I should go with her if I was so bothered about her taking risks with strangers. She said stuff about Cole. About how he never cared about us, especially me, and that he only pretended to so he could keep in with her. And . . . and . . .'

'What?'

'She said she loved him.'

Cole's hand stiffened on my back.

'That was what did it, I guess. I thought she'd told him that and he'd left us anyway. So I took off. She yelled at me to get out.'

'Did you intend to go back?'

'Not until the morning. I thought she'd bring a guy home and I didn't want to be there when she did. She's ill, you see, and that's part of her illness, but she can't see that when she's in the middle of it and –'

The detective held his hand up. 'OK, I get the picture.'

'I think we should take a break,' Gregson said.

Cole leaned forward. 'Do you want to take a break, kiddo?'

'No, I want to get it over with.' And I did. Wanted them to stop asking questions I didn't want to answer. Wanted to stop betraying Mum. I stopped caring about whether they'd charge me or not as long as they left me alone. 'Jenna went back to the house and got some food and blankets. I sobered up a bit after I had something to eat. Then we went to sleep. We were there until the morning.' I stared at the policemen. 'We were asleep. Nothing more. I mean it.'

'You said she left and came back. Can you give us the times?'

'Don't know. Didn't look. I was too out of it. Oh . . . she said something . . . when she first came down. About me being cold and it wasn't eleven yet. She didn't think I should sleep there.'

'So at around eleven o'clock, were you alone or was she there?' His eyes nailed me to the chair.

'I don't know. I told you. If I had to guess, alone probably.'

'Stop there,' Gregson cut in. 'We are straying into conjecture. How is this relevant?'

The quiet one kept watching me as he answered. 'Because at the estimated time of death of the victim, which is eleven o'clock, your client has no alibi. Miss Reed was back at the house.'

'You're surely not suggesting that he left the stables in an inebriated state, wandered down to the canal, happened across the victim and murdered him, before returning and pretending nothing had happened.'

339

'If he was drunk.'

'I assume his girlfriend corroborates that.'

'She's fourteen, Mr Gregson. Young enough to be taken in by a clever act.'

Cole slammed his fist on the table. 'Cut the crap! You know he didn't do it. He's a kid, not a criminal mastermind.'

They ignored him. 'Ryan, did Carlisle jump you again? Was it self-defence on your part? Did it all go too far?'

I sank my head into my hands. 'No, I never saw him after he ran off in the village. I keep telling you.'

The detective leaned towards me. 'I'm going to ask you one final time. Did you kill Steven Carlisle?'

I sat up and looked right back at him. 'No.'

'I think he's made himself clear.' Gregson looked at his watch. 'Are you going to charge him or release him?'

'Neither,' the policeman said. 'I'm going to get a search going for this vodka bottle. I can hold him here until the morning if we need to.'

'He's a juvenile and –'

'And he's NFA.'

I looked a question at Gregson.

'No fixed address,' he told me.

'What if you find the bottle?' I asked.

'If you drank from it and didn't just pour it out then we'll find saliva traces.'

'Won't that take days?'

'Yes. There's secure juvenile accommodation about thirty miles away. If we charge you, you'll go there. If we don't find the bottle then . . .' He shrugged. 'Makes the decision easier.'

Suddenly it was real. It wasn't going away. I wasn't going home. Maybe ever.

Cole made them give us some time alone before they took me down to the cell. He said it was best I did go in there – lie down and get some rest.

'They're never going to make this stick. That guy knows you didn't do it. It's all over his face. But you're all they've got. Come on, if you'd been setting your lass up as cover, you'd have told them about her from the start. He knows that.'

'Cole, will you look after Mum for me?' I couldn't focus on him properly. The colours of his face whirled and mixed to a blur.

He grabbed me and shook me. 'Pack that in. You're getting out of here. They've got to exhaust everything before they let you go. But they will let you go.' He softened his grip and rubbed my arms. 'What Karen said, none of it was true. You know what a bitch she is when she's losing it.' I nodded and he stepped closer and pulled my head to his. 'Worse thing I ever did, leaving you two.'

'What about that woman? Your new one.'

He snorted. 'Lasted all of two months. Just long enough for me to stop being mad at Karen and start missing her.' He ruffled my hair. 'And you.'

'Why didn't you call?'

'Your mother's not exactly the forgiving type when it comes to men who screw up. I didn't think she'd listen.'

'Do you love her, Cole?'

He flushed. I'd never seen him do that before. 'Yeah, always have. Only I never told her.'

'Look after her for me. If I need you to.'

He started to protest.

'Please? I need to know you will.'

He sighed and nodded. 'You get your head down and get some rest. You look all in. I'll be here waiting. I'm not going anywhere till they let you out.'

53 – Jenna

The car wound along the lanes as Dad drove me back from the police station, and I stared out of the window. At the forked roads leading to Strenton, a herd of cows was moving from one pasture to another and filling the lane we normally took. Dad grunted and took the longer route to avoid getting stuck behind them.

I stiffened as I realised where we were heading and he glanced over at me, but he said nothing.

Harton Brook. We never came this way any more.

'Can you stop for a minute, please?' I asked as we slowed to take the bridge.

He pulled over without answering and we sat there with the engine idling. By the side of the bridge, a white rose stood in a tin vase. I frowned at it. Weird – a rose in November.

'Thanks for taking me to the station,' I said.

'Do I need to take you to the doctor?' He stared down into the field where Steven's car had exploded. 'I suppose it's your mother you want to talk to about this.'

'Why do I need to see a doctor?'

'To test . . .'

'What? If I'm pregnant?' I didn't shout — not here. 'There's no need. I told you. I told them. In a police statement. We kissed. We went to sleep. End of. Why can't you believe me?'

The field beside us gave me my answer.

'Dad, I made a mistake when I got into that car. I did something stupid. I knew it was wrong. I knew I couldn't trust them. I knew that all along. But this is different. Ryan's different.'

He slipped the brake off and put the car into gear. A petal fluttered from the white rose in the draught of air as the car passed. I saw it fall to the ground in the side mirror as we drove away.

I went straight upstairs when we got home. Mum came and sat on my bed. 'You've done your best, sweetheart. Let's hope it's enough.'

'You don't believe he did it then?'

'Oh, Jenna.' She sighed. 'You read such awful things in the paper about what teenage boys do to each other. And the people who know them always say they can't have done it.' She shifted position to sit against the pillows beside me. 'But I can't believe it of Ryan, no. Dad told me about the questions they asked. I can't imagine how they can think a boy of that age could plan all that, and then act as if nothing had happened.'

'Unless they think I'm covering up for him. That I wanted Steven dead too.'

She leaned her head against mine. 'I know you didn't.'

We sat for a while in silence, watching the afternoon sun move lower towards the horizon through my window.

'I'm so proud of you,' she said. 'To do that. All those questions and accusations. You've come a long way since . . . A long way.'

Tears welled up in my eyes. I blinked them back. 'He's helped me so much, Mum. None of you understand.'

'I do, Jenna. I see it every day. And if you tell us nothing happened between you that Dad and I need to worry about, then I believe you.' She smiled. 'I'd better go down and think about dinner. You have a rest. I'm sure we'll get some good news soon.'

As she got up, I remembered something. 'Mum, have you ever seen roses flower at this time of year?'

She thought. 'Iceberg does. It's a floribunda. You won't remember, but we had one at our old house.'

'What colour?'

'White. A beautiful milky white. Sometimes ours even had a few blooms at Christmas in a mild winter. A very prolific flowerer – goes right through the summer and on through the autumn if you keep deadheading. They tend to ball in the rain, but that's their only fault. Why?'

'Nothing. Nothing really.'

*

The hours passed and still there was no call. I thought about Ryan, locked up in that place, and I tried not to cry because he wouldn't want me to. But when the sun disappeared and the room slipped into darkness, I couldn't stop myself.

My door opened. 'Jen?'

I scrubbed my face with my hand and turned the bedside lamp on.

My little brother edged towards me. 'Have they let Ryan out?'

'No.'

'Didn't they believe you?'

'I don't think so.'

He crawled on to my bed and sat on his knees. 'Jen, will you come and help me with something? I can't do it on my own.'

'Not now, Charlie. Really, I can't.'

He grabbed my hand and tugged it. 'You don't understand. I-I might be able to help.'

'Charlie, I'm really not in the mood —'

'But it might help Ryan!'

I sat up sharply. 'What do you mean?'

'I don't know. Just come with me.'

I'd never seen my brother like this, quivering with tension, his face pale and strained. Whatever it was, it was better to find out where we couldn't be overheard so I nodded and got up.

We went downstairs together. 'Ponies, Mum,' I yelled, to

prevent any awkward questions as he dragged me out of the front door. 'Back soon.'

Charlie led me around the house and down to the garden shed. Turning the torch on, he opened the door and rummaged on the rack inside.

'What're you doing?'

'Getting a trowel. Come on.'

I stopped him. 'Look, I want to know what's going on. You said you might be able to help Ryan. How? Tell me.'

'I can't tell you,' he said, pulling my arm agitatedly. 'I'm trying to show you.'

This was getting annoying. If this was another of his stupid pranks . . . but he was still white and drawn. 'One more minute, Charlie. That's it – that's all I'm giving you.'

He set off down the garden again and I trudged after him. He'd better not be messing me about.

When we got into the paddock, he turned the torch off.

'Are you ready?'

'No, I'm not going another step with you until you tell me what this is about.'

I couldn't see his face in the darkness, but the strain I'd noticed earlier was replicated in his voice. 'I saw something. The morning after Steven died. Just after you came home. I saw something from my bedroom window,' he whispered.

'You saw what, and why didn't you say anything before?'

'I didn't know about Dad. I didn't know they suspected him. And I don't know what I saw. Not really.'

'Charlie, what are you talking about? This is crazy. Just say it, will you?'

'Just after you came back, after I listened at the door and heard you coming up the stairs, I got back into bed and I saw something out of the window. I got my binoculars out. And I watched . . . Look, Jen, we just need to go and see . . . shut up and come on.'

He scurried off and I stood watching him for a moment. He was infuriating, and this 'I can't tell you' business was grating on my already shredded nerves. But if he had seen something – what I couldn't imagine – maybe it had upset him so much he couldn't bring himself to tell me. Whatever, he was only ten and when he got upset, which wasn't often, he wasn't very good at hiding it. I sighed and followed him through a gap in the hedge into Lindsay's garden. He was definitely upset now so I'd indulge him a little bit longer, but why were we going here?

Charlie crept ahead of me, keeping low, until we came to the rose garden where he stopped and pointed into the darkness.

I squinted and caught a gleam of something pale.

'What?' I whispered. 'What am I looking at?'

'There. In front of you,' he whispered back.

I rolled my eyes, snatched the torch from him and turned it on.

'Be careful,' he muttered and stood behind me.

'What are you doing?'

'Hiding the light from the house.'

'Don't be silly. There's only Lindz's dad in.'

The torch shone on a rose bush which still held a few blooms. Perfect white blooms with a familiar look. I moved the torch slowly over the bush.

'This? This is what you brought me to see?' Ryan was locked up and he dragged me here to look at a bush. I got ready to be angry.

But something stopped me. The way Charlie's voice had sounded, that scared look on his face, and those roses . . . that I'd seen before.

I played the torch over the bush. At the base was a plaque and I crouched down to see it. 'God gave us memories that we might have roses in December,' I read slowly.

A shiver ran up my spine. Something wasn't right here. Not at all.

Charlie pushed me aside. 'Hold the torch and keep watch.' He knelt on the ground and began to dig by the bush. When I cast the torch beam around, I saw it was planted on its own in an island bed, no other plants near it at all. Another shiver ran through me.

'Charlie, what are you doing? What exactly did you see?' I recognised the feeling that started to churn my stomach. It was fear.

'I saw Mr Norman. He was burying something here. It looked like . . . Oh, shush, Jen. I need to find out.' He dug frantically, piling the soil to one side.

I waited, casting glances back up to the house to make sure Mr Norman hadn't seen us. Goosepimples rose on my skin as my brother dug deeper and deeper. Lindz's dad? He couldn't have anything to do with this. It was as crazy as the idea that my dad could –

Charlie recoiled, bashing into my leg, and I dropped the torch. 'Shit! Be careful, you made me jump.'

He scrabbled to retrieve it, but I grabbed it from him again. 'What did you see?' I shone it into the hole. 'Oh God!'

I went cold from head to toe. My brother's face was ashen.

We looked down at a woollen jumper. Even stained from being buried in the soil for weeks, the stiff crust on the wool was clear in the torchlight. A dark, dried crust.

Charlie reached into his pocket and pulled out one of the rubber gloves Mum kept under the kitchen sink. He put it on and pulled the jumper out of the hole.

'Charlie, is that –'

'Yes.'

Underneath the jumper was a pair of beige canvas trousers spattered with the same dark marks as the jumper. And beneath those, shoes and socks stuffed in them. Charlie pulled them out and last of all we saw a box, placed carefully in the bottom of the hole. A wooden casket with a brass plate on the lid. 'Lindsay Norman. Beloved daughter.'

I think I froze for a moment. I could hear the blood drumming in my ears, but I didn't move. Just stared at the box containing Lindsay's ashes, even my eyes paralysed.

'Jen?' Charlie whispered. 'What do we do?'

The torchlight wobbled as my hand shook. 'Put them back. Cover them up. Quick. We've got to get out of here.'

I tried to steady the torch while he worked.

It couldn't be true . . . I couldn't have seen this . . . NO!

But I had. He'd buried those things on top of her. Like a sacrifice. Like he thought this was justice. Steven's blood for hers.

It made me want to cry and never stop, because for a second, something inside said I understood and that it was fair. My heart broke a little bit for Mr Norman then.

I pulled Charlie up as soon as the hole was refilled and switched off the torch. We ran down the garden, fought through the hedge and didn't stop running until we got home. I flung the door open and shoved him in and locked it behind us.

'Jen?' Charlie's voice wobbled. 'I'm sorry. I should've told . . .'

'Why didn't you? Oh, Charlie, God, why didn't you?'

Fat tears sprang in his eyes and fell down his cheeks. 'He used to buy me sweets at the shop. He gave me all his bird-watching magazines. Even his binoculars. Last year, he helped me make the nesting box on the shed.' He buried his head against me. 'He'd never have hurt anyone except him. Never. And I hate Steven. He's wrecked everything. I don't care if Mr Norman killed him. He deserves it.'

And now they'd lock him up, my best friend's dad . . . and that was so unfair because . . . because . . .

'But it's different now. Because of Ryan. I can't not tell, can I, Jen? I don't want to, but we have to, don't we?'

Ryan. Who didn't do it. Who was there now, locked up for something he hadn't done. And so, yes . . . I'm sorry, Mr Norman, so, so sorry . . . we had to.

'Dad! Mum!'

Dad appeared first in the hall, worry creasing his forehead as he looked at Charlie crying, and me . . . because I realised I was crying too.

'You have to call the police, Dad. We know who killed Steven.'

54 – Ryan

I must have drifted off eventually because the clanging of the cell door woke me up. 'Come on, son. Get up.' It was the detective who'd questioned me.

'Did you find the bottle? What time is it?'

'It's after midnight. And yes, we found the bottle a while ago.' He handed me a cup of coffee. 'Get this down you. We found a lot more than the bottle. I'm sorry we've left you down here so long with no news, but something came up and I was called out.' He looked exhausted, his eyes bloodshot.

'So what now?' I took a gulp of coffee to clear my muzzy head.

'You're going home.'

I spluttered into the cup. 'But you said –'

'Got a patrol car coming round to drive you and your parents back.' He smiled, an apology in it. 'I told you something came up. We got who did it. Full confession.'

'Who is it?' I couldn't quite take it in – I was going home?

'The Reeds' neighbour, John Norman. His daughter was killed in the car Carlisle crashed.'

Lindsay's dad . . . 'How did you find out?'

'The Reeds' little boy saw him burying the clothes he was in when he killed Carlisle. He didn't report it until he found out we'd arrested the wrong person.' Carter shrugged. 'He's only a kid and he liked the guy from all accounts – didn't understand he should have told someone. Anyway, we didn't even have to question Norman. He came clean on the lot once he was told we had someone in custody for it. I wanted to come down and tell you myself. You're free to go and there's two people out there desperate to get you home, so let's see if that car is ready, eh?'

The next time I woke up, I was in my own bed. I rubbed my eyes and reached for my phone.

One missed message.

<xxx Call me when u wake up. Not going 2 school 2day>

The last thing I'd done before I collapsed into bed at half one this morning was to text Jenna.

I crawled out from under the covers, my mouth and throat dry.

'Hey, how're you feeling?' Cole asked as I staggered towards the kettle. He and Mum were sitting round the table with a map spread out.

'Need tea,' I groaned and flicked the kettle on.

Mum sprang up. 'I'll do it. You sit down. I'll heat you some soup.'

'Thanks. What's with the map?'

Cole looked away. 'I'll make the tea,' he said to Mum. 'You tell him.'

I met Jenna in the paddock later. She ran down the field and threw her arms round my neck. 'Are you all right? Oh God, was it awful? But you're out. It's over. Did you hear about Mr Norman?'

'Yeah, the police told me.' I held her tight for a moment, then I swallowed hard and pushed her away. 'There's something I need to tell you.'

She looked up at me, big confused eyes. 'What's wrong?'

'We're leaving.' I'm sorry . . . I'm sorry . . . I don't want to . . .

Her head jerked back like I'd slapped her. 'W-what?'

'Mum wants to move on.' I tried . . . I yelled . . . I fought . . . Two hours we screamed at each other.

'When?' But she knew, I could tell.

'Today. Soon. She won't wait. Not after what's happened. She wants to get away from here.' I tried every threat and bribe I could think of, but she won't listen. 'I knew this'd happen eventually. I-I didn't think it'd be so fast. I thought we'd have longer or I'd never have . . . This is why I don't get involved. This is what we do — we move on.' I wiped her tear away with my cuff, but another fell to replace it, and another. 'Don't, please don't. I'm sorry. I should never have got into this, but I thought this time I could make it different. I was wrong.'

Jenna buried her face against me and I held her as tight as I could.

'What am I going to do without you?' she mumbled.

'You're going to go out with your friends. You're going to be happy. You're going to be yourself. And you're going to remember that you don't care what anyone thinks except the people who matter to you.' I stroked her hair — last time — shiny, wheat-coloured silk.

'I can't do that without you,' she snuffled, her fingers knotted into the front of my shirt.

'Yes, you can. I know you can.' I lifted her face between my hands and kissed it — kissed it all over.

'It's not fair,' she said. 'Why does she do this to you? What about you? You've got a job and —'

'She's ill. That's how it is. I can't always do what I want right now. She needs me.'

'I need you!' The tears ran faster down her face.

'Don't make it harder. I don't want to go, but I have to. I tried, but . . .' *Don't, please, or you'll make me cry too and it'll be worse for both of us then.*

She sniffed hard, once, twice. 'I won't forget you.'

I felt like there was a knife in my guts, twisting and tearing me open. I kissed her one last time. 'I want you to forget me.' *I won't ever forget you.* I stepped away from her. 'I have to go. We're leaving soon. She wants to make some distance before dark.'

Jenna scrubbed her sleeve over her eyes.

'Don't call,' I said, and I didn't know how I got the words out. 'It only makes it tougher.'

I looked back once – when I got to the trees. I told myself not to, but I couldn't help it. She was standing in the same spot, watching me go.

Cole stood at the bar and steered the boat down the canal and away from Strenton. I sat with him, leaning against the door and watching the trees disappear as we travelled down the water.

I forgot to say thank you. For believing me all the way through. For going to the police to stand up for me. I should've said that.

55 – Jenna

I forgot to say I love you. I should've said that before you left.

I staggered through the next day at school on autopilot. Beth was all hugs and sympathy, but I couldn't talk about it. When the bus dropped me home that afternoon, I diverted round to the canal and stood on the towpath where *Liberty* had been moored. Hoping against everything that they'd still be there. But of course they weren't.

He'd gone. Not a trace remained that he'd ever been here.

When I took Raggs out that evening, it really hit me. Without Ryan beside me, the loss rose up in my throat, choking me. Suffocating. Too much even to cry at first.

Nobody to tell me it didn't matter who stared. Nobody to make me feel it didn't matter, because he liked my face just fine as it was and other people didn't count. Nobody to make me feel like they needed me too. To make my skin feel tingly when he touched it. To tell me he loved me. To be my best friend.

That night with Raggs felt like the first time I'd gone out alone after the accident. I'd slipped out of our garden gate into the paddock and watched him go crazy around the field while I cowered by the hedge. Checking, checking all the time for anyone who might see me. The paddock had seemed so big and I wanted to run back inside and shut the door on a world I didn't recognise any more. Stay hidden, stay safe, so I'd never have to see how people reacted to my face. The shudders, the revulsion. The thought of people I knew seeing . . .

It choked me like losing Ryan choked me now.

I could go back to how things had been before I met him. But if he knew I was hiding away again, he'd be so mad. I knew what he'd say. 'Whether I'm there or not, it doesn't make any difference. When I was there, I thought you were hot, didn't I? So why do you give a shit over what some dick thinks.'

I didn't want to let him down.

The full story behind Steven's murder came out over the next few weeks. Dad went to see Mr Norman where they'd locked him up in some kind of secure hospital. He told Dad he'd walked down to the crash site at Harton Brook to leave a white rose beside the bridge. He did that regularly. He left the lights and the TV on in the house because this was his private thing and he wanted it kept that way, something nobody should know about but him. That made a kind of sense to me. He must have just got back when Mr Crombie saw him locking up. To have been able to close up the house so calmly after what he'd just done, that made my flesh goosepimple, but Dad said it showed how badly his mind had been affected.

When Mr Norman was returning from the brook, he'd seen Steven on the bridge with his mates as they waited for their lift. They were all joking and messing around. Steven's new girlfriend was there too. Mr Norman watched him kissing her.

Something inside him snapped, he said to Dad. Because Steven was alive to do that and Lindsay wasn't. He watched from the trees until the car picked the others up. Steven waved to them before turning to walk back and then Mr Norman rushed him. Said he found the strength of a man half his age. He grabbed Steven from behind. He didn't give him a chance to struggle, not even to cry out. And he beat Steven's head down on to the stone wall of the bridge.

Once.

Twice.

Steven was dead by then, but Mr Norman didn't stop. He didn't stop until Steven's skull was completely smashed in.

Then he went home.

The police had talked to him too of course, in the early days of the investigation. But he told them he hadn't left the house and they had no reason to doubt that after Mr Crombie's statement.

He'd never wanted anyone else to take the blame. Cocooned in his house and shutting the world out, he hadn't known the police had questioned Dad. He hadn't known about Ryan either.

He said he didn't care what happened to him – he would've confessed except he didn't want to leave Lindsay.

What hurt now, he told Dad, was thinking of her lying alone there with no one to care for her.

'I said I'd keep an eye on the house for him,' Dad said. 'I thought of how I'd feel if it was you and how I felt when I saw you in hospital lying there with your head in bandages. If I was him and it was you buried in my garden, I wouldn't want you there alone with weeds growing up over you.'

'But, Dad, they suspected you at first. Aren't you furious with him for putting you through that?'

He stared into space. 'When I saw his face . . . Jenna, I've known that man for years. Do you remember that Sunday the pipes burst and he came over to help clear up and fix the leak because we couldn't get a plumber to come out? He cancelled his golf engagement, rolled up his sleeves and pitched in without a second thought. And those Christmas parties he used to arrange for you kids down at the village hall. Before his marriage broke up, he was always smiling. He had time for everyone. He made time. Now . . . now he sits there in that place and his eyes are dead. You can't watch someone broken down to that and resent them.'

I remembered Charlie and the binoculars and the birdbox Mr Norman helped him make. How my brother cried when he told the police. Dad was right.

One night, one mistake . . . so many echoes. If only we could turn it all back.

Dad arranged for the house to be secured and shut up. He went over every weekend to check the gardener he'd hired was doing the job right. But he told the man to leave the white rose bush alone. My father tended that himself.

Gradually, Strenton returned to normal. Children went out again without escort. The Carlisles relocated and the house went up for sale. Even Charlie found his smile again, though it took a while. In some way, looking out for him took the edge off missing Ryan. When the village turned on its scanty string of Christmas lights along the main lane and Mum took us to the city to do our Christmas shopping and see the streets lit up with Santas and neon trees and stars, the Charlie we knew began to come back. Every morning, he ran to open the window on his advent calendar and show me the picture hiding behind the chocolate. And then he would eat the chocolate right in front of me with his mouth open about three inches from my face, making disgusting slobbering noises, and gloating that I didn't have any.

When we broke up from school for the Christmas holidays, Beth's parents let her throw a party for her friends. Not a big affair, about fifteen of us including Max. Food and soft drinks and silly party games, the kind you can only play at our age at

Christmas because it'd be too uncool at any other time.

Safe and secure with people who were used to my face, I could forget and get as much into it as they did. Except I could always see Ryan's ghost in the corner of my eye, lounging on the sofa and laughing at me as I lost another round of Pin the Tail on Rudolph. And missing him made the breath tight in my chest.

'Are you thinking about him again?' Beth asked as I helped her plate up the profiteroles in the kitchen. She didn't say his name; it wasn't necessary.

'All the time.'

'You've coped really well,' she said. 'Most people think you're totally over him.'

But missing Ryan was my private thing. I didn't want that on display for others. So I didn't cry over him, except sometimes in the solitude of my own room on bad nights. He wouldn't want me to anyway. But a little piece of me was never there with the rest, like a smashed china vase where the last chip can't be found.

I never let anyone see how many times a day I checked my phone at first, hoping he'd text even though he'd said that would only make it worse. How often I sat there wondering whether to ignore what he'd said and call anyway. How, as the weeks went on and he didn't get in touch, I imagined him finding some other girl and what they might be doing together – I hated her so much, whoever she was. I wanted to shred her face with my nails. At other times I was scared for him that his mum was ill and he was alone, having to cope with that in a strange place. That he needed a hug and there was no one to do that now.

He'd told me to forget him. There was no chance. Every day the wound opened fresh when he wasn't there to tell some funny thing to, or to make me laugh with his stupid random comments.

After we opened the presents on Christmas morning, I was sitting in the kitchen helping Mum with the vegetables when I heard the text tone on my phone. I didn't pick it up immediately. It'd been going off all morning with messages from Beth and Max and the crowd at school. When I did look at it after I put the sprouts in the pan, I stopped breathing for a moment.

One missed message.

Ryan.

<Merry Christmas x>

My thumbs shook as I texted back.

<Merry Christmas 2 u 2 x>

For the rest of the day I kept the phone in my pocket, hoping he'd call, but he didn't and the missing-him wound cracked open again.

56 – Ryan

Late in January, Cole and I sat in the snug of a canalside pub. We'd left Mum on the boat. He wanted to talk to me alone.

'Got some news for you, kiddo, and I want you to be honest with me about how it sits with you.'

'You leaving again?'

He laughed, nervously for Cole. 'No, the opposite.'

'You're sticking around then?'

'Yeah. That all right with you?'

I took a mouthful of my pint. 'Yeah, I guess.'

He watched me carefully. 'Sure?'

I grinned and shoved him. 'Course I am, you stupid git.'

He chuckled and shoved me back. 'Got some other news for you too then. Me and Karen have been talking. About us, about you. Kaz has kind of come round to my way of thinking.'

'Yeah?'

'She's fed up with watching you prowling round the place like a caged bear so we're gonna look for a house and make a base for ourselves. It'll take a while. We've got to find the right spot, get jobs, sell the boat for a deposit –'

I burst out laughing. 'Are you telling me you two are getting a mortgage?'

He grimaced. 'Guess so. It comes to us all, growing up. Just took me and her a bit longer.'

'You really want this?'

'It's time. Long past time. And you can get another job then. Make some mates of your own. She does see that, you know, that you hate the moving on. Or she does now.'

Pity she saw it too late.

'So what do you reckon?' he asked.

I raised my glass to him. 'I reckon we celebrate.'

57 – Jenna

Valentine's Day shouldn't be in February, I've always thought. Not in a month with ice on the wind and stinging rain. It should be in green spring or hot, lazy summer. But what do I know? When other girls were getting cards and cuddly bears, I didn't even bother to check the post.

I sat slumped in front of the TV with Charlie watching mid-morning cartoons.

'Jenna,' Mum called. 'Something here for you.'

I went through to the hall. 'What?'

'A letter,' she said, passing me an envelope and going back to the kitchen.

The name and address on the envelope were mine, but there was no postcode.

I opened it.

A card with a teddy bear holding a big red heart in its hands, no words in the card, just one X.

I turned the envelope over. The postmark was smudged and I couldn't make out where it was from.

Ryan?

Who else?

But he wouldn't know our postcode . . .

I went up to my bedroom to think. If it wasn't him and I texted him . . .

But what if it was?

It took me an hour to decide and hold my breath and send him a single kiss in return.

He didn't reply.

When the roses began to flower again after Easter, I went to the white Iceberg in Lindsay's garden to cut a rose to take to the bridge, and I sat and talked to her for a while.

'I want to tell you something, Lindz. I don't think back when you were alive that I'd have had the courage to say this to you. Or that I even knew it myself. You were always the one who drew people to you. The pretty one. So confident. So sure of yourself. Like the sun, and I always felt bleached out trailing behind you.'

I paused and fingered a perfect bud.

'But you weren't always nice, Lindz. Or kind. The stuff you used to say about Beth and people like her. How you ripped them because they weren't as pretty or popular as you. You never looked beyond that. Never looked at what's great about people inside. If the wrapper didn't look right, you weren't interested.'

I took a deep breath.

'So what I want to say to you is this. Ugly people do have feelings too, Lindz. We're just like the rest of you, and I think everyone should know that.'

Fast-forward

The sun wakes me up early. I smile at the view through the window – wisps of mist clearing to blue sky. It's Saturday and the whole weekend stretches before me.

For now, I have the house to myself, listening to the quiet disturbed only by the birds chirping outside. In half an hour I'll get up and let Raggs out and make breakfast. I'll take him for a walk and then maybe go for a long ride on Scrabble. Until then I sit and listen to the morning.

When I get back from riding, Mum wants me to go into Whitmere with her. We're halfway there when my phone buzzes.

<U busy l8r?>

I stare and stare at the phone screen. At the caller ID display. Then I text <No>

<Canal. 3.30 if u can>

I stare and stare again. Are they passing through on their way to somewhere? I can't believe they could be coming back to stay. I can't let myself because if I do and they're not, that would kill me all over again.

I text him back <K>

And suddenly it's a whole different day, charged with expectation and the torture of waiting.

When it's finally time and I walk down to the canal, I stop just short of the towpath and peek out from the branches. But there's no boat, just a long expanse of orange as far as I can see.

I check my watch. Three o'clock and the sun is heavy and lazy in the blue. I know now how fast narrowboats travel and I should be able to see them if they're coming.

I sit on the towpath with my back against an alder tree and I wait, and wait.

The minute hand on my watch crawls round, but there's still no sign of the boat in the distance.

I wonder if it's a joke. Could he have changed so much that he'd do that to me? It's over six months since I saw him. He could have grown into someone else entirely, got harder, lost that side that makes him care about the people who need him.

My watch reads three-thirty after what feels like hours of waiting. I look up and down the canal again. It's as boat-free as it's been since I got here.

They could be stuck at a lock. But wouldn't he have called?

The hum of insects on the water and the birdsong from the trees are drowned out by the thrum of a motorbike. I notice the new noise half-heartedly. It's a familiar sound, one of those small bikes that the farm lads ride. Probably someone on his way to milking.

The bike stops on the bridge and the rider kills the engine.

I look round in surprise.

A figure comes down the steps. Jeans, heavy boots, a motorcycle jacket under one arm and a helmet under the other. I can't see his face – the sun dazzles it out. But I recognise the walk.

He comes closer. He's a little taller, I think, and broader in the shoulders. As he steps under the shade of the trees, I see that the fairer tints are back in his hair now and he's got that honey tan back.

I can't move.

'Hey,' he says and I see he's nervous. His eyes greet me and flicker away. He reminds me of those moorland ponies again, ready to shy and bolt.

My mouth feels like I'm chewing cotton wool.

He sits next to me, a few inches separating us. My skin tingles and I want to touch him, but I can't move and I don't know if he wants me to.

'I missed you,' he says, looking at his boots. The toe caps are scuffed. Work boots, I think. 'How are you?'

'I missed you too,' I say and my voice is stilted and sticks in my claggy throat.

He turns his face to me and a smile grows there. Slow at first, but it spreads. Infectious, because I feel the corners of my frozen mouth lift.

'What've you been up to?' he asks.

'You first.'

My eyes flit away because his don't leave my face and it's too much and not enough.

'Been busy. A lot's changed. Mum's better, for now at least. Her and Cole are back together.'

I find a smile for that news. It comes unbidden.

'They sold the boat and bought a house.'

My jaw drops.

He gives a little laugh. 'Yeah, I know. I couldn't believe it when they told me either. It's only a small place, but it's got a garden and a real kitchen. Mum's got herself a shop in a craft centre. She rents one out to sell her jewellery and Cole got a job at a garden centre doing the deliveries. Hey, we've even got a TV now.'

So why are you here? To tell me you're never coming back?

'What about you? Your turn.'

I found enough voice to answer. 'Oh, exams. Just finished.'

'They go OK?'

'I think so.'

'Anything else?' His eyes search my face and I don't know why.

'I suppose I've been getting into the loop again. Getting out more. I made some new friends and I see a lot of Beth and Max.'

'They still together?'

I nod.

So does he. 'That's good. They're all right, those two.' He pauses and watches a mallard flap out of the water and waddle along the opposite bank. 'And you? You seeing anyone?'

I shake my head, but he's still staring at the duck and he doesn't see me. 'No.'

'Oh.' And he keeps looking at that duck. 'You got my card, didn't you?'

'Yes.' I want to ask . . . it takes me a while, but . . . 'What about you? Are you?'

'Nope. Haven't wanted to.'

A dragonfly buzzes low over the water and it's my turn to stare out over the canal.

'I got my job back,' he says, facing me again now I'm not looking at him. 'At the marina. Once we got our new place, I went down there. Pete took me on and he's got me on a day-release thing at college to learn the electrical stuff. Bill's getting a bit stiff with arthritis and they could do with another pair of hands for the heavy work. It's a bit of a trek – our house is about twenty miles from here – but Cole bought me the bike. I started back there last week.'

I draw my breath in.

'Oh, and I forgot. Mum and Cole are trying for a baby. She reckons it might not happen. Says she's probably too old, but

Cole says you never know and it's worth a shot. Be good if they do have a kid. He's a great dad.'

Ryan touches my hand like a cat pats for attention, light, a brush and no more. I drag my eyes back to him.

'When I said goodbye, there was something I wanted to say, but I didn't. Because I didn't think it could happen and it wouldn't have been fair.'

'What?'

He smiles and brushes my nose with his forefinger. 'You've got freckles there. Cute.'

My heart thuds inside my ribs so hard I think I can hear it.

'I wanted to say I'd come back if I could. But that might never have happened. And that day was . . . I wasn't thinking straight.'

'No, of course you weren't.'

'I should've said thank you for what you did too. Didn't even get that right.'

I think for a moment he's going to shy away, but he takes my face between his hands. 'Look, I don't know what you want, but I do know what I want. I want to hang out with you again. And if you want it to be just friends then I understand and I'll go with that because it's better than nothing. But I missed you like hell and if you want it like it was before, like I do . . . Oh shit, I'm making a mess of this.'

'You're not,' I whisper.

His grin flashes. 'I'm not? So what do you want?'

'How it was.'

He strokes my cheek. 'It can't be exactly like that, I guess. I'm not on your doorstep any more, but that might freak your dad less. I can see you some nights after work, there's my early finish on Saturdays, and we've got Sundays. You sure you want to make the effort? I do, but do you?'

I hear Lindz's voice in my head, laughing and bright like she used to be with me before her mum left: 'Go for it, girl.' I take the edge of his T-shirt sleeve between my fingers. 'At least you've stopped riding about half-naked. If you came off that bike, you really would be a mess.'

The smug, laughing-eyes grin I remember plasters itself to his face. He lets me go and whips the T-shirt off. 'That better? Does that help you to make your mind up?'

I'm right. His shoulders are broader and he's been working at the yard without a shirt again because his skin is tanned all over. I run my finger along his collarbone because I'm allowed to now. 'I don't need any help making my mind up, but I'm not complaining about having a carrot dangled.'

'Are you calling me a carrot?' He strokes my hair away from my face. 'There's a blackbird up there watching us. I wonder if birds watch us for entertainment, like we watch TV. Maybe we're his *Eastenders*.'

I look at the bird and it looks back at me, head cocked to one side, beady eyes gleaming.

Ryan whispers in my ear, all wicked snigger. 'Want to give it something worth watching?'

I nod and he takes my face again and kisses me long and slow.

The blackbird watches us, me and the Boat Boy, our arms wrapped round each other while the sun sparkles on the dragonfly's wings and glints off the water of the Orange River.

Acknowledgments

Thank you to Debbie Bennett and Kathleen Reid for helping with the research for this book. And to John Booth for asking some vital questions in the early stages. Shoshanna Einfeld, you held my hand across the ocean when I needed to keep believing the book would make it onto the shelves – thank you for keeping me strong and making me laugh. Berni Stevens, you were my first writing friend and you've supported me so much through the writing process, finding an agent, selling the book – thank you for being such an awesome cheerleader.

To very generous Simon Trewin, thank you for monitoring my baby steps into the world of publishing. And I owe a huge debt of gratitude to Felicity Carter, without whom I don't think I'd be in print yet – thank you so much for all your help and advice when I was starting out as a writer.

Thanks to two very important people: my editor at Egmont, Stella Paskins, for pushing me to achieve the best I could for this book and making it so much better than I ever could on my own; and my fantastic agent, Ariella Feiner, for taking a chance on me and being the best agent I could wish for. To the rest of the team at Egmont, and Jane Willis at United Agents – more thanks.

And finally, a big thanks to my mother for reading and rereading the early drafts, and to Paul, for patiently putting up with me during the edits.